TIME TUNNEL:
THE EMPIRE

RICHARD TODD

Time Tunnel: The Empire
By Richard Todd
Copyright © 2019 Richard Todd Miller
All rights reserved.
Pre-publish edition
Not for resale

Print Edition ISBN: 978-1-7331936-0-3
Kindle Edition ISBN: 978-1-7331936-1-0
Library of Congress Control Number: 2019907714

This book is dedicated to Laura

[CLASSIFIED]

Department of Justice
Federal Bureau of Investigation
Counterterrorism Division

J. Edgar Hoover Building
935 Pennsylvania Ave NW
Section D, Routing 12
Washington, DC 20535

EVIDENCE

CASE#: 2992888211
Marriott Hotel, Newark International Airport
Room 466
Newark, NJ

AGENT: John C. Turner XF8586957

> PDB: BIN LADEN DETERMINED TO STRIKE IN U.S.
>
> PDB: BIN LADEN DETERMINED TO STRIKE IN U.S.
> UNITED AIRLINES 93 HIJACKERS
> TARGET: WHITE HOUSE

DEPARTMENT OF JUSTICE
CASE #: 2992888211
CLASSIFICATION: X CLASSIFIED ___ DECLASSIFIED
FILED:
BY:

[CLASSIFIED]

7 West 75th Street
New York, NY
September 11, 2001
20:12 hours
Timeline 002

Padma Mahajan watched TV in a dark room. Images from the oversized flat-screen TV saturated her face, already swollen and wet with tears. Padma hugged her bare legs to her chest. Her long black hair fell on her shoulders, shrouded in one of Kyle's white dress shirts. She buried her face in the unbuttoned sleeves. She could smell Kyle, as though his arms were in the sleeves wrapped around her.

Behind the sofa, on a small table stand by the black apartment door, sat a tiny blue-skinned ceramic figurine of Krishna playing a golden flute. A votive candle flickered next to the porcelain deity. Bright marigold blossoms surrounded the shrine.

Padma had stared at the TV screen for hours. The same images and sounds repeated—harrowing videos of American 11 missing the World Trade Center's North Tower by mere feet. The roar of the 767's overtaxed engines and the screams of the crowd could be heard as the airliner hurdled toward the North Tower, suddenly tilting on its side to skirt the building at the last microsecond before impact.

The action videos were interleaved with interviews with American 11 passengers and crew. Then there was the one static picture that punctuated the videos—the one of her fallen husband, Major Kyle Mason, the heroic Delta Force soldier who had helped lead the charge against the hijackers.

In the picture, Kyle was wearing his Army officer's uniform. It occurred to Padma that she had never seen him dressed in his officer's uniform before. His chiseled jaw framed an easy smile. Green eyes pierced through the screen and met Padma's dark brown eyes.

He is so handsome, she thought.

Padma broke down again. *He **was** so handsome.*

The day before, on September 10, Padma had stepped out of their SoHo Grand honeymoon suite for a cigarette and coffee. When she returned, she expected to find her Adonis the way she had left him—naked in bed. Instead, Kyle was fully dressed and rapidly packing his bag. She saw the pained look on his face, reflecting her own expression of surprise. Kyle told her that he had been recalled for a mission that he could not discuss with her. Though Padma understood that "the unexpected" came as part of the package of marriage to a Delta operator, she could not mask the deep pang of disappointment of being abandoned on her honeymoon. Mixed with the pain was fear for her man. When most people left for work each day, the certainty was virtually 100 percent that they would be home for dinner. With Kyle's job, the odds were real that he would never return.

Before he left, Kyle made a strange request.

"I need you to promise me something," he said.

"Of course, love, anything," replied Padma.

"Promise me you won't go to work tomorrow."

Padma laughed. She thought Kyle was joking. Padma was a rising-star investment banker at Cantor Fitzgerald. Twelve-hour days at her Twin Towers office were routine for her. Taking a day off for her honeymoon was already a stretch. Taking a second day off for no apparent reason was impossible. In Padma's business, time was money.

Padma saw that Kyle was serious.

"What's going on?" she asked.

"I can't tell you," Kyle replied. "Promise me you'll stay home."

Kyle kissed her goodbye. She could feel urgency on his lips. To Padma, it felt like a last kiss.

Padma watched the hotel door shut behind him. She turned to the lonely remains of their empty love nest. The tossed bed linens and pillows lay on the bed. A tray with wheat toast, coffee, and a bowl of berries sat on the end of the bed. A half-eaten slice of toast rested on the tray—Kyle's hurried breakfast. She worried that Kyle had not had enough to eat before facing whatever dangers lay ahead.

Padma honored her promise to Kyle and went home to her Upper West Side brownstone apartment, a stone's throw from Central Park. With her honeymoon cut short, she suddenly found herself with time to kill—unprecedented for her.

Padma's apartment was spartan. Her job left her little time to do more in her dwelling than sleep, shower, and change clothes.

The apartment's plain white walls held no art, save a single framed charcoal sketch of a leaf floating in a pool of water—the drawing she had made as a teenager. A Tarom Persian rug in the living room covered the dark hardwood floors. The rug's crimson and burnt orange were interwoven with violet accents. An iron coffee table stood atop the rug. A clay-colored leather sofa and contemporary dark wood sideboard completed the ensemble. Padma's one indulgence, a brand new 2001 plasma TV, was mounted on the wall over the sideboard. She had no time for entertainment—she used the TV to monitor news and market conditions as she got ready for work in the morning.

Padma walked to her apartment's sole bedroom, kicked off her boots and unbuttoned her crimson blouse, tossing it on the bed—queen-sized with contemporary head and footboards decorated with right-angled black iron bars. A single onyx-colored nightstand with a simple lamp bounded the bed. Padma's long black hair fell down her naked brown back, nearly touching the waist of her jeans.

She opened a cramped closet. In addition to her signature jet-black business suits, blouses, jeans, and a handful of dresses, a few changes of Kyle's clothes hung in the closet. She took one of his white dress shirts off its hanger and put it on, buttoning it up partway and leaving the sleeves undone.

From her second-floor balcony, Padma gazed at Central Park in the afternoon. The park was a gorgeous eruption of summer green. She marveled at its beauty. A fleeting thought challenged her work-life balance choices over a cup of coffee as a summer breeze wafted across her balcony.

That evening, Padma slid off her jeans and climbed into bed wearing only Kyle's shirt.

At 1:05AM on September 11, the phone rang. It was Kyle.

"I'm sorry to wake you," said Kyle.

"I'm not," replied Padma, groggy.

"Honey, I've gotta work late again tonight."

"What's the excuse this time," replied Padma, sharpening up.

"Gotta save the world," said Kyle.

"There's always something," said Padma.

There was a pause.

"Come to my bed," said Padma.

Kyle sighed. "You're killing me."

"Hey, I'm not the one who had to go save the world."

"Right about now, I'm thinking your bed is worth a court martial."

"My bed's worth a firing squad," said Padma.

"You are making me crazy."

"Good," said Padma. "Then quit the Army and come home."

"You know there is no place else I want to be," said Kyle.

Another pause.

"Are you being careful?" asked Padma.

"I am," replied Kyle.

"That's good," Padma said, "because I really don't think I can live without you."

"I wouldn't live without you," said Kyle.

After they hung up, Padma tried without success to get back to sleep. The words cycled in her mind.

I wouldn't live without you.

Padma eventually dozed off, arriving in a dream where she tried to find Kyle in an office maze of hallways and cubicles. She ran toward glimpses of her husband, though she could never reach him. Someone or something always interrupted her, slowing her down. Each time she arrived at the place she had sighted him, he was gone.

At 6:00AM, Padma rose from bed and started her morning routine, making coffee and flipping on the TV to scan the day's financial news.

At 8:35AM, her phone rang again.

"Are you at home?" Kyle asked.

"Yes, I'm exactly where you told me to be," Padma replied cheerfully. "I miss you. When am I going to see you again?"

Her question was met with silence.

Padma sensed trouble. "Kyle? What's wrong?"

"I'm not coming home."

"Oh God! *No*," she gasped. "No! No! *No!*"

Though Padma knew the possibility of Kyle's untimely death was a risk that came with marriage to a Delta soldier, she had assumed she would have more than 48 hours of married life with him before she was widowed.

Padma sobbed on the phone, unable to speak.

"I am so sorry," Kyle said. "I wanted to live with you. You don't know how much I wanted to live with you."

"I do know," said Padma, crying.

Padma tried to pull herself together. "I need to be strong for you," she said. "What can I do for you? Tell me what you need."

"I was supposed to be the one to protect you," said Kyle.

"I know that you already have," said Padma.

"Beloved," Kyle said, "know that if there is any way I can be with you, I will. I promise I will. There is no other place I want to be."

"I am selfish, but I don't want you to rest. I want you to haunt me forever," she said.

"I will be your ghost. I feel sorry for the next guy who tries to date you."

Padma laughed through the tears.

"I don't," she said. "I want to see the look on his face when you rattle your chains."

"I am so sorry, love. I have to go now," said Kyle.

Padma sobbed.

"Goodbye, my love."

"Goodbye, beloved," Padma cried. "Please take my love with you."

"I will, love. Always."

Padma dropped the phone. She raised her hands to her face and cried into them.

Minutes later, news of American 11's near miss of the North Tower flashed across her TV. *Was this connected to Kyle's warning for her to stay home?*

News trickled out over the following hours. *Kyle was on the plane!* He had died while leading a charge to retake the plane from Muslim extremist hijackers.

Padma realized that Kyle had given his life so that Padma might live in a world without Kyle. The irony was maddening to her.

More news began to flow. Bizarre reports. Stories of murdered young Middle Eastern men in hotel rooms in New Jersey, Boston, and Virginia—was there a connection? Though FBI agents had instantly swarmed the crime scenes, squelching news, rumors filtered out from first responders about assassination-style killings and strange notes left at the scenes, suggesting American 11 was not an isolated incident but instead part of a broader terrorist conspiracy involving as many as four airliners. The implications were chilling. Speculation churned overtime on news networks.

Among the interviewees were Kyle's parents in Palo Alto, California. The press had wasted no time flushing the two grieving middle-aged parents out of their home and into a phalanx of cameras and microphones.

Kyle and Padma had not yet told their parents that they had eloped two days prior. No one knew Padma was the brave Delta Force operator's widow. As she watched Kyle's parents struggle to maintain their composure in the strange, alien world that had landed on their front lawn, Padma was thankful her 48-hour marriage was a secret. No reporters would be waiting for her when she emerged from her brownstone.

Padma knew her own parents would call when they saw the news. She dreaded the call. Padma's parents knew their daughter was in love with the Army Special Forces soldier—someone they considered beneath her station. They hoped the infatuation would pass and that their daughter would marry a doctor or lawyer.

"You should not be alone right now," said Padma's mother.

"There is a very nice man you should meet. I think you would enjoy his company."

"Are you serious?" Padma responded in a deep voice, as though her measured words coiled like a serpent to strike. "I've lost the love of my life and you're trying to fix me up? What the fuck is the matter with you?"

"He's a lawyer at Skadden Arps," her mother added.

"Mother! Love is not a pedigree!" Padma cried.

She hung up. The phone rang again. She yanked the cord out of the wall and screamed. Orange rage mixed with her other colors of pain. Padma wondered if she too would lose her mind when she grew older, as her mother clearly had.

At that moment, Padma heard the lock of her apartment door unlatch. Someone pushed the door open.

Padma spun around as the door closed shut. A man stood in front of the door behind the sofa. The stranger was illuminated only by the TV and the solitary candle —too dark for Padma to see clearly.

Wearing nothing but Kyle's shirt, Padma's sense of vulnerability swelled in the intruder's presence.

"Who are you?" demanded Padma. "What are you doing here?"

The man stepped toward Padma. He was a big man, over six feet tall, wearing black. He carried a backpack in one hand. He dropped the pack on the floor with a thud.

Padma screamed and covered her face with her hands.

Kyle Mason was standing in her living room.

7 West 75th Street
New York, NY
September 11, 2001
20:13 hours
Timeline 002

Padma shrieked at the ghost standing in her apartment. She buried her face in her hands and began to sob. She felt Kyle's hands around her wrists. Instinctively, she jerked her hands and pulled away.

"No! You're dead!" she screamed. "You're *dead!*"

"Beloved," Kyle said softly, "I'm here. I'm really here."

Padma pulled her hands from her eyes, eyeing the man with suspicion.

Kyle pulled up his sleeve to show Padma the Sanskrit tattoo of her name on the inside of his arm. "It's really me."

Padma looked at the tattoo in the dim light. She reached out and touched it cautiously with her forefinger.

She withdrew her finger. Her gaze returned to Kyle's face.

"I don't understand," said Padma in a breaking voice. "How can you be here?"

"It's a long story," said Kyle. "For the moment, can you trust that I am?"

"Not if it's only for a moment," cried Padma. "If you're here, you have to stay here. You can *never* leave—*ever!* Can you make that promise to me?"

"Yes. I can make that promise. I will never leave you again."

Padma wrapped her arms around Kyle and kissed him hard. The moment she touched him, she felt something strange.

Noli me tangere.

The Latin words flashed in her mind—Jesus after his crucifixion admonishing Mary Magdalene to "touch me not" because of his unrisen state. Padma's body was rejecting something about the man she was holding. There was something foreign about him.

But the man she was holding and kissing *was* Kyle. She recognized his face, his body, his voice. She dismissed the false voices in her head, hoisted her body up onto his and wrapped her legs around his waist. He carried her into the bedroom, laid her on the bed, and pulled her shirt open, ripping off the buttons and exposing her naked body.

She looked up at him with molten dark chocolate eyes. "Come to me," she said.

7 West 75th Street
New York, NY
September 12, 2001
02:47 hours
Timeline 002

Padma looked at the man sleeping soundly next to her. Candlelight and shadows moved across his body. Though hours of lovemaking had exhausted them both, the warning voices in her head persisted, keeping her wide-awake. She took the votive candle from the nightstand and held it close to his right arm to view his tattoo more closely.

She gasped.

The fresh tattoo, which had been crisp, black, and bordered by red inflamed skin the previous day, was completely healed. Age had blurred it and faded the black ink to dark patina. She instinctively held her hand to her mouth, squelching a shriek. Her heart raced.

The man to whom she had given herself was an imposter.

She felt a bolt of dread in her stomach. Tentacles of fear fired through her arms and legs. Frantic, conflicting, terrified thoughts overwhelmed her mind. The man sleeping next to her looked like Kyle. He knew things that only Kyle could know. And yet, he was not Kyle.

Padma carefully slid out of bed, put Kyle's white dress shirt back on, and exited the bedroom.

7 West 75th Street
New York, NY
September 12, 2001
06:30 hours
Timeline 002

Kyle Mason opened his eyes. Next to him was the cavity of a vacant white pillow. The head that had rested there was gone. In its place, a strand of long black hair lay tucked in the pillow's ample folds.

He got out of bed.

"Padma?" he called as he began to walk through the apartment. Morning light was beginning to stream through the windows. Kyle found Padma in the kitchen. She was sitting at the small wooden kitchen table. A mug of coffee sat on the table in front of her. Her forehead rested on the table, her long black hair splayed across it. Kyle noticed that his backpack rested on the floor next to Padma's chair. It was unzipped.

"Padma?" Kyle asked, standing naked in the kitchen doorway.

Padma slowly raised her head off the table. She then lifted Kyle's Glock 9mm pistol from her lap, pointing it directly at him. Kyle froze.

"Who...are...you?" asked Padma.

Kyle took a breath, unprepared for the confrontation. "You're not going to believe me."

"I'm not going to believe you?" asked Padma hysterically. "What part, exactly, am I not going to believe? The part about my husband dying then magically resurrecting? Or the part about the fact that you look and sound exactly like my husband, and you know things that only my husband knows, but you are *not* my husband."

"Do you mind if I put some clothes on before we have this conversation?" asked Kyle.

Padma raised the gun. "Do you mind if I put two rounds in your heart and one between your *fucking* eyes like my husband taught me?" Padma shouted, "Sit the fuck down and start talking!"

Kyle pulled out the wooden chair opposite Padma and sat down. He folded his hands on the table, took a deep breath, and exhaled.

Kyle turned the inside of his arm toward Padma. "You remember the day I got this tattoo—it was three days ago—the day we were married. It was the happiest day of my life.

"The thing is that, for me, that day didn't happen three days ago—it happened seven years ago.

"Forty-eight hours after we were married, on September 11, 2001, four commercial airliners were hijacked by Muslim terrorists. Two of the planes hit the Twin Towers. The towers were completely destroyed. You were killed when the North Tower collapsed."

Padma's burned out expression didn't flinch. Her eyes were locked on Kyle. The gun was aimed directly at his chest.

"You tried to call me to say goodbye before you died," Kyle continued. "I was on the flight back to Fort Bragg after our honeymoon. You couldn't reach me, so you called a stranger to make sure I got the message. You told the stranger to tell me that you loved me. That was all.

"I went to Afghanistan to hunt the terrorist responsible for the attacks. His name is Osama Bin Laden. My mission failed. Bin Laden escaped."

Kyle's gaze left Padma's eyes and descended to her coffee cup on the tabletop.

"I broke down. I was a wreck. Years later, I was recruited by my mentor, General Craig, for a mission…"

Kyle paused, taking a breath.

"It's crazy… It's so crazy that I don't believe it myself. I don't believe that I'm actually here with you," he said.

"Keep talking," Padma said.

"There's a facility at Area 51 that General Craig runs… It can send people through time."

Kyle looked up from the table into Padma's eyes. Her expression was frozen.

"The mission was to prevent 9/11 from happening. '9/11' is what we call it in our time. I was sent with a partner back from the year 2008 to this year—2001.

"That's when everything went wrong. We arrived late and my partner was DOA. We were supposed to arrive several weeks before 9/11 so we would have plenty of time to kill the terrorists. Instead, I arrived alone the morning before.

"In order to complete the mission, I recruited my younger self. The day before yesterday, when you stepped out of the SoHo Grand for a cigarette, I was across the street, watching you. When you went for coffee, I went up to your room and met Kyle. The mission Kyle told you about when he left—those orders came from me.

"I knew where all the terrorists were supposed to be sleeping that night. Kyle and I divvied up the list and went hunting."

"On the news—the assassinations—that was you?" asked Padma.

Kyle nodded. "Both of us—yes. Something went wrong. I don't know what. He wasn't supposed to be on that plane yesterday. I don't know what happened. I can only assume that he couldn't get to everyone on his list. He must have improvised. I would have.

"I was supposed to return to 2008 after my mission. There's a gadget that sends me back. It's in my pants pocket. I disobeyed my orders. I couldn't leave you.

"I understand this is crazy, but there's evidence of everything I'm telling you, starting with Kyle's body in the morgue. There's also the keycard log from when I entered your hotel room, the gadget that sends me back to 2008, as well as this guy I abducted in Weehawken…"

Padma's eyebrows rose.

"…It's another long story."

"There's one more thing," Kyle said. "Reach into the side pocket of my backpack."

Padma kept the gun aimed at Kyle while she carefully reached into the backpack. She pulled out a piece of paper, folded in quarter.

"Open it," Kyle said.

Padma unfolded the paper. It was the drawing of a leaf floating on a pool of water she had made as a teenager.

Padma got up from her chair.

"Don't move," she said.

She ran into the living room and snatched the framed drawing of the leaf on the pool of water from the wall. She walked back into the kitchen and set the two drawings on the table side-by-side. She dropped into her chair.

"Holy fuck," she said.

"I took it when I left for the mission," Kyle said.

"So…I am your husband, but I am not your husband. You are my wife, but you are not my wife."

"So you're a time traveler from the future?" said Padma.

"That's right."

"And you're the one who got my Kyle killed?"

"Yes."

Tears welled and flowed down Padma's face. She held up the gun.

"Why shouldn't I kill you right now?"

"Because I'm the only Kyle you have left."

Padma held the gun for a full minute, then slowly lowered it and set it on the table. She raised her hands to her face and began to cry.

"You killed my Kyle," she sobbed through her hands. "My Kyle is dead."

Kyle watched Padma, feeling sick. Her tears seared a hole in his chest. Though he had saved thousands of lives, he had wounded the life he valued the most. After what seemed an eternity, he finally spoke.

"Beloved, your Kyle is still here."

Padma did not move. Her face was planted in the palms of her hands.

"I am older than I was when I got this tattoo, but I am still that man. Every memory, every feeling, everything that makes Kyle is here. Both of us loved you completely. One of us remains, here, now, still completely in love with you."

Padma lifted her wet, swollen face from her hands.. Tangled strays of long black hair hung in front of her eyes. She looked at Kyle's face and naked torso, examining him. He didn't look a day older than when she last saw him two days before. His face was that of the handsome young soldier in dress uniform whose picture had been shown on the news. His powerful body was every bit as taut as she remembered. Still, she heard something in his voice and felt something in his touch that was foreign.

"So, you're 40 years old?" she asked.

"Yes."

"You age well," she said, managing a smile.

It reminded Kyle of the conversation he'd had with his younger self two days before.

"I've had some work done."

Padma nodded. "I want your doctor when the time comes."

They smiled, meeting eyes.

"How are you different than my Kyle?"

Kyle looked down at the table. His expression turned to pain.

"This one has some wear and tear."

Padma reached across the table, lifting Kyle's chin. She looked into his green eyes. This Kyle's face looked identical to her Kyle's, though she could see the hurt in his eyes and hear it in his voice. She took his hand. He grasped hers and held it tight. Tears began to well in his eyes.

"Your Kyle is still in here," he said, placing his hand on his chest. He choked up. "I came back to save you, beloved. I would do anything for you. Please believe me."

Tears streamed down Padma's face. She rose from her chair and came to the wounded warrior. Standing next to him, she cradled his head against her chest.

"I know that," she said. "I know your pain. I lived it too."

Kyle wrapped his arms around Padma's waist, held her tight and cried into her shirt. Padma held his head and stroked his hair. She had never seen this vulnerable version of Kyle before. The Kyle she knew was superhuman—an elite Special Forces operator, powerful, smart, and confident. She felt enormous pride for Kyle the warrior. The exposed man in her arms was summoning unfamiliar feelings from her.

Like Kyle, Padma was a super-achiever. She had never been attracted to men she considered weak. Her nurturing reaction to Kyle's defenselessness surprised her. She held her man close, protecting him.

Padma kissed the top of Kyle's head, then leaned down to kiss his lips. Kyle raised his face to meet hers, returning her warm, loving kisses. She took his hand to lead him back to the bedroom.

"C'mon," she said.

7 West 75th Street
New York, NY
September 12, 2001
11:30 hours
Timeline 002

Kyle and Padma lay in bed, intertwined. Though bone-tired, neither wanted to sleep. They had both lived through the other's death. Neither wanted to miss a single moment.

Padma kissed Kyle, then sat up. She reached into her nightstand and pulled out a pack of American Spirit cigarettes and a small brass elephant-shaped lighter. Before she lit up, she turned to Kyle.

"Do you mind?" she asked.

Kyle smiled. "Not one bit."

Padma loved a cigarette after sex. She found this cigarette, after sex with a time traveler, to be particularly satisfying.

The Kyle of 2001 had hated it when Padma smoked. It was the only thing about her he wanted to change. The 2008 edition of Kyle embraced every atom of Padma, including the blue-white smoke that blew from her gorgeous full lips. Padma smiled, acknowledging the changed man. She wondered what else was different about this Kyle.

"I'm getting some ice water—can I get you anything from the kitchen?" he asked as he got out of bed.

"I'll have a sip of yours," she said.

Kyle returned from the kitchen with a glass in one hand and his Glock pistol in the other. Padma's eyes widened. He sat the glass down on the nightstand, then ejected the gun magazine and checked the chamber. It was empty.

"For future reference, the next time you want to shoot me, you'll want to chamber a round."

"Good to know—thanks," she said with a wink.

Kyle sat the pistol and magazine on the nightstand next to the brass elephant. Padma rested her cigarette on a glass ashtray and took a sip of water. Kyle climbed back into bed. Padma turned and rested her head on his chest. Kyle stroked her hair.

"Kyle?" she asked.

"Yes?"

"You know the future," she said.

"I know *a* future, not this future," Kyle answered.

"But you know the broad strokes—companies, economics…"

"Yes—what are you getting at?"

"Tell me some big things that happen."

"Let's see…Apple becomes one of the world's biggest companies."

"Shut the fuck up! Apple is dead!" Padma exclaimed.

"No, really—next month they launch something called the iPod, then they'll come out with iTunes—it totally changes the music industry. CDs become obsolete. In a few years, they launch the iPhone. The stock is trading at a couple hundred dollars in 2008. I think the stock split in 2005."

Padma's eyes grew wide. That morning, on September 12, 2001, Apple stock was circling the bowl at $17. If the stock would trade at $200 in 2008 after a split, its valuation would have increased by 23 times!

"What else?" she asked.

"In 2007, the housing market collapses. Lehman Brothers goes bankrupt in 2008…"

"Wait a minute—back up. Lehman Brothers goes bankrupt?"

"Right."

"That's crazy!"

"Well, I time traveled here from 2008—Lehman Brothers going bankrupt doesn't seem like the craziest part of this story."

"I'm not so sure about that," replied Padma.

"Something called 'credit default swaps'?"

Padma's face blanched. Kyle could feel her heart race against his chest. She began breathing rapidly.

"What's wrong? Are you OK?"

Padma put her hand on her chest. She sat up and looked Kyle in the eye.

"Do you have the slightest idea what this means?"

"Not really, no."

"It means we're going to be the world's first trillionaires."

Harpo Studios
1058 West Washington Boulevard
Chicago, IL
September 11, 2008
10:10 hours
Timeline 002

Padma stood in the stage wings of *The Oprah Winfrey Show*, waiting to join Oprah for her interview. It was the seventh anniversary of the American 11 incident and the death of her husband, Major Kyle Mason.

Padma was wearing her signature jet-black pant suit with a white Nehru collar blouse. Her long black hair, normally pulled into a tight ponytail at work, was set loose to flow freely down her back.

Padma was now 42. She had grown even more beautiful with time—almost imperceptible lines and shadows made her face blossom. Her physical appearance was enhanced by a serene, majestic countenance that she had grown into as the world's most successful CEO.

A producer, a bearded man dressed in black with a skullcap of receding red hair and a headset, stood with Padma in the shadowed wings. Oprah made Padma's introduction.

"I am very honored to have with us today the CEO of Wild

Industries. As you know, Padma Mahajan is not only the wealthiest woman on the planet, myself included…"

The audience laughed.

"…she is the also the widow of Major Kyle Mason, the hero of American 11. Padma was married to Kyle for only 48 hours before his life and their marriage ended tragically on September 11, 2001. Padma has never spoken publicly about her relationship with Kyle until now. Please welcome Padma Mahajan."

The producer standing next to Padma signaled for her to go onstage. Padma walked out into the bright stage light and applauding audience. She beamed and waved to Oprah's excited audience of fellow women.

Oprah hugged Padma, and they took their seats.

"I want to thank you for being here today and sharing your story," said Oprah.

"It is my pleasure," replied Padma. "Thank you for having me."

"Before we talk about Kyle and your relationship, I'd like to talk about you, because you are one phenomenal woman."

"You are very kind," Padma said, smiling, as the audience applauded.

"You are the CEO of Wild Industries, one of the world's largest companies, and you are also the world's wealthiest woman. Forbes estimates that you are worth, wait a minute, I need to check to see if I'm reading too many zeros here—there are a lot to count, let me tell ya…"

The audience laughed again.

"You are a trillionaire—*a trillionaire!*"

The audience gasped.

"How much is a trillion?"

"A trillion is a thousand billions," answered Padma.

"Whew," Oprah said, fanning herself with her hand, "that's a lot of money."

"I have been very fortunate."

"How'd you do it, Padma?" Oprah asked. "How on Earth did you make so much money, so darn fast?"

"It's a combination of homework, common sense, and just plain luck. For example, when Steve Jobs returned to Apple, it was a good bet that he was still the genius that he was in his first tenure. I didn't bet on the company. I bet on the man.

"In our most recent housing crisis, the conventional wisdom was that housing prices would go up forever. I thought that was ridiculous and I took a short position."

"Tell me what that means," asked Oprah, "because I hear words like 'derivatives' and 'credit default swaps' and it absolutely makes my eyes glaze over."

"I think financial people make this much more complicated than it actually is," answered Padma. "A credit default swap is simply insurance—in this case, insurance against a loan defaulting. What happened in this particular situation is that Main Street banks made home loans to people who couldn't repay them. Those loans were bought up by Wall Street banks and sold to investors. Though the loans were junk, credit agencies gave them triple-A ratings, which meant the cost of insuring them was very cheap—only pennies on the dollar. I bought a lot of that insurance."

"And the insurance companies and investment banks went bust when the music stopped playing," said Oprah. "The insurance companies couldn't pay up."

"That's exactly right."

"The American taxpayer," Oprah continued, "ended up footing the bill to keep those big companies afloat—you took some heat for making so much money from American taxpayers."

"I fully appreciate taxpayers' frustration, though I think it is important to keep a couple things in mind—the first is that I didn't create the perfect storm—if the big investment banks had not pushed these junk products onto their clients while the credit reporting agencies were simultaneously giving them junk triple-A ratings, none of this would have happened. The other thing to be aware of is that these big banks sold this stuff to their investors while simultaneously betting against their own clients by buying their own credit default swaps. I think it's one thing to take advantage of a perfectly legal situation. It's another thing entirely to perpetrate a fraud—I think that's just unconscionable."

The audience applauded again.

"You have become very influential in American politics," said Oprah. "Some call you the most powerful woman in America. Some even call you the 'Empress of America.'"

"I wish people would stop calling me that," said Padma, laughing. "It's true that I'm an advocate for causes that I believe are important to the country, like clean energy and education, though all citizens have a right and obligation to speak and have their voices heard. I am no different in that respect."

"Let's talk about Anderson Wild," said Oprah.

"OK," said Padma, taking a nervous breath.

"The mysterious Anderson Wild—who is he? There is almost no public information about him—"

"And most of that information is wrong," Padma interrupted.

"No one has even *seen* him before! He's the other richest person on the planet besides yourself—who *is* Anderson Wild?"

Padma hesitated, smiling. The audience laughed nervously.

"Obviously, he's a recluse—" Padma began.

"Why is he so secret?" Oprah interrupted. "What's he got to hide?"

"He doesn't have any rattling skeletons that I'm aware of," said Padma. "However, to say he's painfully shy is an understatement."

"What can you tell us about him—how old is he?"

"He's about my age."

"Which is?"

"I'm 42."

"Wow! Wow! You are gorgeous!" Oprah said to the audience's applause. Padma smiled, embarrassed.

"What does he look like? Is he good looking?"

Padma looked away, embarrassed, laughing. The audience laughed with her.

"Yeah, I think he's good looking," Padma said.

A whoop erupted from the audience as the crowd burst into laughter and applause.

"So, have you two hooked up?"

"Oh my God!" Padma exclaimed, laughing and holding her hand to her face. "No."

"Uh huh," said Oprah, unconvinced.

"We haven't! Oh my God!" laughed Padma. The audience roared.

As the laughter died down, Oprah continued. "Let's talk about Kyle."

Padma nodded. "OK."

"It was seven years ago today that you lost Kyle when he stopped the hijackers on American 11 and saved the lives, not only of the passengers on the plane, but also thousands of people at the World Trade Center. Tell us about Kyle."

Padma looked down for a moment, preparing.

"Some of us are fortunate enough to meet the one love of our lives," said Padma. "Kyle was that love."

Tears began to well. A pin drop could be heard in the studio.

"Tell us about the 48 hours of your marriage."

Padma paused.

"Do you need a moment?" asked Oprah.

Padma shook her head. "We eloped. My parents did not approve of Kyle. They wanted me to marry a doctor or lawyer. When Kyle died, I hadn't yet gathered the courage to tell my parents we were married.

"We were married in New York's city hall. No witnesses—just the two of us. The day we were married, Kyle had a tattoo done of my name in Sanskrit."

Padma pointed to her arm. "It was on the inside of his arm.

"We spent the rest of that day and the following morning in a suite at the SoHo Grand. Kyle didn't make a lot of money in the Army, and he spent every last cent of his savings on that room and this ring."

Padma held up the sparkling diamond ring, still on her left ring finger.

"You've never taken that ring off?"

"No. And I never will," Padma replied. Tears began to stream down her cheek.

The camera cut to crying women in the audience.

"You'll never remarry?"

"Not a day goes by when I don't think of him. He was already bigger than life in my eyes and my heart before he became the hero of American 11."

"He was…he was extraordinary," Padma said, looking at Oprah. "He was strong and courageous and funny—"

"And not bad to look at," said Oprah.

"My God, he was a hunk!" Padma exclaimed. The audience laughed through their tears.

"No man could compete, even before American 11. Then he went and raised the bar even higher that day," Padma said. "So, no, I can't begin to imagine another man who could turn my head. I don't just love him. I am every bit *in* love with him as I was seven years ago."

Oprah was speechless. There wasn't a dry eye in the room as the audience rose to its feet in a standing ovation. Padma, visibly moved, clasped her hands and bowed to the audience in a Namaste blessing. Several audience members returned the blessing.

Oprah turned to the camera. "We'll be back," she said, wiping tears from her face.

League City, TX
September 17, 2008
18:30 hours
Timeline 002

A television ad blazed onto screens across Texas at dinnertime.

On the screen, an American flag waved against a blue sky.

As the flag waved, a male intoned in a deep voice: "Our founding fathers sacrificed their lives for the one thing most precious to Americans...

"...Our liberty..."

The skies behind the flag grew cloudy and dark.

"That liberty has been taken from us—by an outsider..."

The visual cut to a close-up picture of Padma. Her image had been photoshopped to further darken her skin. Her brow was furrowed and the corners of her lips pulled down into an angry visage. Errant strands had been added to her normally disciplined straight hair.

"Someone with a foreign agenda who has taken your hard-earned tax dollars from the AIG bailout and used that money to buy politicians. She's bought congressmen, senators, even the president!

"She wants to take away your Second Amendment constitutional right to bear arms. She wants to take God out of our classrooms. She wants us to obey Sharia law. And she wants to destroy our oil and gas industry, eliminating tens of thousands of jobs.

"But there's one man who can't be bought by foreigners..."

A plump middle-aged Caucasian man, wearing jeans with a rodeo buckle, cowboy boots, a button-up shirt, and a cowboy hat, hoisted an AR-15 assault rifle and began shooting at watermelons perched on wooden posts. The watermelons exploded into red fruit and rinds.

"Since 2002, Senator Jonah Jones has fought to protect Texans from tyranny. He's willing to stand up to foreign forces that would take away our liberty and destroy our way of life."

The image cut to a group of white men wearing jeans, boots, button-up shirts, caps, and straw cowboy hats. They were holding assault rifles. One held an American flag. Another held the lone star flag of Texas.

"2 Corinthians 11:14 tells us that 'Satan disguises himself as an angel of light.' Don't be fooled by darkness. This November, stand with Senator Jones in the fight against tyranny."

The commercial ended with a twanged voice: "This is Senator Jonah Jones, and I approved this message."

One World Trade Center
New York, NY
September 22, 2008
10:05 hours
Timeline 002

The Twin Towers gleamed in the sunlight on a beautiful fall day in New York City. Giant signs trumpeted the owner's name— Wild Industries—in white letters against a blue background on all four sides of each tower.

Senator Jonah Jones sat in a windowless anteroom on the first floor of the World Trade Center's North Tower. Like all of his Senate and House colleagues, he had made the requisite pilgrimage to the new Mecca of American politics.

Called "The Bunker" by everyone who set foot in it, this concrete and reinforced steel fortress inside the World Trade Center contrasted with the airiness of the rest of the building, where sunshine poured through floor-to-ceiling glass. The bunker was a building within a building—ten floors above ground and five below. It was virtually impervious to conventional weapons and surveillance, and had been built to withstand the ridiculously unthinkable contingency of the tower's collapse. The bunker was the inner sanctum of Wild Industries, housing Padma's office, her apartment, and offices for select staff. The bunker was completely self-contained, with its own electricity, water, and recycling infrastructure. It even housed its own private subway garage behind a reinforced steel vault door.

The mysterious Anderson Wild had bought the World Trade Center towers in 2005. He had appeared from nowhere in 2001, becoming the wealthiest man on the planet in a few short years. Earth's other wealthiest person, Padma Mahajan, was the mastermind behind the couple's vast reserves. That the two were a "couple" was pure speculation. Anderson and Padma were not married, and no one had ever seen them in public together. Indeed, no one had ever seen Anderson Wild at all. As Padma's wealth skyrocketed, the gorgeous financial prodigy drew increasing media attention. In 2007, after poring through New York City's hardcopy public records, one enterprising reporter stunned the world when she broke the story that Padma had married the hero of American 11, Major Kyle Mason, only two days before he lost his life on September 11, 2001.

The day after September 11, Padma abruptly quit her investment banking job at Cantor Fitzgerald and began making uncannily prescient investments—going long on some stocks like Apple and shorting others. Padma's sixth sense for investment seemed clairvoyant, drawing suspicion from both the press and the government. She and Anderson had been investigated multiple times by the FTC for insider trading. Each time, not a shred of evidence could be found to support the government's suspicions. If the couple was cheating, they were exceptionally good at it. By the end of

2005, the couple was worth in excess of a quarter trillion dollars. Though Anderson had been subpoenaed multiple times in the course of government investigations, he'd ignored all requests to appear. Contempt warrants were issued. Wild offices were searched—no one could find Mr. Wild. Eventually, Wild Industries' infinitely funded legal team eroded the government's resolve. Warrants for Wild's arrest were torn up.

At the beginning of 2006, Padma suddenly and inexplicably shifted her focus away from stocks, instead plowing over $100 billion into exotic derivatives—specifically, credit default swaps.

To Wall Street sharks, Padma's move was madness. In 2006, housing prices were soaring. Padma was betting on a collapse—and a catastrophic one at that.

She bought credit default swap insurance for pennies on the dollar. In some cases, she actually paid only *one* penny on the dollar, meaning a billion in cash insured $100 billion in bad debt. By the time the housing market began to crash in 2007, Padma was holding over $5 trillion in insurance—insurance AIG was unable to pay. When AIG and the investment banks began to fail, the American taxpayer stepped in, paid off Padma's insurance and bailed out the investment banks. The one bank denied the taxpayers' largess was Lehman Brothers. Just as Kyle had predicted seven years earlier, the iconic investment bank filed for bankruptcy in September 2008.

Padma and Anderson were trillionaires, worth more than the next million wealthiest humans *combined*.

Credit default swaps were not all the couple were buying.

Anderson and Padma also invested heavily in state and federal elections, stacking the decks in their favor. The conventional wisdom in politics was that it was now impossible to win an election without the power couple's finger on the scale.

Wild Industries no longer needed lobbyists in Washington. Instead, lawmakers made pilgrimages to New York to pay homage and receive marching orders. Padma took meetings with the president, governors, and senators. House members were met by others on Padma's staff. Legislation was written by Wild, passed by Congress, and signed into law by the president. The two most recent Supreme Court justices, including the chief justice, had been hand-picked by Anderson and Padma. The high court only took cases that were in the couple's business or personal interests.

Senator Jones looked at his watch—seven minutes past the hour. Padma was late for their meeting. He chuckled at the slight, though it didn't bruise the Texas senator's lone star-sized ego.

Jones looked around the anteroom. The walls were concrete, shaped into simple geometric block patterns. Mid twentieth century-style black sofas and chairs with efficient square edges surrounded a copper coffee table. Across the room, a receptionist worked at her desk next to a locked heavy metal door—the gateway to Padma's office. A guard stood outside it. The buff guard was Caucasian, over six feet tall, with a blond crew cut. He wore a perfectly tailored black suit, accessorized with a matching black MP7 submachine gun.

The guard was an employee of Wild Industry's Dark Star subsidiary. Formerly known as Blackwater, the private military and security consulting company had been acquired by Wild in 2005. Over the years, Wild had paid top dollar to recruit the very best Special Forces operators from Delta, the Navy Seals, Green Berets, and Army Rangers. Over time, Wild had assembled the world's best private army. Padma's personal security exceeded that of any world leader.

"Ms. Mahajan will be with you shortly," said the receptionist, noting that Jones had checked the time. Diane Galovan was always watching, even when she appeared distracted. She was an attractive brunette in her thirties. She wore an expensive crimson haute couture suit. Wild Industries bucked the conventional corporate American trend toward casual wear in the office. Wild employees were expected to look as though they were paid as well as they actually were.

Unbeknownst to Senator Jones, Galovan's desk was fitted with a reach-in compartment with a loaded Glock pistol and a panic button. When pressed, the panic button would secure the steel door to Padma's office with two-inch bolt locks, while simultaneously summoning a platoon of the guard's colleagues. Galovan had been selected for her job in part for her gracious attention to detail, part for her crack aim.

Galovan sized up the senator. He was in his fifties, 5'9", overweight, with slicked-back silver hair. His signature cowboy boots sprung from the pant legs of a brown rack suit.

"Did you take the train from DC, Senator?" asked Galovan.

"No ma'am," replied Jones. "I flew."

"The Wild maglev train is so much faster," said Galovan. "It takes only 30 minutes."

"I prefer to fly."

Galovan smiled at Jones. Her gaze returned to her computer screen.

The door to Padma's office opened, and a woman emerged. She was a petite woman in her early sixties, with quaffed dyed brown hair, a navy Chanel suit, and a resigned expression. On the lapel of her suit, she wore a United States Senate pin. California Senator Barbara Anastasio saw her expansive fellow senator splayed on the sofa and instantly turned on her best gleaming politician smile. Jones' big gap-toothed smile reflected back at Anastasio. To Anastasio, the fat senator in his cheap brown suit looked as though a dinosaur had taken a dump on the sofa.

"Barbara!" Jones exclaimed as he launched himself off the sofa with a boost from both hands. He extended a hand to shake Anastasio's hand, then gave her an unsolicited sloppy kiss on the cheek. Both Barbara's smile and her contempt for Jones never wavered.

"You here to kiss the ring too?" Jonah asked in a twanged voice that was way too big for the room.

"I'm here to listen to the opinions of a concerned citizen," replied Anastasio, putting a politic face on the total collapse of American democracy.

Jones let out a belly laugh. Anastasio's glistening Botox smile remained fixed.

"You know you are the smartest person I know?" asked Jones.

"I did not know that. I must say I am flattered, that coming from someone as erudite as yourself," replied Anastasio, wondering whether Jones knew what "erudite" meant.

"You are as kind as you are beautiful!" replied Jones.

Galovan interrupted the senators' faux love fest. "Senator Jones, Ms. Mahajan will see you now."

"Gotta go—can't keep the empress waiting!" exclaimed Jones with a laugh. "Let's you and me have lunch."

"That sounds lovely," replied Anastasio, revulsed at the thought of watching Jones eat a Flintstones-sized portion of rare prime rib.

Galovan opened the door for Jones. Behind the door was an enormous office—100 feet long and 75 feet wide, with a ceiling nearly three stories high. As was the case in the anteroom, the walls were untreated concrete, though the floor was hardwood. On one wall hung Rembrandt's *The Night Watch*. Padma had strong-armed Amsterdam's Rijksmuseum into selling the gigantic Dutch masterpiece.

The facing wall was covered with high-resolution LCD panels. Padma normally used them to monitor aspects of Wild Industries' operations, as well as her portfolio performance. Today, those sensitive metrics had been replaced by a live video feed of Lower New York Bay from the World Trade Center's South Tower.

At the far end of the office, Padma stood in front of a large Onyx-colored desk. She was wearing a jet-black pantsuit with a white Nehru collar blouse. Her long black hair was pulled into a tight ponytail bound by a silver cuff. Her hands were folded neatly in front of her.

"Empress Padma!" Jones exclaimed as he bounded into

the office.

Padma smiled politely as she watched the buoyant Jones bounce cheerfully across the expanse of the room. While her left brain understood the duplicity of politics, her mind was not able to fully reconcile the cartoonish image of the fat, gap-toothed senator with his hateful television messages targeted squarely at her.

Padma shook Jones' hand, then deftly moved out of range before he was able to plant a wet kiss on her cheek. She motioned for Jones to take a seat as she sat behind her desk.

Across the desk from Padma sat the one man her political engine had failed to defeat. Senator Jones had narrowly eked out a win in the 2002 election and returned to the Senate for a second term. Padma knew the election had been rigged—the polls had clearly favored her candidate. The media reported Jones' victory as the greatest political upset since Truman had defeated Dewey in 1948. Padma's political machine had been in its infancy in the 2002 election, with a fraction of the money and apparatus she now had at her disposal. In 2008, she fully intended to dislodge the Texan bull nettle from her side.

Padma and Jones were now fully engaged in a pitched and ugly battle for control of Jones' Senate seat. Padma's super PAC had poured tens of millions of dollars into state advertisements and PR to promote her progressive candidate, Wendy Davis, and expose Jones' close association with big oil and banks.

From the content of his ads, a visitor from another world might have deduced that Jones was running against Padma instead of Davis. His ads spared any pretense of civility. The racism levied against Padma was full-throated, rallying white Texans against the brown-skinned woman whom he accused of being a Muslim with a foreign agenda. Jones called upon his base to take back their country from a dark, evil caliphate. It was red meat for conservative Texan voters who had sported "secede" bumper stickers on their pickup trucks long before Padma came to power. Padma was astounded by the irony—a party traditionally in the hip pocket of big business railing against the biggest business of all.

"May I offer you something to drink, Senator?" Padma asked.

"Iced tea, if you have it," said Jones.

Padma picked up a small black remote on her desk and spoke into it.

"Please bring an iced tea for the senator and a black coffee for me—thank you."

Moments later, a side door opened and a uniformed waiter emerged with a tray. He set a cup of black coffee in front of Padma. In front of Jones he placed a silver tray bearing a tall glass of iced tea on a coaster and a silver sugar bowl. Jones shoveled sugar into his glass, carelessly sprinkling some onto Padma's otherwise pristine black desk. Padma's gaze and serene poker face never left the senator's face as the errant sugar crystals skipped across her desk.

Jones took a gulp of iced tea, egested a satisfied "ahhh," then set the glass on Padma's desk, missing its coaster. Condensation began to run down the glass and puddle on Padma's desk. Though the senator's Cro-Magnon manners irritated Padma, she knew better than to let Jones think he could get under her skin.

"I want to thank you for making the trip to New York, Senator,"

Padma said with a cordial smile.

"It is my pleasure," said Jones with a chuckle. "Thank you for seeing me."

"I must say, I'm a little surprised you accepted my invitation to meet," said Padma. "Your schedule has never permitted a meeting over the years."

"Yes, well, representing the interests of my Texan constituents is a full time job," said Jones. "I saw you on *Oprah*. It looks like you're busy yourself on the talk show circuit these days."

"Yes. It's leaving me less and less time for my day job," replied Padma.

"I hear you've got a book deal in the works too."

"Your hearing is excellent, Senator."

"Well, America loves you, there is no doubt about that. If you ran for president, you'd win in a landslide."

"I much prefer my current job."

"I don't doubt it—your job is much more powerful than the president's."

"I doubt that seriously."

"Oh, come on. Everyone knows you and the mysterious Anderson Wild run this country. Every member of Congress, every governor, even the president comes here to kowtow to the empress and get his marching orders. They know they can't get elected without the backing of Wild Industries."

"You did."

"Yes, I did," said Jones. "The people of the great state of Texas march to a different drummer."

"That's one possible explanation," said Padma. "It's interesting that the people of Texas said one thing to pollsters and another thing entirely at the voting booth. Does that mean the people of Texas are also…disingenuous?"

"You mean, are we liars?"

"That's a severe way of putting it."

"What it means is that polls can be so unreliable sometimes."

"You overcame a 15 point spread in three separate polls where the margin of error was 3 points. That can't be explained by science."

"I'm not a big believer in science. The Lord works in mysterious ways."

"So your explanation is divine intervention?"

"I'm a United States senator. I don't believe I'm required to explain myself to you."

Padma paused and took a sip from her coffee. Her gaze didn't leave Jones.

"I am sorry Senator," Padma said, placing her coffee mug on her desk. "We're getting off to a bad start. I had hoped we could try to find common ground. I realize we have differing visions regarding this country's direction."

"Well, common ground is all well and good, but where I come from, those in elected office get to decide the country's direction," Jones said with a toothy grin.

Padma smiled politely and nodded. She knew well that Jones fully understood the absurdity of his comment. They both knew that the issue was not "whether" corporate masters, but instead "which" corporate masters.

"Perhaps it might be helpful," continued Jones, "if you shared some of your priorities with me so I can let you know whether or not I can be of service to a concerned citizen like yourself. You are a citizen, right?"

Padma's face did not betray her anger at the suggestion that it was OK to question one's citizenship because their skin color was not white.

"I am a citizen—thank you for asking," replied Padma with a smile. "Are you a citizen too?"

"Touché! Touché!" Jones said with a hearty laugh. "Indeed I am."

"I'm also not Muslim, as your ads claim," continued Padma, exposing the elephant in the room, "though I'm not clear why it would matter if I were."

Jones chuckled. "I think we both understand the realities of the world in which we live."

Padma felt a sinking void in her chest. Yes, she fully understood the hate and ignorance that still pervaded America, despite her very best efforts to eradicate it through education and opportunity. She also understood those who were all too eager to exploit America's dark side and target the innocent for personal gain.

"To your question, Senator, Wild Industries has an interest in a government research facility at Groom Lake, Nevada. We believe it might be in the country's best interest if this particular facility was under private management."

The smile evaporated from Jones' face. Padma had caught him off guard.

"You're talkin' about Area 51," he said.

"A portion of it, yes," she responded.

"That's a mighty big ask," said Jones.

"If it were a small ask, there would be no need for you and me to talk, would there?" Padma replied, smiling.

Jones paused for a moment, then raised his hands from his armrests and pressed his fingertips together. "You know, funny thing about the American people—they have a very low tolerance for tyranny."

"As well they should," affirmed Padma.

"America is a democracy, not an empire," said Jones. "We don't take our orders from mystery men no one has ever laid eyes on… or their exotic servants."

"Actually, Senator, America is a republic," corrected Padma, "and this particular 'exotic servant' wishes to ensure that the American people are well represented."

"I am indeed sorry if I offended you," said Jones with a big grin, noting that his epithet had scored its mark.

"Senator," Padma said, leaning forward, "how could someone like you possibly offend someone like me?"

The senator laughed. He took another gulp from his iced tea and set it back in the puddle on Padma's desk. He stood and extended his hand to Padma. Padma stood and shook his hand. It was clammy and wet from the tea glass.

"Thank you for your time," said Jones with a broad smile. "This has been…illuminating."

"Senator," Padma acknowledged as Jones turned, strode the length of the office to the door, and exited.

Padma stared at the empty tea glass in its pool of water on her desk. She wiped her hand on the pant leg of her suit.

Another side door in the office opened. Kyle Mason entered the room.

One World Trade Center
New York, NY
September 22, 2008
10:30 hours
Timeline 002

At 47, Kyle, aka "Anderson Wild," was in remarkable shape. Only touches of gray at the temples of his collar-length hair hinted at his real age. The contours of a superhero's body shaped the black long-sleeved V-neck shirt that descended into his jeans.

Padma saw the incensed look on his face.

"No, you can't kill him," Padma preempted.

"Would the world really miss him?" Kyle asked.

"Maybe not, but I'd like to think we still have some shreds of a moral compass left intact. He probably believes he's in the right."

"But he's not. We are."

"Everyone believes they own the high ground."

Kyle's concern for Padma drew a loving smile from her. She turned her chair to face Kyle and extended her hand.

"Love, come here."

Kyle walked over and sat on her desk, taking her hand.

"It kills me that I can't be at your side," he said.

Years earlier, on September 12, 2001, once the couple had finally emerged from Padma's bedroom, Padma suggested that they have dinner at a neighborhood favorite on the Upper West Side, an Indian restaurant at Columbus and 75th. At first, she didn't understand Kyle's pained expression in reaction to her simple suggestion. Then she realized...

Kyle can never be seen in public again.

In their timeline, Kyle Mason was dead. The news networks had relentlessly beamed his visage into every living room, etching the image of his handsome face onto virtually every brain in the modern world. Compounding the problem was Padma's plan to leverage Kyle's knowledge of the future for financial gain. The wealthier she became, the more attention she would draw. In some file cabinet, somewhere in New York City Hall, was a public record of her marriage to Kyle. It was only a matter of time before someone discovered it. The world's wealthiest woman, arguably also the world's most beautiful, would be shadowed by paparazzi day and night. Disguises were no good—she could never be seen with anyone who even remotely resembled Kyle. Padma's gaze dropped from Kyle's anguished face as she processed the epiphany. The man she loved came with an immense price tag.

Padma knew that the Kyle of 2008 was well aware of the burden he had placed on their union. One difference Padma recognized between the old Kyle and the new was the hefty bag of guilt this one hauled around. This Kyle's spirit was haunted by the death of one love, combined with the sacrifice of another, imprisoned by his anonymity. As heavy as Padma gauged that load to be, she sensed there was still more that Kyle had not shared.

"Everything I've done has been to protect you," Kyle continued. "The bunker, Dark Star, it's all been to protect you from harm. No one can hurt you here, but someone like Jones can run an ad and…"

Kyle paused. His face scrunched in pain and frustration. Padma gripped his hand tighter.

"I want to protect all of you. I want to protect your feelings."

"Love," she said, "it's not your job to protect my feelings."

Padma kissed Kyle's hand and sighed.

"I have a question for you," she said.

"What?"

"Kyle, are we having fun yet?"

Kyle looked down and sighed.

"We're the richest people on the planet. We run the country. We can do anything we want, except for everything that everyone else can do. We can't go to a restaurant together. We can't go to the movies. We can't go dancing. We can't hold hands in public. We can't go to Disneyland, for Chrissakes!"

"Disneyland?" asked Kyle.

"Yes—Disneyland! You know, Tomorrowland, Frontierland. If I have to choose between running the country and Space Mountain, I choose Space Mountain in a heartbeat."

Kyle's expression went sad. "I choose Space Mountain too. All this time together, I never knew you liked Disneyland."

Padma smiled. "Listen to me—had someone given me the choice on 9/11 between living the rest of my life in a prison with you, or living in the sunlight without you, the choice would have been simple. It still is, love."

"We may still be able to have what we want," said Kyle.

"The Time Tunnel?" asked Padma.

Kyle nodded. "It's our only way out."

Mission Control
Time Tunnel Complex
Area 51, NV
October 13, 2008
10:00 hours
Timeline 002

General Aaron Craig watched CSPAN on the giant screen in the Time Tunnel's mission control center with his mission director, Gus Ferrer. The gavel had fallen on the US Senate's vote on House Resolution 7081, the Strategic Research and Development Act. The vote was 99 to 1 in favor. The sole dissenter was Jonah Jones from Texas. Having cleared both houses by overwhelming margins, the measure was on its way to the president's desk for signature.

The general shook his head in disbelief.

"General, I am sorry," said Gus. "I'm speechless. This is truly incredible."

"In what universe does America's most secret military research facility get handed over to a private company?" asked the general.

"This one, apparently," answered Gus, shaking his head.

H.R. 7081 handed the keys to the Time Tunnel over to Anderson Wild and Padma Mahajan.

"How long until the transition?" asked Gus.

"They fast-tracked this sucker—my guess is a week, maybe," said the general.

The general looked at the huge ultra-high-resolution mission control screen. "Why didn't we ever use this thing to watch football?"

Gus laughed. "We still could."

"Dammit!" said the general. "I sure wanted to take the tunnel for a spin."

Even the vessel of the general's steel-belted discipline could not contain his crushing disappointment. The Time Tunnel was his crowning achievement. He had worked for a decade to wrest control of the complex from General Patterson, then to transform it and bring the Time Tunnel online. It was now fully operational. The only question was how to use it. The history team had not produced any obvious inflection points in time to fix. In 2008, America was a juggernaut—it was at peace with the world, and its economy was at full throttle. Though the general would not be able to forgive what Anderson Wild and Padma Mahajan had done to him this day, he could not deny that America's emperor and empress had made some very smart moves. America's shiny new energy, communications, and logistical infrastructure was sparking a third industrial revolution, leaving other world economies in the dust. Unemployment was low, and test scores were up. Americans were happy and adoring of their unofficial empress. Many advocated simply legitimizing the empire—sweeping away America's wasteful and corrupt branches of government.

"What do they want with the Time Tunnel?" asked the general.

"They can't know what's really down here—no one on the outside does."

"Maybe a leak?" speculated Gus.

The general shook his head. "No one knows. Even the president's knowledge is limited. He knows the Grays and their craft are here, but not much else. He doesn't know they're from the future, he doesn't know their craft is a time machine, and he sure as hell doesn't know we've built a damn time tunnel down here. Unless… wait a minute."

"What is it?" asked Gus.

"Maybe they know exactly what's down here."

"I don't understand."

"What if we've already used the Time Tunnel?"

Gus' face went white. "Anderson Wild?"

The general nodded. "You think he and Padma Mahajan became trillionaires just because they're smart? What do we know about Anderson Wild?"

"The same thing that everyone else knows—nothing," said Gus.

The general picked up a phone from one of the mission control consoles. "Page Roger Summit and Aysha Voong. Have them come to mission control on the double."

Minutes later, mission control's vault door opened, and Roger and Aysha entered. Before either could say a word, the general began.

"When does Anderson Wild show up in history?" he asked.

"That's a question that gets asked a lot and does not have a high-precision answer," said Roger, stroking his salt-and-pepper beard.

"The earliest document we can find on him is from January 2002. That's when official documents begin to appear."

"Fake documents?"

"They must be," said Roger. "Whoever he is, he didn't just change his name—there is no one prior to 2002 to connect him to. He appears out of nowhere."

"Or no-*when*," the general said.

"General?" Roger asked, confused.

"Padma Mahajan was married to Kyle Mason for 48 hours. He dies on American 11 preventing a terrorist attack on the World Trade Center. Other terrorists in Virginia, New Jersey, and Boston are found dead in their hotel rooms the same day—coincidence?"

"There are no coincidences," said Gus.

"What about the notes at the crime scenes?"

Roger and Aysha sat down at their terminals at the history hive, under the rose-colored TVA light cube. In seconds they punched up the assassins' notes on the big screen. The note cards were classified and had not been released to the public. They all referenced the President's Daily Briefing, or PDB, of August 6, 2001, prepared for President Bush by the CIA. The PDB warned of a terrorist attack by Osama Bin Laden. The note cards referenced other planes to be hijacked, as well as their targets. The cards were all handwritten by the same hand.

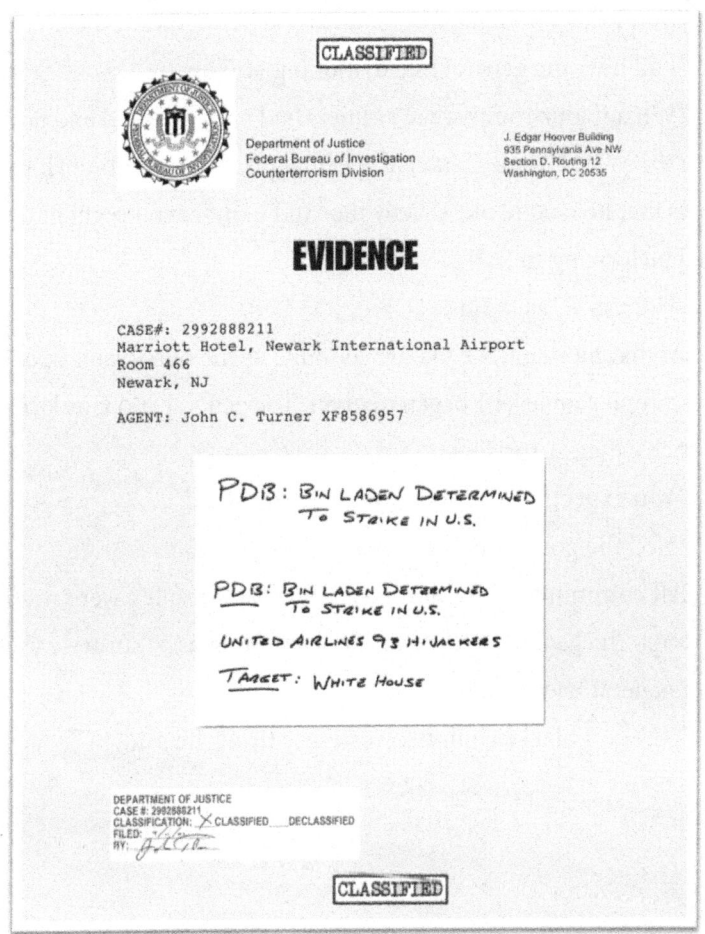

"Why was Kyle Mason on that plane?" asked the general.

"No one knows," said Roger. "There was never an explanation."

"Why does a Delta Force major who's honeymooning in New York end up on a flight from Boston to Los Angeles? And it just happens to be the one flight that gets hijacked by terrorists?"

"Again, no coincidences," said Gus.

"But, I don't understand," said Roger. "Kyle Mason died."

"Did he?" the general asked, looking at Gus.

"What if four commercial airliners had been hijacked and flown into the World Trade Center, the Pentagon, and the White House? Does that not sound like exactly the kind of inflection point in time we'd be looking to fix?"

"Holy shit!" said Gus.

At that moment, the klaxon sounded as the outer vault door to the complex on level 1 began to open. The general and Gus looked at each other, surprised.

"You expecting visitors, general?" Gus asked.

"No," the general replied coldly.

All communications and visits into the complex were routed through the general. There was no such thing as a "surprise visit." The general had been blindsided.

"The son of a bitch didn't waste any time," he said.

Mission Control
Time Tunnel Complex
Area 51, NV
October 13, 2008
10:17 hours
Timeline 002

A woman's voice came over the PA system. "Attention, General Craig and senior staff, please come to the main entrance on level 1 immediately. Repeat, General Craig and senior staff, please come to the main entrance on level 1 immediately. Please acknowledge."

"God damned son of a bitch!" exclaimed General Craig.

"Do we have options?" asked Gus.

"None that I can see, unless we want to take the tunnel out of time," replied General Craig.

"There's not enough time to fire it up," said Gus. "It takes two hours from a cold start."

"Attention, General Craig and senior staff, please come to the main entrance on level 1 immediately. Repeat, General Craig and senior staff, please come to the main entrance on level 1 immediately. Please acknowledge," repeated the voice on the PA.

"I think that's it," said General Craig. "Either we come out peacefully or they'll drag us out."

General Craig picked up a phone on one of the consoles "Craig here. On my way."

"OK, let's go," he said.

On the elevator ride to level 1, the general said to the team, "Don't repeat what we've discussed here. I think your lives may depend on it."

The team nodded.

The elevator doors opened on level 1 onto the enormous cream-colored mezzanine that circled the giant atrium. The general saw that the rest of his senior staff was assembled outside the main vault door. The vault door was open. Two dozen armed soldiers in desert fatigues stood near the staff. An officer, a general, stood with the soldiers.

They came prepared, the general thought.

Lara Meredith, wearing her signature lab coat, gripped the handles of Strangelove's wheelchair. John Kaomea, looking confused, pushed his glasses onto his nose with one finger, and held onto his laptop computer with the other hand. His second in command, Zhang Li, stood next to him, her poker face intact. Two of the soldiers appeared to be guarding Annika Wise. She was dressed in camo pants and military boots, with her arms folded over a black tank top. Her trademark scowl was on display. Annika's guards eyed her closely—the general surmised that she had already had a dust up with the intruders.

Several of the soldiers peered over the railing at the giant atrium and park below, marveling at the fantastic underground city. The general standing with them did an effective job of masking his stunned amazement. General Craig recognized the three-star general as James Patterson, the man from whom he wrested control of the complex in 2002. The last time General Patterson had seen the complex, it was little more than an underground concrete bunker, a fraction of the size of the 2008 Time Tunnel, with none of its present creature comforts.

General Patterson had not taken his ousting well. Prior to General Craig's arrival, he had been busy weaponizing the Grays' antimatter reactor with the giddy excitement of a schoolboy playing with cherry bombs. He envisioned the world's most gargantuan explosions that would make hydrogen bombs puny by comparison. He fantasized vaporizing entire rogue nations with a single device. He'd had difficulty containing his excitement, which sometimes breached his rigid, square-jawed exterior.

General Craig had crushed Patterson's dreams of big blow-ups. Patterson's grudge had festered over the years. Now, another of Patterson's fantasies, delivering a brutal payback to General Craig, was becoming reality.

General Craig considered General Patterson a dim-witted functionary of the highest order, someone whose vision of the battlefield was restricted to three dimensions and a race for the biggest bomb. General Craig grasped the enormous potential of adding a fourth dimension—time—to the battle theater, making conventional weapons completely irrelevant.

"General," said General Patterson. He did not extend his hand. He observed General Craig's informal khaki pants and polo shirt dress. "Casual Friday?"

"I've got four stars in my pocket," General Craig replied. "That's about as formal as I need to be."

General Patterson smiled, ignoring the dig at his subordinate rank. "I see you've made some renovations in my absence."

"A little paint. A few flowers," replied General Craig.

General Patterson smiled curtly, then pulled a folded piece of paper out of his hip pocket, unfolded it, and began to read aloud.

"General Craig, it is my duty to inform you that, per the articles of the Strategic Research and Development Act, management of this facility is now under civilian control," said General Patterson in an unnecessarily loud and officious voice. "You stand relieved of your command and will exit the premises immediately. The following members of your former senior staff will also exit the premises at this time: Colonel Annika Wise, Gus Ferrer, and John Kaomea."

The general nodded. "I'll collect my things."

"That won't be necessary, General," said General Patterson. "Your personal effects will be shipped to you."

General Craig was stunned by the complete absence of decorum. It was one thing to be relieved of command—it was another thing entirely for a four-star general to be kicked out of his house, with his belongings tossed out on the front lawn. He hid his indignation behind an incredulous smile.

Paybacks are tough, he thought, looking directly at General Patterson.

General Craig turned to the staff members he was leaving behind.

"Well, it looks like this is goodbye. It has been a rare privilege working with you," said the general. "Good luck to you all."

The general shook hands with Roger, Aysha, and Strangelove. Their expressions were shocked. Lara hugged him. She felt his big warm hands on her back. She also felt fear and sadness, as though her father was leaving.

"General, what in God's name is going on?" she whispered.

"A ghost has returned from the dead," he replied.

Lara looked at the general's face, perplexed. The general shook his head and turned to leave with the exiled members of his staff. He patted Annika on the arm, guiding her out.

"You already managed to get yourself in trouble?" he asked.

"I'm pretty sure I'm not the one who's in trouble," Annika replied. "Are you going to explain this to me?"

"I don't know any more than you do," the general replied.

"Right," said Annika. As she turned to leave, one of the soldiers poked her in the back with the barrel of his assault rifle.

"Let's go, sweet cheeks," the soldier said.

Annika wheeled in the blink of an eye, snatching the rifle out of the soldier's hands, flipping it, and pointing it directly at his heart.

"That's *Colonel* Sweet Cheeks to you, Corporal, and how'd you like to know what it's like to breathe through your rectum?" snapped Annika.

"No ma'am, I don't want to know what that's like," replied the soldier, shaken. He had never seen anyone move so fast before.

Annika pointed the rifle at the other soldiers. She had caught them all flatfooted, with their weapons lowered. General Patterson looked uneasy.

"Anyone else want some of this?" she asked.

Annika tossed the rifle back to the soldier, turned, and strolled out the great vault door to the elevator platform. The general was at her side.

"Someday that temper of yours is going to get the best of you, Colonel Wise," said the general, enjoying the moment.

"That day is not today," replied Annika.

One hundred feet above the Time Tunnel complex, Kyle and Padma waited in their black armored SUV in the ground level hangar. Their ride was one in a phalanx of SUVs and armored personnel carriers parked both in and outside the hangar. The couple had arrived with 200 Special Forces soldiers from their Dark Star subsidiary.

Red strobe lights fired in the hangar, signaling the ascension of the hangar elevator. Kyle and Padma watched as the enormous platform reached the surface, with General Craig, Annika, and the rest of the Time Tunnel outcasts, guarded by General Patterson's armed squad.

As the group stepped off the elevator platform, Padma watched Annika closely. Annika looked directly at Padma's SUV—straight into Padma's eyes, as though she could see through the SUV's blackened windows.

Mission Control
Time Tunnel Complex
Area 51, NV
October 13, 2008
14:00 hours
Timeline 002

The senior staff was assembled around the big conference table at the base of the mission control amphitheater, in front of the giant screen. A new member of the team, mission director Colin James, had assembled the team after General Patterson and the soldiers left. The other members of the senior staff looked at Colin, waiting for an explanation for the seismic change to their subterranean world.

Colin was a slight man with fair skin, receding blond hair, and wire-rim glasses. He wore a permanent smile on his face, no matter how challenging the circumstances. Colin had come to the Wild family through one of the conglomerate's many acquisitions of defense and technology companies. Over the years at Wild, Padma had found Colin to be an outstanding manager—somehow able to turn complex projects in on time and under budget without burning out his staff.

"We are waiting for a couple more people to join us," Colin said.

The mission control vault door opened, and two people entered—a man and a woman. As they descended the steps to the conference table, the original Time Tunnel staff members gasped. It was Padma Mahajan, the empress of America, accompanied by her husband, Major Kyle Mason, the dead hero of American 11. Padma wore her trademark black pant suit with a crimson Nehru collar blouse. Kyle wore jeans, boots, and a white dress shirt. They descended the mission control amphitheater steps and took their seats at the center of the table.

That the world's most secretive couple could emerge from the shadows in the Time Tunnel complex was owed to the vice grip controls the general had established on security and communications. Kyle knew the general had made sure that all communication and access to the complex was controlled by a single person. Now that Kyle held the keys to the Time Tunnel, no word of his existence would leave the underground city.

"Thank you for joining us," began Padma. "I gather from your expressions that introductions are not necessary?"

The stupefied staff members slowly shook their heads.

"Good, then let's begin," Padma said. "I realize some explanation is in order. I am going to let my husband start us off."

It was the first time in over seven years that Padma had referred to Kyle as her "husband" to others while he was in her presence. Though their circumstances were deadly serious, she could not contain a sparkling smile as the words left her lips. She turned to Kyle. His smile mirrored his wife's.

"Since the Time Tunnel became operational a few months ago,

Roger and Aysha's history team have been trying to identify a key inflection point in time to target an operation," Kyle began.

Roger and Aysha glanced at each other, noting Kyle's apparent familiarity. He spoke as though he knew them well.

"The reason you have not been successful is because the inflection point you're looking for has already been corrected," Kyle said.

The original staff members rocked back in their chairs, stunned.

"You know me from the American 11 story," Kyle said. "However, I am not that Kyle Mason. The Kyle Mason from your time died on American 11 on September 11, 2001. As you know, 14 Middle Eastern men were found dead in various hotel rooms in Boston, New Jersey, and Virginia that same day. Notes were found in their rooms suggesting that American 11 was not an isolated incident, but part of a wider conspiracy to destroy the World Trade Center towers, the Pentagon, and the White House. Those men were killed by me and the Kyle Mason of your time.

"In my timeline, the terrorists succeeded in destroying the World Trade Center towers and part of the Pentagon. The attack fundamentally altered this country's trajectory. In effect, it punctuated the beginning of the decline of the American empire.

"We refer to the terrorist attack as '9/11.'"

The faces of the other staff members were ashen. They struggled to grasp two bombshells—that time had already been changed, and that the Twin Towers had been destroyed. Both seemed beyond comprehension.

Lara Meredith managed to speak first. "You didn't return to your time."

"No," Kyle replied. "In my timeline, my wife died when the World Trade Center's North Tower collapsed."

Kyle looked at Padma. "The North Tower was the American 11 hijackers' target. When I knew the Kyle from your time was dead, I chose to stay and reunite with my wife."

The staff sat in stunned silence.

Suddenly, Strangelove slapped the conference table with both hands, startling the others.

"It works!" he exclaimed in German-tinted English. "This is fantastic!"

"You are unbelievable," said Lara, shooting Strangelove a sharp look.

"What? It works—isn't that marvelous?" replied Strangelove, genuinely confused by Lara's reaction.

"We're all trying to absorb the fact that this AWOL soldier from the future, whose doppelganger is dead, has changed time, reunited with his dead wife, become a trillionaire and de facto emperor, and, by the way, made us all artifacts of a new timeline," Lara said. "All you can think about is that your toy actually works."

"Well, I think it is a little more than a toy," Strangelove said, looking down, embarrassed and disappointed that no one else shared his elation.

"Sweetheart, I'm saying it's a lot to take in. We need a minute, OK?"

"OK, OK, I get it," Strangelove said. "It just seems like a really great thing, that's all."

"It's a great thing, honey," Lara said, patting his sleeve. "You did good. Or, at least, the other Strangelove did."

"So, why are you here?" asked Roger.

"The other Time Tunnel is fully operational," replied Kyle. "They may choose to leave this timeline alone—or not. Depending on the choices they make, this timeline and everyone in it could cease to exist and be replaced with a new timeline, just as it was before. Everything could be erased and started over at the inflection point they choose."

"We no longer live in ignorant bliss," said Roger. "You've shown us our sword of Damocles."

"Which brings me to the reason I'm here," said Kyle. "I'm here to disable the other Time Tunnel so this timeline can endure."

"You mean, so *you* can endure," said Lara.

"I mean so *we* can endure," Kyle replied, taking his wife's hand. "Fortunately, the byproduct of our selfishness is that it potentially saves the living realities of nearly seven billion people in this timeline."

Zhang Li spoke, a rare event that turned all heads at the table, "The other Time Tunnel is in a distinct parallel universe," she said. "We have no way to go there."

Strangelove's white brows furrowed as he considered the problem. "Major Mason…"

"Actually, it's colonel now, but please call me 'Kyle,'" interrupted Kyle.

"Congratulations," said Strangelove. "Do you happen to have…"

"This?" Kyle said, holding up his temporal transponder.

"Ah, yes," said Strangelove.

Kyle slid the metal box across the table to Strangelove. Strangelove picked it up, thrilled to be holding an artifact from another universe and time.

"It might be possible to triangulate the other universe with this," said Strangelove, his mind already immersed in the challenge.

"Wait a minute!" said Lara. "Before we boldly go to universes where no one has gone before, I think we need to reality check this. These people land here, kick out the general, who is even more of a father to me than my bio father was, then we're told we need to invade another universe. Is this particular crazy thing something we should really be doing?"

"The implications of another adjustment to this timeline by the other Time Tunnel are real," said Roger. "We've already been 'reset' once by that tunnel. We have no awareness of it, because our experiences changed. We aren't the people we were. It would be one thing if we didn't know about what could happen, but we do. We know the tsunami might come."

"Why did you kick them out? asked Lara, referring to the general, Annika Wise, and John Kaomea.

"The general was my mentor," Kyle continued. "He gave me my silver star. But the bottom line is that I disobeyed the other general's orders so I could be with my wife. There was potential for conflict, and I couldn't risk confusion in the chain of command—particularly if something goes wrong."

"Travelling to another universe—what could possibly go wrong?" Lara snarked.

"If you were one of the two temponauts in your timeline, that means Annika was your partner," deduced Roger.

"Yes," answered Kyle.

"What happened to her?" asked Roger.

"She died during the jump," said Kyle. "Hence the reason why John is not with us."

The group went silent, reminded that time travel was not a risk-free venture.

Central Park
Time Tunnel Complex
Area 51, NV
October 13, 2008
21:15 hours
Timeline 002

Kyle and Padma walked in the great atrium park under a starlit sky. The stars and constellations of the northern hemisphere glimmered on the atrium's enormous faux skylight above the park. A sliver of waxing crescent moon accented the crystal-clear night sky.

Padma wore a simple cream-colored halter dress and pump sandals. Gold hoops glittered from her ears. For the occasion of their first dinner date in public, Kyle layered a black dress coat atop a white dress shirt and jeans. They held hands as they strolled the park's stone paths through the trees, illuminated by perfect replicas of the iron Henry Bacon lamps that lit the way in New York's Central Park. Padma enjoyed an ice cream cone Kyle had bought her from a park stand after dinner. She beamed with joy.

"We're holding hands in Central Park," Kyle said.

"I still can't believe it!" replied Padma giddily, kissing Kyle on the cheek. She wiped ice cream off the side of his face with her hand.

Earlier that evening, the couple had dined on Italian at one of the Time Tunnel's restaurants. They held hands across the table, covered by a classic red and white-checkered tablecloth. They scarcely touched their food. Instead, they gazed into each other's blissful eyes as the light and shadows of a wax-drenched Chianti bottle candle moved across their faces.

The denizens of the Time Tunnel complex tried to avoid staring at the celebrity couple on their date. Ironically, after years of living in the shadows, Kyle and Padma relished the attention. Those that stole glances could plainly see that the couple was head over heels in love. The warmth of their adoration washed over the complex, melting the cold edge of General Craig's abrupt departure.

"I can't stop smiling," she said. "I'm *so* happy!"

Kyle's smile mirrored Padma's. His joy at being with Padma in public was multiplied by witnessing her happiness.

Kyle and Padma stopped at the park waterfall. Kyle pointed at a constellation in the artificial night sky, anchored by stars arranged in a square.

"That's Pegasus," Kyle said. "Do you know how he got there?"

"I do not know," replied Padma.

"Pegasus was involved in many heroic adventures in ancient times. The most famous was when Bellerophon rode Pegasus into battle against the dreaded Chimera, a monster that breathed fire. Bellerophon slayed the Chimera with the help of his trusty winged steed.

"Zeus rewarded Pegasus for his many heroic deeds by making him a constella—"

Padma interrupted Kyle, grabbing his face with both hands and planting a warm kiss.

"That's fascinating," Padma said between kisses.

"I wasn't finished—" said Kyle.

Padma kissed him again.

"Pegasus can wait," he said.

Padma looked around to see if anyone else was within eyeshot at the large waterfall-fed pond. She peeled off her dress, kicked off her shoes, then dove off the rock embankment into the pond. After a few moments, she surfaced, running her hands back along her long black hair.

"The water's perfect!" she said.

Kyle quickly shed his clothes and joined her. They held each other in the water. Kyle nodded to a rock cave behind the waterfall. They felt the pounding waterfall as they swam beneath the surface into the hidden cave. Inside the cave, they found rock footing. The waterfall roared in the cave opening. Moonlight scattered through the water onto their faces and exposed shoulders. Padma wrapped her arms around Kyle's neck and her legs around his waist. He held her buttocks, pulling her close. As they rose and fell in the water, echoes of the lapping waves ricocheted off the cave walls. Padma dug her nails into Kyle's back. The pain shot through Kyle's body, releasing his animal id. He grabbed Padma's long hair in one hand, wrapping it around his fist at the base of her neck, pulling her head back. Padma clenched her teeth, then released a long, satisfied sigh.

She cradled his head with her hand. He felt her pounding heart and the rise and fall of her chest. Her breath was warm against his cheek as she pressed her wet face against his. When she finally spoke, she whispered one word.

"Perfect."

• • •

Later that evening, Kyle and Padma lay in bed in their Time Tunnel townhouse apartment. Padma rested her head on Kyle's chest. A night view and sounds of the South Pacific Ocean rushing gently against the pylons of a Moorea overwater bungalow played on the wall screen next to the bed. The view was partially obscured by sheer white curtains waving gently in an artificial breeze.

"We live in Disneyland," Padma said. "We held hands and made love in Central Park, and now we're sleeping in Disneyland."

"We just need Space Mountain and it will be perfect," Kyle replied.

Padma reached up and kissed Kyle.

"It's already perfect. It's beyond perfect," she said. "I'm happy here. I don't need to leave. Can we stay here?"

"I hope so," Kyle said. "We need to be prepared to go through with the plan, just in case."

Padma turned over and reached for a pack of American Spirits on the nightstand.

"There's no smoking in the Time Tunnel," Kyle said.

Padma shot him a glance and lit up. She sat up against the headboard, exhaling as she pulled the sheets over her breasts.

The image of Annika Wise's cold stare in the hangar flashed through Padma's mind.

"You've never talked about Annika Wise," she said.

Kyle felt his abdomen tighten.

"You two weren't just partners," she finessed.

"No," Kyle answered, piercing the perfect evening. "You were dead. Her husband was dead. We didn't plan it. It wasn't love at first sight."

Padma stared ahead. She drew on her cigarette, taking in the revelation with the smoke. Since meeting Kyle, she had never been with another man. Words and feelings cycled within her. The words of her cosmopolitan mind reminded her wounded feelings that, technically, Kyle had not cheated—he was widowed when he met Annika. Her feelings simply hurt in reply.

"Do you love her?" asked Padma.

"That person is not the Annika I knew," he said, glancing avoiding the question.

"Do you love her?"

"I love the memory of a person who's dead. She's *dead!*" Kyle shouted. "Just like you were—*dead!*"

Kyle tossed off the sheets and got out of bed. Padma's questions had driven a lightning rod into his darkest place—his horror at hearing the news of Padma's death, his failed attempt to avenge her, his breakdown, the years of crippling depression that followed. Yes, he had loved Annika and mourned her loss, though he had never stopped loving his fallen bride.

Kyle picked his jeans off the floor and began stuffing his legs into them.

"I didn't cheat. I was never *anything* but completely, totally, unconditionally in love with you. You were *dead!* Even if our mission succeeded I wasn't going to be with you. I could bring you back to life, but I couldn't be with you.

"Don't you get it?" he shouted. "You were going to be with another Kyle! I was saving you for *him!*"

Kyle sat on the bed and began pulling on his boots. Padma got out of bed and moved to Kyle's side, sitting next to him. She put her hand on his back. She had never seen Kyle so agitated, on the ragged edge of unhinged.

"I trust that you love me," Padma said softly. "I trust you completely."

She placed her hands on his face, turning it to meet hers. "Don't you trust my love too? I just needed a minute," she said, smiling.

Kyle turned and embraced her. In an instant, Padma had released an enormous weight from Kyle's shoulders, sharing some, dismissing the balance. The dark burden rose to the ceiling with the smoke from her cigarette, burning on the nightstand.

"I'm so sorry," Kyle said. "I didn't want to hurt you." His anger had surprised and embarrassed him. Though exorcising his secret had exhausted him emotionally, he felt lighter, happier. Prior to his disclosure of his past with Annika, he had not believed it was possible for him to love Padma more. He was wrong. He held her tight.

"I don't think it's possible for you to hurt me, love," she said, holding his head.

United States Army Central (ARCENT)
Shaw Air Force Base, SC
October 22, 2008
09:00 hours
Timeline 002

General Craig sat at his desk in his office at Shaw Air Force Base. His hands were folded against a black leather blotter atop a shiny wood veneer desk with a reddish tint. A similar artificial wood product credenza flanked his office chair. Flags of the United States and the Third Army bookended the credenza. A small round table with four chairs completed the office ensemble.

The walls were white plastered sheet rock. A white drop ceiling with fluorescent light panels hung overhead.

The general wore standard-issue fatigues. Four stars gleamed from his lapel. He stared over his folded hands into space, clinically depressed, unable to fully comprehend or accept his new world.

General Craig had been given command of ARCENT, formerly the Third Army, as a consolation prize for losing Dreamland. Normally, command of Patton's army would be considered the achievement of a lifetime. To General Craig, it felt as though he had been tossed off Mount Olympus and landed squarely in Sumter, South Carolina.

There was a knock at the door.

"Come in," said General Craig.

A young woman, a corporal in fatigues, opened the door.

"General, there is someone here to see you," the woman said.

"Do they have an appointment?"

"No sir," replied the corporal.

"Then they don't have an appointment," replied the general. "By the way, do I know your name?"

"My name is Corporal Jennifer Ryan, sir," replied the corporal. "I'm your secretary. I'm the person who sits at the desk in front of your office."

"Good to know. That will be all, Corporal," said the general.

"Yes sir…Sir, I think you may want to see the person who is waiting to see you," Jennifer persisted.

"Why do you think that?" asked the general, glaring at the young corporal with sullen eyes.

"He's a senator, sir," she replied.

The general's glare didn't budge. The very last thing he wanted was a futile conversation about the state of readiness of the world's most powerful army at a time when said army had nothing to do but drill and polish weapons. The country's energy policies had completely transformed its military priorities. Now energy independent, the US no longer imported oil from the Middle East. As a result, the country's strategic interests in that part of the world had largely vanished. America was far less preoccupied with which despot, mullah, or fanatic ran which particular oil-rich Arab state.

Jennifer shifted uncomfortably under the general's withering stare. After an awkward moment, the general capitulated.

"Very well," he sighed. "Send him in."

The general felt as though the gravity had been turned up in his office as he rose unenthusiastically from his desk. At the moment he reached apogee, Senator Jonah Jones bounded through the office door. His flab-filled white dress shirt lapped over the waistline of his brown suit pants like a soufflé. Dark brown cowboy boots thumped the floor. A fat blue tie with a sloppy knot was the coda to the high-speed fashion wreck.

The senator laughed as he entered the general's office and extended his hand.

"My apologies, Senator," said the general as he shook Jones' hand. "Somehow your appointment did not make it onto my calendar."

"The apology is mine, General—I'm ambushing you with a surprise visit," shouted Jones with a projectile guffaw. He shook the general's hand exuberantly.

The general gestured to a chair in front of his desk, then returned to his own.

"To what do I owe this unexpected pleasure?" asked the general.

"Well, General, may I first offer my heartfelt congratulations on your appointment to commander of ARCENT," Jones said. "It is quite an honor, and I can't imagine anyone better qualified."

"Thank you, Senator," deadpanned the general. "I appreciate that."

"I want you to know that my lone vote against the Strategic Research and Development Act had nothing to do with my estimation of your qualification to lead the Third Army," Jones said.

"Thank you," the general said, wishing Jones would get to the point and get out of his office.

"I hear the emperor and empress have taken up residence in Area 51," Jones said.

"That is my understanding as well."

"I am burning with curiosity about what on Earth those two wanted with that facility. Can you shed any light on that?"

"Even if I could, you know I wouldn't be able to share that with you," replied the general.

"I know, I know—you can't blame a guy for trying," giggled Jones.

The general attempted a courtesy grimace in response.

"I have to tell you though, I just shudder at the thought of the two richest and most powerful people on earth with their hands on the levers of some of our military's most classified research projects," Jones said.

You have no idea, thought the general.

"I share your concern," he said.

"You see, General, I believe the power of the people has been usurped by these two individuals," said Jones. "I believe this government is now a democracy in name only. As such, I believe Anderson Wild and Padma Mahajan have committed crimes against the constitution and need to be held accountable."

"I don't disagree with your assessment," said the general, "though I don't know what this has to do with me."

"General," Jones said, leaning forward, "you now command the world's largest army."

The general's eyes went wide in disbelief. "Senator, I say this with all due respect: You must be insane."

"What I am suggesting is that we take back our country from these dictators and restore the freedom and liberty bequeathed to us by our founding fathers," explained Jones.

"Restore democracy through a coup d'état," the general replied.

"Only temporarily," said Jones. "As you know, there is precedent for imposing martial law in these United States. Lincoln suspended habeas corpus in 1861, and Congress did it again in 1863."

"Lincoln was president," the general said. "What you are suggesting is treason."

"Is it, General?" Jones asked. "Is it treason to restore democracy that has been taken from us by these despots? There are many in Congress who share my view."

"Look, Senator, may I speak frankly?"

"Well, since we're speaking treason, we might as well speak frankly."

"Even if your argument had an ounce of merit, I think we both know you have no interest in restoring democracy. You see an opportunity to exploit, and you're going for it. Maybe you think that because I run the Third Army and was kicked to the curb from my former command, the stars might be aligning in your favor.

"Honestly, Senator," the general continued, looking him dead in the eye, "do you think I earned four stars for my flag by disobeying the chain of command? Do you think that I'd consider for one cold minute the possibility of overthrowing my own government?"

"You could have anything you want," Jones said.

"You have nothing to offer that I want—certainly nothing that would make me betray my country."

"What if you could get Dreamland back?" said Jones.

The general rocked back in his chair.

Jones had his attention.

Physics Lab
Time Tunnel Complex
Area 51, NV
October 22, 2008
10:00 hours
Timeline 002

Kyle walked along the wide, gently curving hallway on the blue-colored level 2. He reached a large steel door marked "Physics Lab." He held his access card up to the card reader, and the door slid open.

The lab was huge—over 100,000 square feet, with computer racks with flashing LED lights, conference tables with white boards, and large interactive displays. Lab stations with exotic-looking apparatus were scattered about. Cable trays were suspended from the ceiling, packed with power and telecommunication cables that dangled into the lab stations via ribbed black plastic conduit pipes. Arcane mathematical formulas filled white boards. Scientists in lab coats sat at computer terminals and gathered around science stations.

Kyle heard banging on a glass window. He turned and saw Strangelove rapping on the glass wall of a conference room, gesturing him to enter. Parked around a conference table were

Strangelove and Zhang, as well as two people Kyle had not met.

"Good morning everyone," Kyle said as he entered the room.

"Good morning Colonel," replied Strangelove. "Colonel Mason, you already know Dr. Li. Let me introduce two of my colleagues—Dr. William Min and Dr. Kristin Ahn. They have been assisting Dr. Li and me in this very interesting problem you have brought to us. Shall we begin?"

"Yes."

"To restate the problem," Strangelove began, "it is in two parts. One, is it possible to locate the original Time Tunnel. And if so, two, is it possible to go there and safely return to our own."

"Dr. Min, would you mind displaying our first graphic?"

Dr. Min clicked a button on a remote on the table. An image of two universe planes appeared. Squiggly lines joined them.

"As we know," continued Strangelove, "the theory of multiple universes was just that—a theory—until we encountered our Gray friends and their time machine. Up to that time, there were multiple theories that contemplated the possibility of multiverses.

"One of those was the so-called M-theory, which unified all

superstring theories. That theory proposed that our universe is a three-dimensional 'brane' that exists with many others on a higher-dimensional brane or 'bulk.' In that model, particles are bound to their respective branes except for gravity. This M-theory model has been proven by the Grays.

"The temporal transponder you brought with you uses gravitons to interact between universes. Gravitons, which carry the force of gravity, are not bound to a particular universe. Because gravitons can move freely between universes, they are an obvious choice to use for inter-universal communication or telemetry. The challenge, obviously, is getting the gravitons to do what you want them to do. Because they are not bound to a particular universe, they have a nasty habit of disappearing from the universe at inopportune times. Managing gravitons was one of the many breakthroughs our Gray friends managed to achieve.

"In effect, the temporal transponder is a graviton beacon, sending gravitons back to its universe of origin to give the other Time Tunnel the transponder coordinates. From that point, the tunnel is reactivated, and a new space-time wormhole is created to retrieve the traveler.

"One of the challenges associated with this problem was locating the other universe without alerting the other Time Tunnel. It would have been comparatively easy to follow the graviton breadcrumb trail to the other universe, though that would have been detected. Ultimately, we were able to devise a way to shield the gravitons from escaping our universe, while still providing sufficient information regarding their destination. I am pleased to report that we have succeeded in locating the other Time Tunnel."

"Excellent!" said Kyle. "Where is it?"

Strangelove and his colleagues exchanged awkward looks in reaction to Kyle's question, surprised that the answer was not as intuitively obvious to him as it was to them.

"The universe is here," Strangelove replied.

Kyle appeared confused.

"All of the universes occupy the same physical space," explained Strangelove. "As we speak, similar conversations are happening around this same conference room table."

Strangelove knocked on the table for effect.

"In other universes, different people are assembled around the table. In others still, the Time Tunnel doesn't exist. The possibilities are infinite, though all the possibilities exist in the same place."

Kyle's expression was blank as he realized he was sinking in the deep end of the science pool.

"Would you like an explanation of how we manipulate the gravitons?" asked Strangelove.

"Would I understand it?" replied Kyle.

"I don't believe so, no."

"Let's move on, then."

"As for the second part of the question, as we can retrieve people from another universe, we can also reverse the process and send them there as well."

"We are limited to two travelers at a time?" asked Kyle.

"Yes, the tunnel's capacity is currently two people, with a very limited quantity of baggage, though we can send multiple groups of two."

"That's a problem," Kyle said. "Two people beaming inside the complex will not be sufficient to overcome resistance if their security force puts up a fight."

The group went quiet, pondering the problem.

"Does the temporal bubble extend beyond the physical walls of the complex?" asked Kyle.

"Yes. The temporal bubble is a sphere. The complex is a cylinder. If you imagine a cylinder within a sphere, you can get a sense of where there is more and less space outside the complex."

"How much space is there outside the main vault door?"

Strangelove turned to Dr. Ahn, who began typing on her laptop computer. She punched up an image that showed the Time Tunnel complex within the sphere of the temporal bubble. The edge of the bubble sliced through the elevator shaft.

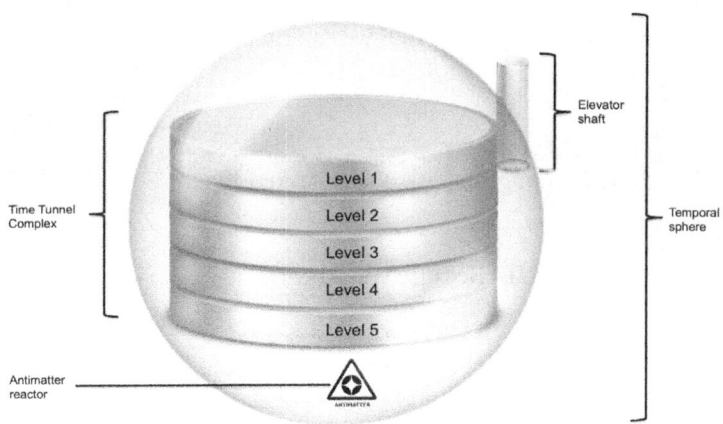

"Not much," she said. "The vault door is near the top of the cylinder and the edge of the bubble. I estimate about 15 meters."

"Enough to encompass part of the main elevator?" Kyle asked.

"Yes."

"So, conceivably, we could assemble a team at the elevator platform, sending them two at a time, then enter at once through the vault door."

"Yes, that could work," said Dr. Ahn, "though it would require pinpoint accuracy. A few meters off and you would end up nowhere—literally. From what I understand, you were miles off target in your first jump."

"We have identified and corrected the errors responsible for the problems with Colonel Mason's previous jump," said Zhang, "including the time-space anomalies, as well as the proximate cause of Colonel Wise's death. In the process, we have boosted the output of the Time Tunnel by 33 percent—sufficient to transport weapons or light equipment with each team."

"How confident are you that we can hit this target accurately?" Kyle asked Zhang.

"Very."

"Confident enough to risk a life?" asked Kyle.

"Yes."

"Good," Kyle said. "Because you'll be joining us on this mission."

Time Tunnel Complex
Time Tunnel Chamber
Area 51, NV
November 7, 2008
08:55 hours
Timeline 002

A team of 10 Dark Star commandoes was assembled in the anteroom outside the Time Tunnel chamber. They wore black fatigues and helmets, with utility vests containing ammunition, stun grenades, and their temporal transponders. Their HK416 assault rifles were slung at their sides. Each soldier also packed a compact infrared spotlight, to be used to blind surveillance video cameras. As she had projected, Zhang Li had boosted the output of the temporal reactor sufficiently to enable the troops to bring weapons and gear on the mission.

Zhang waited with the commandoes for Kyle to join them. The petite bookish engineer looked distinctively out of place next to the black-clad Velcro supermen standing next to her. Unlike the soldiers, she wore her regular civilian attire—blue jeans, sneakers, and a long sleeve pullover shirt.

Zhang's purpose for joining the mission was to disable the Time Tunnel in timeline 001 once the commandoes had secured the facility. The details of her mission were tricky. She needed to sabotage the other Time Tunnel's ability to send people through time and space, while preserving the temporal bubble that kept its parallel universe inflated and its inhabitants alive.

In Kyle and Padma's townhouse, Kyle was finishing up in his dressing room.

In the bedroom, Padma called after him, "Honey, you're going to be late for your inter-universal Time Tunnel sabotage mission." She sat on their bed wearing jeans and a China-blue blouse.

Kyle emerged from the dressing room. She expected to see him in ninja-commando wear. She was instead surprised to see him wearing a very sharp black Hugo Boss suit with a black tee.

"Is this the executive commando look?" she asked.

"I'm feeling a little anxious about meeting the general again," he replied. "I guess I just wanted to look nice."

"Seriously? That's what you're nervous about?" Padma replied, incredulous. "I'm worried sick about whether or not you're going to come back to me alive, and all you can think about are your wardrobe choices. Need I remind you that the mortality rate with this Time Tunnel contraption is 50 percent?"

"We've talked about this, love," Kyle said. "The team has fixed the Time Tunnel. It's been battle tested. It's safer than riding in a cab in NYC."

"That's supposed to be comforting?" she asked. "What if someone takes a shot at you when you get to the other side?"

"As you insisted, the Dark Star guys are going in first," he said.

Kyle moved between Padma's legs. He reached for her face and kissed her.

"I'll be back before you know it," he said.

Padma clamped her legs around his.

"You'd better," she said.

Kyle smiled and turned to leave. Padma maintained her grip on his legs.

"I'm serious," she said.

Kyle put his hand on Padma's cheek. "So am I."

Padma released Kyle and watched him exit, remembering what happened the last time he left for a mission.

Mission Control
Time Tunnel Complex
Area 51, NV
November 7, 2008
09:00 hours
Timeline 002

Mission control was a beehive of activity as the team prepared for the first in its series of inter-universal jumps.

Colin stood above his mission director console on the center mezzanine of the mission control amphitheater. On one portion of mission control's big screen, he saw the first two commandoes enter the Time Tunnel's glass sphere. They were assisted by two technicians, who wore white clean-room overalls, hoods, and booties. The balance of the big screen was filled with system status readouts—statistics and graphs.

When the technicians exited the chamber, Colin began the countdown.

"All staff, time is T-minus five minutes. We are at final system check," said Colin. "Respond when called."

"Reactor," Colin said.

"Reactor go," replied an engineer. "Power at 30 percent. Go for throttle up."

"Temporal engine," said Colin.

"Temporal engine go," replied another engineer.

"Navigation."

"Temporal navigation go."

"Bio."

"Bio go."

"Transponder."

"Transponder go."

"All systems, all staff, punch your status buttons now," said Colin.

At that moment, the hundreds of people throughout the complex tied to the operation of the Time Tunnel pushed one of two buttons—green or red. A single red button would abort the jump. Gus watched the board for results.

System	Status
Reactor	Green
Temporal engine	Green
Navigation	Green
Bio	Green
Transponder	Green

Percentage of respondents: 100%

Percentage green: 100%

Percentage red: 0%

"Throttle power to 60 percent," ordered Colin. "Retract Tunnel moorings."

Colin watched the live video feed of the Time Tunnel chamber on the giant screen. The cables supporting the donut ring detached and retracted into the ceiling. The platform that supported the sphere retracted into the floor. The ring and sphere, supported with magnetic repulsion, floated in space like a man-made Saturn.

Colin noticed the two commandoes glance at each other as the chamber floated away from its moorings.

Colin removed two lanyards from his neck. They held rectangular blue and red anodized keys. The keys both had hourglass cutouts. The red key was formerly the general's. Now Colin possessed both keys and could unilaterally initiate a Time Tunnel jump.

Colin inserted the keys into his panel and turned both simultaneously.

The status lamp next to the ARMED indicator turned from green to red. A red ARMED indicator flashed on all monitor displays. A klaxon alarm sounded. A large button on Colin's panel marked "COMMIT" flashed on.

"Reactor—throttle power to 100 percent," said Colin.

"Throttle to 100—Roger that," came the reply.

The command to throttle up threw the Time Tunnel's energy reactor into overdrive, annihilating matter and antimatter in equal parts, releasing monstrous energy.

Colin pressed the COMMIT button.

The giant monitor beamed a blinding white light from the video feed of the chamber, forcing the mission control staff to turn away. Moments later, the light faded, as system power levels dropped to zero. The monitor flickered back to life. The Time Tunnel chamber was empty. The first two commandoes were gone.

Two by two, the commandoes filed into the chamber and

disappeared in a blinding flash. Kyle and Zhang were the last to enter the chamber.

The vault door to mission control opened, and Padma entered, descending the steps to Colin's mezzanine level. She stood next to him, watching the giant display with great concern as her man stepped into the chamber with Zhang.

"It's going to be all right," said Colin.

Padma nodded bravely. "I'm sure you're right."

Inside the chamber, Kyle turned to Zhang. Zhang's face betrayed no more emotion than if she were eating a day-old ham sandwich. Taking a trip to another universe through the Time Tunnel appeared to be simply one more task to check off her to-do list.

"Any last words?" asked Kyle.

The normally mute Zhang replied with a Chinese proverb.

"It is better to live as a dog in an era of peace than a man in times of war."

The blinding light crescendoed, then faded. Kyle and Zhang were gone.

Main Vault Door Elevator Platform
Time Tunnel Complex
Area 51, NV
October 27, 2008
08:15 hours
Timeline 001

The blinding white light faded. Kyle and Zhang saw the 10 commandoes facing them on the yellow circle that marked the Time Tunnel's freight elevator pad. The exterior walls of the elevator shaft were painted red. "Level 1" was painted against the red walls in giant white letters. Recessed LED lighting illuminated the room. Behind the commandoes was the enormous steel vault door to the complex, approximately 20 feet by 20 feet, with two giant hinges on the left. An area of the floor in front of the door, also 20 feet by 20 feet, was painted with yellow and black hazard stripes, denoting the swing area of the door. A series of blue strobe lights hugged the door's perimeter.

Kyle looked at Zhang. Disoriented, she began to take a step backward. Kyle grabbed her arm as the commandoes pointed and shouted for him to stop her.

"Listen to me," Kyle said. "Don't turn around. Take three steps forward with me."

As instructed, Zhang walked forward with Kyle toward the commandoes and the vault door.

Zhang saw the relief in the commandoes' faces as they approached.

"OK," Kyle said to Zhang. "Now you can turn around."

Zhang turned to see the edge of the freight elevator platform disappear into a darkness unlike any she had seen before. It was beyond black. What lay beyond the gentle curve of the Time Tunnel's tiny bubble universe was void of everything—the edge of forever. She gazed at dark space with awe. Something about its complete stillness seemed perfectly attuned to the tranquility she guarded at her core.

Kyle noted the fact that this jump did not have the crushing physical effects of his first trip through the tunnel. More importantly, none of the team members were dead. Zhang's new and improved Time Tunnel had delivered the team safely, as promised, and with laser-precision accuracy.

"The cameras are blinded, sir," said one of the commandoes, nodding to the high-intensity infrared lights assembled to blind the security cameras set behind the smoked Plexiglas bubbles protruding from all four walls.

"Excellent," replied Kyle. "Are we good to go?"

"Yes sir," the commandoes replied in unison.

"Zero casualties, right?" checked Kyle.

"Roger that."

"OK, let's go."

Kyle walked to the authorization console to the right of the vault door.

"Authorize," said Kyle.

"Authorize," replied the console.

"Colonel Kyle Mason, Radius, Nine, Five, Five, Three, Four,

Aquarius, Authorize," he said.

The black panel lit up, scanning Kyle's face and eyes.

"Authorized," replied the console.

A loud klaxon sounded, and the door's brilliant blue perimeter lights began to strobe. The soldiers normally stationed inside of the vault door were gone. Because there would be no "outside" after the tunnel's move outside time, there was no need to post guards. The general was not expecting visitors.

As the door opened, the team could hear cheers from inside the tunnel as the complex's inhabitants celebrated their successful mission to prevent 9/11.

The commandoes rushed into the level 1 mezzanine, setting up infrared spotlights to blind the security cameras. The team ran to the mission control elevator. Kyle swiped his keycard and authorized the descent to mission control.

The elevator doors opened. A single guard was posted in the anteroom outside mission control. Shocked by the appearance of the commandoes, he scarcely had time to reach for his weapon before the brilliant red targeting laser lights of the commandoes' assault weapons lit up his chest.

"Gun down," one of the commandoes ordered. The soldier complied, placing his rifle on the floor. The commandoes rushed in, laying the soldier face first on the floor and securing his wrists and ankles with plastic binds. With the room secured, the commandoes nodded to Kyle, who proceeded to the authorization panel.

Kyle took a deep breath. "Here goes," he said, opening the vault door.

The door swung open to reveal a packed mission control room.

Video images of the Twin Towers, fully intact in the revised timeline, streamed across the giant mission control screen. The celebration of the mission's success, a joyful party only moments earlier, had turned to confused concern when the vault door's klaxons sounded. Kyle saw the general, who stood by Roger Summit in the history hive next to the illuminated rose-colored TVA cube. The general's jaw dropped at the sight of Kyle Mason, aged seven years in less than a minute and wearing a beautifully tailored suit.

The room went quiet as Kyle strode to the general and extended his hand. The general refused to take it. He glared at Kyle, realizing that the Delta soldier had disobeyed his orders and remained in the past.

"You've got a lot of nerve, soldier," the general said grimly.

The commandoes swarmed into mission control, followed by Zhang. The Zhang from timeline 001 saw her doppelganger, eliciting a rare emotional reaction as her eyes widened.

Kyle turned from the general and walked down the steps to John Kaomea's console.

"May I see your glasses?" Kyle asked Kaomea.

John removed his eyeglasses and handed them to Kyle, confused.

Kyle took them, folded them carefully, then punched Kaomea in the face, breaking his nose. John cupped his hands around his nose and screamed as blood poured from between his fingers. Several in the room gasped.

"That's for Annika," Kyle said, tossing Kaomea's glasses on his console.

"My team has some work to do," Kyle continued, "so I'm going to ask you all to return to your quarters and remain there until you receive further instructions. The information network and communications are being taken offline temporarily. They'll be restored when we're done."

Kyle turned to the general. "General, I'll brief you in your quarters shortly."

The mission control staff began filing out. Lara Meredith pushed Strangelove's wheelchair. Kaomea, whimpering, held his bleeding nose. The general gave Kyle a final withering look before exiting.

Zhang from timeline 001 hesitated as she watched the new Zhang approach her workstation. The two stared momentarily into each other's even brown eyes. Zhang 002 understood that her counterpart knew exactly what she was up to. The stare was a silent throwdown—001 would defeat whatever sabotage 002 effected.

Zhang 001 turned and followed the others out the vault door. The commandoes followed the staff out, making sure they arrived at their apartments before locking their doors.

Zhang 002 began typing at her workstation. After deactivating the information network and other internal communications, she began the tricky work of disabling the Time Tunnel's ability to send people through time or space without jeopardizing the temporal bubble that enabled the complex and its citizens to exist. She knew that her counterpart would anticipate her methods of sabotage and encryption. She had to get creative, though not creative in the way 001 would expect.

Kyle joined Zhang.

"Have you got this?" he asked.

Zhang turned slowly and looked at Kyle without saying a word.

"OK, good," said Kyle. "I'm going to visit the general before we leave."

• • •

In his townhouse apartment, the general paced. After giving orders for years, he suddenly found himself without a command. Restless, he sat down at his laptop computer and began typing.

-- TOP SECRET --

DEPARTMENT OF THE ARMY
DREAMLAND RESEARCH FACILITY
GROOM LAKE, NEVADA 89044

MEMORANDUM THRU   27 OCT 2008
                                                         TIMELINE 001

GENERAL AARON CRAIG
COMMANDING GENERAL
DREAMLAND RESEARCH FACILITY

FOR FILE

SUBJECT: Time Displacement Mission, 27 October 2008

The purpose of this memo is to acknowledge the mishap that occurred on 27 October, 2008 in the course of the first time displacement mission, as well as to outline preliminary contingency steps. The cause of the accident is unknown at this time. Due to compromised security at the Time Displacement Complex that occurred as a direct result of the accident, a thorough review of the cause is problematic in the short term. It is unknown whether the cause of the problem lies in the time displacement technology or is the fault of human error or lapses in judgment.

The first priority of this office is to secure the facility. Once this is accomplished, senior staff will be directed to execute a comprehensive evaluation of system and personnel in order to determine the proximate cause of the accident. Once the cause is identified and resolved, recommendations will be solicited from senior staff regarding options to correct the damage caused as a result of the accident.

At this time, the status of Lieutenant Colonel Annika Wise is MIA. It is not known at this time whether Lieutenant Colonel Kyle Mason has knowledge of the Colonel's location or present status.

The events that transpired today are a direct result of my orders. I assume full responsibility.

Respectfully,

                                    Aaron T. Craig
                                    FG, USA
                                    Commanding General
                                    Dreamland Research Facility

-- TOP SECRET --

He didn't know why he wrote the memo. He needed to do something.

The general heard a knock at the door.

"Come in," said the general. Kyle entered.

The general was seated at his desk. He swiveled his chair to face Kyle. Kyle closed the door behind him.

"I'm here for my debriefing, sir," Kyle said.

"Where is Colonel Wise?" asked the general.

Kyle picked up a chair from the kitchen table, set it in front of the general, then sat down. He folded his hands in front of him.

"Annika didn't make it."

The general's face turned to pain.

"Everything went wrong," Kyle continued. "Annika was DOA. We were way off course. We arrived on September 10 in a hotel room in Weehawken, New Jersey."

The general shook his head.

"I had to make a decision whether or not to abort. I improvised and recruited the Kyle from 2001. He and I divided up the list and went hunting.

"Something went wrong. The Kyle from 2001 ended up on American 11. He died during the attempt to retake the plane from hijackers."

Kyle paused.

"The Kyle in that time was dead," he said. "I couldn't leave my wife.

"I'm sorry, General," Kyle continued. "You believed in me when I didn't believe in myself. You are my commanding officer, and you are the closest thing to a father any man could hope for.

"I thought I was a better soldier, but I'm not. When it came time to choose between my orders and my wife..." Kyle trailed off.

"You changed time," the general said.

"Well, yeah, that was the point, right?"

"What are you doing to the Time Tunnel?" asked the general.

Kyle took a deep breath. "I am disabling it."

The general's eyes went wide.

"You asked me once whether or not I thought we could do a worse job than the people running our government," said Kyle. "We did a better job. We did a way better job."

"I accomplished my mission. I prevented 9/11. I turned the country around. I reunited with my wife. I don't want things to change," said Kyle.

"You call me a father," said the general. "Yet you don't trust me."

"I should trust you," said Kyle. "I'm sorry. There is too much at stake."

"Get out," said the general.

Kyle rose from his chair and left.

As the door closed, the general thought about an explanation Strangelove had given him once about the randomness of quantum mechanics. Einstein was convinced that the universe must behave according to a set of orderly laws. He was unable to accept the possibility that an aspect of the universe was unpredictable, exclaiming that "God does not play dice with the universe."

Seeing what he had set in motion less than an hour earlier when he'd sent two temponauts back in time, the general acknowledged that Kyle Mason was living proof that Einstein was dead wrong.

Mission Control
Time Tunnel Complex
Area 51, NV
November 7, 2008
09:15 hours
Timeline 002

Moments after Kyle and Zhang disappeared, an alarm sounded in mission control. It was the temporal transponder. Padma held prayerful hands to her lips.

"Transponder alarm," called out a voice from a console.

"Roger that," said Colin. "All systems go for jump?"

Colin watched the display as all stations reported systems "green."

"Jump on my mark, three—two—one…"

"Go."

Colin punched the commit button. A blinding light flashed in the glass Time Tunnel chamber. When it faded, Kyle and Zhang were standing in the sphere. The staff in mission control erupted in applause. Padma, enormously relieved, smiled and hugged Colin. On the video feed from the Time Tunnel chamber, Kyle gave a thumbs up—the mission was a success.

NRG Stadium
Houston, TX
October 25, 2008
19:00 hours
Timeline 002

Over 70,000 Texans sang the lyrics of Lee Greenwood's "God Bless the U.S.A." as it soared over the PA system at the massive NRG stadium, home of the Houston Texans. As the final strains wound to a close, cheers erupted from the crowd as a plump man emerged onto the football field below, waving to the crowds as he walked to a stage in the center of the field. Red, white, and blue buntings hung from the mezzanines. Images of the American and Texan flags waved on the stadium's giant screens. Jonah Jones scaled the steps to the stage and walked to the podium.

As was the case when the junior senator was first elected in 2002, he was down in the polls going into the election. He was once again running into a stiff headwind whipped by Padma's super PAC media storm. Though Padma's ads and PR had moved the hearts and minds of independents, they had failed to dent Jones' impenetrable bedrock conservative base.

"Thank you, thank you…God bless you, my fellow Texans," Jones spoke into the microphone. His twang echoed off the stadium walls. "God bless the USA!"

The crowd roared its approval, preventing Jones from speaking. Jones put his hand over his heart. Tears welled in his eyes.

"Thank you! God bless you!"

The crowd continued cheering for another minute. Jones beamed, his hand on his heart as he soaked up the adoration.

"My fellow Texans, do you know how much I love this great country of ours?"

The crowd roared again.

"You do, don't you?"

Roar!

"You know that I would give anything to protect and defend these United States from all threats, both here and abroad. You know I would sacrifice my very life to protect this country from harm. You know that, don't you?"

Roar!

"You know what the one most important thing is about America? You know what our Founding Fathers fought and died to secure for us?"

"Liberty!" came shouts from the crowd.

"Liberty!" affirmed Jones. "Blessed liberty!"

"My fellow Texans, that liberty that our Founding Fathers sacrificed for has been taken from us!"

The crowd booed.

"It has been stolen from us by an outsider, an invader, someone who pretends to love this country…"

On the giant stadium displays appeared the same darkened,

angry, photoshopped image of Padma used in Jones' ads.

The crowd booed and jeered.

"...but she doesn't. She doesn't love this country. She's *infected* this country! She's taken your hard-earned tax dollars and used that money to buy politicians. She's bought congressmen, senators, even the president!

"2 Corinthians 11:14 tells us that 'Satan disguises himself as an angel of light.' Well, we know better, don't we? This woman isn't an angel of light. Does this woman look light to you?"

Epithets shrieked from the crowd.

"Arab!"

"Muslim!"

"Nigger!"

"So what are we gonna do about this, my fellow Texans?"

"Kill her!"

"Lynch her!"

"Thomas Jefferson said 'The tree of liberty must be refreshed from time to time with the *blood* of patriots and tyrants.' Are there any patriots out there willing to shed their blood to refresh the tree of liberty?"

The crowd roared.

"I know I am. Are you?"

Roar!

"Are there any patriots willing to shed *tyrants'* blood to refresh the tree of liberty?" Jones said, pointing at Padma's image.

The crowd howled its approval, drowning out Jones. A chant began to form.

"Kill her! Kill her! Kill her!"

Padma and Kyle sat on their townhouse bed, watching the spectacle. Padma clicked the remote off. Her gaze remained on the blank screen.

Kyle turned to her. His face was pained.

"Beloved…" he began. He was lost for words, overcome by the orgy of hate directed squarely at the woman he loved.

"I am so sorry," was all he could manage.

Padma remained silent, staring at the screen. Up to that point, she had successfully blocked Jones' hate ads from her feelings, though the collective blood lust of 70,000 people screaming for her death now swarmed her mind, overwhelming it.

"I want to kill them all," Kyle blurted.

"So do I," said Padma.

Pennsylvania Avenue
Washington, DC
November 21, 2008
08:00 hours
Timeline 002

Pedestrians walking to work in the brisk sunny morning in the nation's capital were the first to know that this day would be unlike any other.

Over the usual sounds of rush hour car engines and footsteps on the pavement, they heard a hum in the distance. They could feel a vibration beneath their feet. The hum erupted into a roar as dozens of charcoal-gray Apache helicopters buzzed low as they flew northwest down Pennsylvania Avenue toward the Capitol building and the White House. A phalanx of desert-tan camouflaged M1 Abrams tanks barreled down the avenue behind the attack helicopters. Humvees and armored troop transports joined the procession of tanks. The engines of the hulking tanks roared as they raced toward their target. Their metal tracks, designed for soft ground, clattered against the cement road.

Commuters watched anxiously from their cars as the approaching column of tanks grew larger in their rearview mirrors. Most tried to pull over to avoid the hulking machines. When the lead tank reached its first traffic jam, a soldier opened the hatch and scanned the line of cars in front of him. He then pulled the bolt of his .50-caliber machine gun and fired into the air. Pedestrians screamed and fled as the soldier pointed the machine gun directly at the silver Honda Civic in front of him.

Panicked, the driver, a white man in his thirties with glasses and curly black hair, stomped the accelerator, crashing into the black Lexus sedan in front of him. The line of cars wriggled uselessly as they bumped and crashed into each other. The soldier on the tank shouted something into his headset microphone. The tank revved its 1,500 horsepower gas turbine engine and edged up to the rear of the Honda Civic. With a roar of its mammoth engine, the tank climbed up the trunk of the car and onto its roof, crushing it as its driver narrowly escaped. The doors of the other cars in the jam swung open and their occupants fled with horror as their rides were compacted under a train of 68-ton tanks.

Dozens of Blackhawk helicopters joined the Apaches cruising toward their targets. Soldiers manned their side-door machine guns.

Around the country, citizens watched TV with stunned amazement as images from news copters streamed identical scenes of tanks, troops, and attack helicopters swarming all major US cities. "Special report" chyrons announced the invasion over shocking images of tanks crushing cars and soldiers firing their weapons.

Suddenly, every TV screen in America went dark. At the same time, all radio broadcasts went static. Every Internet page froze. Phone conversations were cut mid-call. America was blind and silent.

An image replaced the dark screen. It was Jonah Jones, seated behind the president's desk in the White House Oval Office. He wore a custom navy-colored military-style tunic, with two columns of bright brass buttons and a high collar. He faced the camera and hundreds of millions of citizens around the world with a smarmy expression.

"My fellow Americans," Jones began, "soldiers from the Third Army have occupied all major American cities and secured key infrastructure, including communications, energy, and transportation. These patriots have joined me to liberate this country from the despots that have seized control of our blessed nation. I am referring to Anderson Wild and Padma Mahajan.

"Mr. Wild and Miss Mahajan have used their influence to corrupt our government, sweeping aside our blessed democracy and replacing it with totalitarianism.

"I am here to assure you, my fellow Americans, that their treasonous acts will no longer be tolerated by these United States.

"I have assumed custodianship of the government of the United States while Mr. Wild and Miss Mahajan are apprehended and brought to justice for their crimes against the Constitution. They will be tried by a military tribunal, along with any co-conspirators who have aided and abetted their efforts to undermine our democracy. This tribunal shall have complete authority to thoroughly investigate and prosecute anyone suspected of being associated with this treasonous plot. Any persons found guilty of treason by the tribunal will face severe punishment.

"It is known that many in this government have aided and

abetted these traitors. It will take time to root out the cancer that has infected our great country.

"During this transition period, to maintain order, I have suspended Habeas Corpus and declared martial law. During this time, President Bush and President-Elect Obama shall be kept under house arrest, pending an investigation by the tribunal regarding the extent of their involvement with Mr. Wild and Miss Mahajan.

"I wish to assure all Americans that this period will be as brief as possible—just long enough to restore freedom and liberty to America. During this time, I have assumed the temporary position of Consul Pro-Tem.

"While martial law is in place, curfews will be established, as well as rules regarding proper behavior. Dissent against the United States government, in any form, will not be tolerated. Our soldiers have complete authority to maintain order.

"For our neighbors around the world, be advised that this is not a time to challenge the strength or resolve of these United States. The world's most powerful military is under my command, including our formidable nuclear arsenal. Do not test our borders. Do not provoke us. If you do, you will find that the United States will shoot first and ask questions later.

"My fellow Americans," Jones said, smiling to the camera. "I realize this may be a confusing and stressful time. Be assured that what is being done is for your best interests, and for the best interests of these blessed United States. You have my assurance that I will protect our citizens and restore greatness to this country. God bless you and God bless the United States of America."

Mission Control
Time Tunnel Complex
Area 51, NV
November 21, 2008
08:30 hours
Timeline 002

Padma and Kyle stared at the giant mission control screen as the image of Jones' face cut to a modified emblem of the president. The president's same American bald eagle held arrows and an olive branch in its talons, though the words encircling the eagle had been changed to "SEAL of the CONSUL of the UNITED STATES."

Padma raised her hands to her lips. "Oh my God."

Kyle was silent.

"They're coming for us!" she said.

Kyle nodded. "Yes."

"How much time do we have?" she asked.

Kyle shook his head. "To prepare an assault on the complex? A couple of weeks, at least. General Craig has his hands full right now consolidating power.

"Breaking into the Time Tunnel isn't easy," added Kyle, trying to comfort his wife. "We're in a steel-encased underground fortress. We've disabled all the vault door entrance codes. The logistics of an assault are very tough. It's hard to break in without destroying the complex."

"They could just nuke us," Padma said.

Kyle was silent for a few moments. The words of Jones' NRG Stadium hate speech replayed in his mind. He felt a chill in his center.

"Jones wants you alive," Kyle said.

He shook his head, returning to the present. "Even if Jones opts for nukes, General Craig won't risk destroying the Time Tunnel. The general is holding the keys to the army—at least for the moment.

"The bottom line is that it's time for Plan B," Kyle said. "We have to make some decisions—where and when to go. We agreed that we need to go a time and place with reasonably modern medicine, a place that is tolerant, and one where we can rebuild our fortune."

"I still can't believe we're going to do this," Padma said.

"Love," Kyle said, taking Padma by the shoulders. "We have to go."

Padma nodded. "I understand. I just can't wrap my head around it."

"We talked about the fifties—post-war, Eisenhower era," Kyle said. "It's a boom time. Maybe go back to New York?"

"Sure," replied Padma. "With my gender and skin color, I'll have no trouble landing a job cleaning toilets."

They were quiet for a moment, thinking.

"Kyle," Padma began, "I have a crazy idea."

"What?"

"What about the sixties?" she said. "San Francisco."

Kyle smiled. "The summer of love?"

Padma nodded, smiling back at him.

Kyle looked at Padma's face. It was easy to see flowers in her beautiful long dark hair.

"It's perfect," Kyle said.

Washington DC
November 28, 2008
09:30 hours
Timeline 002

General Aaron Craig sat in the back seat of a black Lincoln Town Car as it drove down Pennsylvania Avenue toward the White House. The green hat of his dress uniform rested in his lap. He wore a long black wool topcoat over his uniform.

A black-uniformed driver, wearing a flat-topped military-style cap, sat behind the wheel. Another identically uniformed man sat beside the driver.

The driver gripped the wheel with black leather gloves. A shiny black patent leather shoulder strap of a Sam Browne belt passed through the right epaulet of each man's black tunic. A silver star gleamed on each epaulet. On each of their right shoulders was a patch—a fist gripping a sword in front of a red shield with a gold-accented eagle—the insignia of the newly minted Praetorian Guard. They had replaced the president's secret service, most of whose members had died during the White House gunfight that ensued when the army apprehended the president. The rest of the president's secret service detail had either fled or been imprisoned.

The general noted the consul's penchant for ancient Rome. In addition to their MP7 submachine guns, Guard members also wore a ceremonial short sword in a black leather sheath on their right thighs.

Though the Guard was initially charged with the responsibility of protecting the consul, its scope was widening rapidly to include police and military responsibilities. The Guard was growing stronger by siphoning soldiers and weapons from the army. General Craig had already been ordered to transfer two full regiments to Guard control. He knew he was running out of time.

As they drove down Pennsylvania Avenue, the general saw banners that lined the avenue, hanging from lampposts. The banners alternated between the American flag and an image of the consul.

The consul's image was an eighteenth-century-style bust portrait. The consul appeared in his uniform, looking up and slightly toward the left. A divine light shown on his face from above, illuminating an expression that attempted to balance defiance, bravery, and supplicant humility. The consul's right arm crossed his chest, his hand over his heart. The general noted that the consul's physique had been generously sculpted by the artist, molding his enormous potbelly into a powerful barrel-shaped chest. At the base of the portrait, "Liberty" was written in gold Times Roman letters.

"Would you like to listen to the radio, General?" asked the driver.

The general didn't respond. The driver turned on the radio. A man's voice read the news.

"In today's news, units of the consul's elite Praetorian Guard stormed the World Trade Center buildings this morning in the hunt for the fugitives Anderson Wild and Padma Mahajan..."

The two Guard members smiled and nodded toward each other.

"...Though neither of the fugitives were found in the buildings, our valiant Guard members uncovered additional evidence of the fugitives' treason in the form of computer records and files. The fugitives' financial assets have been seized and will be used for one of the consul's preferred charities..."

The charity of the personal enrichment of Jonah Jones, thought the general.

"...In another victory for our glorious Praetorian Guard, commandoes thwarted an attempt by Muslim terrorists to detonate a high explosive device onboard a passenger airline last night. Richard Paul, America's newly appointed minister of security, had this to say:

'My reaction to this attempt to kill innocent Americans is the same as that of all Americans—utter abhorrence! While we in the Ministry of Security realize that not all Muslims represent terrorist threats, we believe that in the interest of public safety, we must embrace certain prudent measures to keep our citizens safe. The Ministry of Security has issued an edict, effective today, that all Muslims are required to register with the Ministry. At that time, they will be issued a pin displaying a star and crescent, the symbol of their religion, which they will be required to wear on their clothing at all times while in public. Law enforcement and Praetorian Guardsmen are authorized to stop and question anyone suspected of being Muslim who does not comply with these simple requirements. Those found in violation of the law will be detained for further questioning and possible charges.'"

The news anchor continued, "That seems like a sensible precaution from our minister of security, one that is fair, yet still protects Christian Americans.

"And finally, in a triumph for morality and family values, the Supreme Tribunal unanimously struck down Roe v. Wade, making abortion illegal in the United States. The penalties for committing the atrocity of abortion will be severe, ranging from a minimum incarceration period of ten years in a patriot re-education facility to death by hanging. In its first step to enforce the law, Praetorian Guardsmen closed dozens of Planned Parenthood centers and arrested hundreds of doctors and employees..."

The driver began surfing stations. All radio, TV programming, and Internet websites were now managed by the new Ministry of Information. Radio choices were limited to propaganda news and talk shows, Christian music and talk radio, and other bland music considered inert by the ministry.

The general was unaware that he was gripping his hat tighter. He realized Jonah Jones had studied the fascist playbook well. America's consul had wasted no time putting it into action in the very last country on earth expected to succumb to totalitarianism.

The general knew he bore the responsibility for making this nightmare possible. He suppressed his shame, driving it deep within him. He reminded himself that the ends justified the means. Regaining control of the Time Tunnel was the only thing that mattered. Once he had done so, he could easily reset America with a time jump, erasing Jones' takeover and making everything right again.

As the general's car pulled into the White House driveway, he noticed several differences between the consul's White House and the home of the former democratically elected president. Dozens of black-uniformed Praetorian guards carrying M16 rifles stood at the iron fence bordering the White House grounds. Two banners flanked the White House portico—the same two that lined Pennsylvania Avenue, as well as hundreds of other streets in America.

As the town car rolled to a stop in front of the White House portico, another Guard member saluted by pressing his right fist to his heart, then extended his arm parallel to the ground with his hand extended. The general knew the Nazis had fashioned their similar salute on that used in ancient Rome. The guard opened the car door. The general climbed the red-carpeted steps to the White House entrance. Guards on either side of the entrance greeted the general with the same Roman-style salute.

Inside the White House, the general was escorted to an elevator where another guard stood watch. The guard saluted, then inserted a key into a panel next to the elevator doors. The doors opened, and the general and his escort entered. The guard inserted his key and pressed the basement button. The general realized their destination was the White House Situation Room.

Outside the Situation Room entrance, yet another guard saluted. The general's escort returned the salute. The guard opened the door for the general. He stepped into an administrative anteroom outside the Situation Room. Women sat at three separate desks—two Caucasian and one African American. They were attired identically, each wearing an inappropriately short dress with a column of shining buttons running up the front of the left side. The style was similar to the military tunic worn by the consul. The general couldn't help but notice that all three women were breathtakingly beautiful. Though computers sat on each of their desks, the women sat with their white-gloved hands folded in their laps. A static emblem of the Consul of the United States was displayed on their computer screens.

The general looked at the African American woman. She looked up from her desk, meeting the general's gaze with beautiful green eyes that peered from beneath long bangs. Her long straight bobbed hair framed her face. She smiled at him. The general looked away, embarrassed, as he removed his topcoat and hat.

"May I take those for you, General?" asked the woman. The general avoided looking at the woman, as she gave the hem of her short dress a slight tug over her thighs as she rose from her seat.

One of the Caucasian women, a fair-skinned woman with long blond hair, giggled at the general's awkwardness. He gave her a sharp look.

"The consul is expecting you, General," the woman said, smiling, impervious to his glare. "Please go in."

The general did not return the woman's smile. He handed his coat and hat to the woman of color and entered the Situation Room as the three women giggled in his wake.

The White House Situation Room was a rectangular conference room with a long wooden conference table and large computer displays on the wall. One display showed a world map with icons depicting US and foreign military assets. Another was a helicopter view of the World Trade Center. Another was a satellite view of Area 51.

At one end of the table sat Jonah Jones, the consul of America. Seven other Caucasian men sat at the table. With one exception, all of the men wore the same navy-colored military tunic as Jones. The exception was a young man in his twenties, who wore a black Pretorian Guard uniform. He wore four stars on his epaulet shoulder boards. The long brown partially grown sideburns of an adolescent grew on a face bursting with pimples.

"General," said Jones, "You're right on time. Please have a seat. General, I would like you to meet the chiefs of our ministries."

General Craig instantly recognized one of the men.

One by one, Jones introduced the men—Hunter Williams, minister of information; Brent Walker, minister of education; Chase Reed, minister of energy; Charles Hammer, minister of economics; The Reverend Gerald Wainwright, minister of morality; Richard Paul, minister of security.

"...and I believe you know our new minister of defense..."

The former General James Patterson smirked at General Craig.

"General," he said.

The general noted that several former agencies were no longer represented by the cabal, including the Environmental Protection Agency, the Department of Veterans Affairs, and Health and Human Services.

Jones turned to the Praetorian guard sitting to his right. "And this is my son, Joshua Jones. I am very proud to announce that Joshua has been appointed the new general of the Praetorian Guard."

The others seated at the conference table applauded. Joshua made an entitled smile, lifting his hand in a wave. General Craig's sullen expression did not budge.

"One of General Jones' tasks over the coming weeks will be to liaise with you to coordinate the transfer of assets from the Third Army to the Guard."

The remark caught General Craig like a sucker punch. After handing the keys to the United States to Jonah Jones, he was now expected to hand over his army to his brat.

"Before we get down to business," said Jones, "Reverend, would you like to lead us in prayer?"

Reverend Wainwright was in his forties, and wore his red and gray hair very short and parted on the side. A neatly trimmed goatee surrounded his mouth. He was the founder and pastor of the First Calvary megachurch in Dallas, Texas, leading a flock of some 50,000 Southern Baptists.

"Dear heavenly Father…" began the reverend as the men around the table lowered their heads and closed their eyes. It was General Craig's second awkward moment since arriving at the White House. He bowed his head, but he kept his eyes open, staring at the grains in the wood conference table.

"…we thank you for delivering the blessed consul to us. We ask you to protect your Christian warrior and bestow your blessings upon him as he restores greatness to these United States of America. Please help him as he reclaims America—wrests it loose, oh Lord—from the grasps of the wicked. Enable him to punish those who have chosen to deviate from your glorious shining path while showing your eternal love to those that follow your way—the only way.

"We ask this in the name of your blessed son, Jesus Christ. Amen."

"Amen!" echoed the men at the table. General Craig remained silent.

"Thank you for joining us, General," began Jones. "The reason we've invited you here today is to get a progress report."

Expectant eyes fell on the general.

"As you know, the objective of the operation's first phase—" began the general.

"The liberation," interrupted Jones.

The general continued, "…the objective of the first phase was to secure the federal government, the Pentagon, major cities, and all communications, including broadcast television and cable, radio, and Internet. The first objective was accomplished on day 1.

"As part of phase 1, the army also secured major financial institutions and infrastructure to prevent the transfer of funds outside the country.

"The army has since moved to the second phase, which was to assume control of the other branches of the military. Our army has secured all domestic Air Force installations, Marine bases, and Coast Guard bases. We have secured all domestic naval bases, though several aircraft carrier battle groups remain at sea, as well as ballistic and tactical submarines.

"Though the ballistic submarines carry nuclear missiles, those weapons cannot be enabled without the launch codes, which we have secured.

"The army has now entered phase 3, securing the country's energy infrastructure—all energy production facilities and transport infrastructure. Completion of this phase is expected by end of day."

"What resistance are you encountering?" asked Jones.

"Limited. Sporadic," replied the general. "Our greatest concern was resistance from the other branches of the military. Our goal was to achieve the element of surprise, which we succeeded in doing. Communications to leadership was severed at the outset of the operation, which created confusion in the chain of command."

"Some isolated groups of civilian fighters have attempted to stage resistance here and there, but all communications are closely monitored. When we detect insurgent communications, we freeze their bank assets and raid their homes. Though there have been attempts to encrypt communications, we control all the companies used for encryption. We can freely eavesdrop on all communications.

"In a few instances, when resistance has been well organized and armed, instead of risking soldiers' lives, we'll simply drop a Hellfire missile from a predator drone.

"Though some survivalists have stockpiled significant stashes of weapons, ammunition, food, and supplies, they've been cut off from their funds and are now draining their caches. The vast majority of citizens are terrified of the consequences of lending support to the insurgence. Most of the preppers will exhaust their resources within the year."

"Excellent work, General. You and your soldiers are to be

commended," said Jones. "Now, what do you have to report regarding your progress in apprehending the fugitives Anderson Wild and Padma Mahajan. I must say I'm a little disappointed it's taking so long."

"My apologies, Consul," replied the general. "My army and I have been a little busy over the past few days."

"Your sarcasm is not appreciated here, General," snapped Jones. "The American people demand justice, as do I."

The general glared at Jones, summoning the full measure of his will to contain his inner contempt for the fat dictator.

"My staff and I are preparing the attack plan," replied the general coldly. "Taking over America was easy. Taking Dreamland is another story."

"And why is that, General?" asked Jones. "You have the most powerful army in the world."

"Dreamland is an underground fortress encased in hardened steel," replied the general. "Breaking in without destroying the facility is challenging."

Jones fantasized about a public show trial for the couple, followed by an execution for Wild and a lifetime sentence of servitude for Padma at the consul's beck and call.

"Give them an ultimatum," said Jones. "If they don't come out, nuke Dreamland."

"That would be a mistake," replied the general.

"What the hell did you say?" snapped Jones. "I'm the consul! I don't make mistakes. But you sure as hell just did!"

"I think you should know exactly what you're nuking before

you do it," replied the general coldly.

"So, tell me, General, what exactly is at Dreamland?" asked Jones.

"It would be best if I shared that with you in private."

"I have no secrets from these men," said Jones.

"After I tell you," said the general, "you'll wish you did."

Jones and the general stared at each other for a few tense moments. Jones blinked.

"Gentlemen, please excuse us," said Jones.

The men rose and began to file out of the room. As General Patterson reached the door, General Craig called out to him.

"Oh, General Patterson, there's just one thing before you go," General Craig said. "You didn't tell him, did you?"

Panic flashed across General Patterson's face. Jones looked confused.

General Craig turned to Jones. "You see, Consul, you may not have any secrets from these men, but one of these men is holding back a secret from you."

General Craig pivoted to General Patterson. "I'm not the only man in the room who knows what's at Dreamland. General Patterson knows what's down there too… You see, Consul, General Patterson ran Dreamland before I did."

Jones glared at General Patterson, stunned.

"Consul, I…" General Patterson stammered, "I was trying to find the appropriate time."

Jones looked at General Craig, then turned to Joshua Jones.

"General Jones," Jones said to his son, "please have your men escort General Patterson to the Praetorian Guard detention facility.

I'll have some questions for him later."

"Yes, Consul," replied Joshua Jones, motioning for Praetorian guardsmen to escort General Patterson out of the situation room. Two black-uniformed guardsmen entered and took General Patterson by each arm.

"Consul, no!" yelled General Patterson. "Please! I can explain!"

All eyes were on General Patterson as he was pulled from the room. Only General Patterson saw General Craig's Cheshire grin as the door slammed shut.

Jones and General Craig were alone. Jones turned to the general.

"This had better be good," warned Jones.

"In 1947," the general began, "it was reported that a spacecraft crashed in Roswell, New Mexico—"

"Oh goddammit! Roswell's a myth!" interrupted Jones.

The general stared forward. His expression didn't flinch.

"You're shittin' me!" said Jones. "Roswell was real?"

"Roswell was real," confirmed the general.

"The aliens are at Dreamland?"

"The remains of four are at Dreamland," replied the general, "as is their spacecraft."

"Jesus!" exclaimed Jones.

"We reverse engineered much of their technology," continued the general. "Their power source is of particular interest. They use antimatter to power their ship."

"What in the Sam Hill is 'antimatter'?"

"The short answer is that it's the most powerful weapon on this planet," replied the general. He placed his hands on the chair in front of him. "An antimatter bomb with the mass of this chair could destroy Europe."

"God Almighty!" exclaimed Jones. "And Wild and Mahajan know this?"

"They do," replied the general. "Which is why the ultimatum won't work. They know I'll never destroy Dreamland."

"So those two are the most powerful people on the planet," deduced Jones.

"They are."

Jones chuckled. "Now I understand why you wanted Dreamland so bad, General. Whoever rules Dreamland rules the world, right?"

The general was silent.

"Well, General, you are right that we're not going to nuke Dreamland," said Jones. "But when you go in, you can be damn sure that I'm coming with you."

Apartment 343
Time Tunnel Complex
Area 51, NV
December 5, 2008
00:01 hours
Timeline 002

A violent shudder woke Kyle and Padma from a sound sleep. Alarms sounded within the Time Tunnel complex. Strobes flashed with the alarms. The townhouse phone rang as the complex shook again.

"This is Kyle," he shouted into the phone. "What's going on?"

"We have uninvited guests upstairs," shouted Major Tony Darwin, the leader of the company of Dark Star commandoes. "We're under attack."

Kyle paused.

"Colonel, it's time for you and your wife to go," said Tony.

"Tony…" Kyle began.

"Kyle, we've got this. We've got your back. Go."

"Thank you, Tony," Kyle said, choking up. "No words. "

"It's been a privilege knowing you, Colonel."

"Godspeed"

Kyle hung up the phone and speed-dialed another number.

"Colin here. What's going on?"

"It's time to go," replied Kyle.

"Understood. We'll be ready."

Kyle hung up. Padma was already pulling on her jeans—bellbottoms. Kyle grabbed a black Kevlar vest from under the bed and tossed it to her.

"Put this on," he said. "Have you got your getaway bag?"

Padma drew a large black backpack from under the bed. "Right here!" she replied. She pulled a jade turtleneck over her body armor, then threw on a long-fringed leather vest and quickly tied a leather band around her head to complete the chic hippie ensemble.

Kyle heaved a larger, heavier backpack on top of the bed as he threw on flare jeans, boots, an Illya Kuryakin-style black turtleneck, and suede jacket.

One hundred feet above the Time Tunnel complex, in the midnight darkness, General Craig stood in the gun turret of his desert-camouflage Humvee. His ride was parked with his armored regiment, 100 yards outside the Time Tunnel's freight elevator hangar. Over 100 tanks, along with dozens of attack helicopters and 1,500 soldiers, had begun their assault on the complex.

One side of the Time Tunnel's ground-level hangar was ripped open, shredded by a barrage of tank shells.

Parked next to the general's desert-camo Humvee was another Humvee, painted black, with the insignia of the Praetorian Guard on each side. Joshua Jones stood in his gun turret, keeping an eye on the general. Jones wore a black helmet and body armor with his standard Guard uniform.

"Fire," General Craig said calmly into his helmet headset.

Simultaneous yellow cannon blasts from dozens of tanks lit and shook the desert, shattering the hangar. The general noticed Joshua jerk in reaction. The concussion of the powerful blasts rattled the junior Praetorian Guard general. He shivered with fear. He realized he was out of his depth, but could not risk disappointing his father, who sat inside their Humvee.

The elder Jones also wore a helmet and had managed to stretch a flak jacket around his pot-bellied girth. He gasped as the barrage of tank blasts pummeled the hangar.

Standing near the Jones' Humvee were two platoons of Praetorian Guard troops. Though 2,000 of General Craig's battle-hardened soldiers had already been transferred to the Praetorian Guard's command, both Joneses had chosen to use handpicked Guard members for this assignment to avoid conflicts of loyalty between their old and new commanders. The 30 Guard members under Joshua's command were a discordant mix of mercenaries and inexperienced personal friends.

General Craig's regiment vastly outnumbered and outgunned the Praetorian Guard's troops. The general had prepared for two battles—one for the Time Tunnel, and another with the Guard. He had lied to the Joneses about the size of the force he was bringing to the engagement. Under the cover of darkness, the Joneses did not begin to realize the full scope of General Craig's army until the first barrage was unleashed on the hangar.

A crane truck drove into the shredded hangar building toward the elevator well. A pallet was hanging from the crane—it looked like a giant hockey puck. The general spoke into his headset, and the crane lowered the pallet into the elevator well.

"What are you doing?" shouted Joshua Jones from the Humvee.

General Craig spoke to one of his officers, a colonel, standing beside his Humvee.

"Colonel, please explain to the boy what we're doing," said General Craig.

The colonel walked over to Joshua's Humvee.

"We're lowering daisy cutter bombs into the freight elevator well," the colonel shouted to Joshua. "These bombs have been specifically designed for this mission. They're encased in armor, with one end exposed—the end facing the vault door. The objective is to breach the vault door to the complex while minimizing damage to surrounding structures as much as possible. It'll still make a helluva mess, though. No way around that.

"The bombs are lowered to level 1 and detonated. After we breach the vault door, Special Forces will rappel into the elevator well and enter the complex. That's when your troops go. Get ready."

"Will it work?" shouted Joshua.

"Yes sir, it'll work," replied the colonel. "The only question is, how many bombs will it take to knock down the front door. I'm betting on four."

The colonel turned back toward the general's Humvee.

"Fire in the hole!" crackled a voice over the radio.

"Fire!" said the general.

A blast rocked the earth and shot a geyser of orange fire into the air, blowing the roof off the hangar. A second crane truck moved into position with its payload.

The massive explosion rattled the complex, though it had not yet breached the vault door. Dark Star commandoes massed on the level 1 mezzanine, preparing to repel the attackers.

• • •

Kyle and Padma ran to the elevator. As they descended to the Time Tunnel chamber, the complex shook again violently. The elevator lights flickered out momentarily, then came back on.

The doors opened onto the mission control anteroom. The Dark Star guard opened the vault door.

Inside, a skeleton crew frantically prepared the tunnel for a jump. Colin barked out orders to his team. Kyle waited for a pause.

"Where are we?" Kyle asked.

"By the book, it takes one hour to jump-start the tunnel," said Colin.

The complex shook again.

"I don't think we have that long," said Kyle.

"You think?" replied Colin. "You and Padma get to the chamber. I've got the miracles covered."

Kyle nodded.

"C'mon," Kyle said to Padma.

They ran to the Time Tunnel chamber's anteroom. Moments later, the door opened and two technicians in white clean-room suits hurriedly guided Kyle and Padma up the steps to the glass sphere chamber. The technicians secured the door, removed the steps and exited the room. Kyle took Padma's hand.

Colin's team was executing Plan B, a contingency that had been drilled dozens of times. Plan B had been positioned to the staff as the ultimate defensive measure. In the event of an attack, the Time Tunnel emergency jump would take the complex out of time, into its parallel universe, leaving the enemy behind. A byproduct of Plan B was Kyle and Padma's escape into the past—insurance in case the enemy breached the Time Tunnel fortress.

The record time to execute a jump from a cold start was 30 minutes. Ten minutes had elapsed since the first explosion shook the complex.

In mission control, Colin yelled for system status over the din of his team members. Most of the system status lights showed red. Firing up the Time Tunnel on short notice was like turning a super tanker on a dime.

Kyle and Padma felt the Time Tunnel chamber shake as another bomb exploded at the vault door. Padma looked at Kyle, anxious.

"We're going to be fine," Kyle said, reassuring her.

The lights went out in mission control. Emergency lights came on. Auxiliary generators instantly kicked in to keep vital equipment online.

On level 1, another bomb exploded, cracking the vault door. The concussion from the blast seared through the fracture. Tony called mission control.

"Colin here."

"Estimate five clicks before the vault door goes," shouted Tony. "Maybe ten before they get to mission control."

"Thank you, Major," said Colin. "Godspeed."

"Roger that, Darwin out."

Colin looked at the clock. *Not enough time*, he thought.

Colin looked at the status board. All of his vital system status statistics showed red.

System	Status
Reactor	Red
Temporal engine	Red
Navigation	Red
Bio	Green
Transponder	Green

Tony shouted into his helmet microphone, "Kill the lights, except in mission control and the tunnel."

The complex went dark. Tony's team lowered their night vision goggles.

Another explosion cracked the vault door in half. Special Forces operators from General Craig's army rappelled into the smoking elevator shaft. Jonah and Joshua Jones stood on the rim of the elevator shaft, peering at the Special Forces soldiers on the smoking elevator platform 100 feet below.

"Are you gentlemen joining us?" asked General Craig.

The Joneses, startled, watched as General Craig rappelled into the elevator well.

"He wouldn't go down there with the lead soldiers if he didn't have a good reason," shouted Jonah. "We can't let him take control of Dreamland. We have to go!"

Jonah and Joshua looked at each other. Both attempted to mask their fear.

The Praetorian guardsmen hooked a harness to the winch cable on their Humvee.

"I'm going first!" shouted Jonah. Though terrified of what lay below, his covetousness of the Gray's antimatter weapon trumped his fear.

The guard helped the fat consul into harness straps. He sat on the edge of the shaft, took a deep breath and pushed off. Dangling over the edge, the winch motor was snapped on, slowly lowering Jones into the shaft as Special Forces operators sped past him on their rappel ropes.

Inside level 1, a grenade was tossed through the vault door opening onto the mezzanine.

"Grenade!" shouted Tony.

The grenade exploded, hurling steel fragments in all directions. The Dark Star commandoes, huddled behind columns protruding from the mezzanine walls, were not injured, though smoke filled the mezzanine.

Two more grenades landed on the mezzanine. The blast concussions rocked Tony's team. They aimed their rifles' infrared targeting pointers at the gap in the vault door. The first of General Craig's commandoes leapt through the gap. Exposed on the mezzanine, they were instantly cut down by Tony's team.

In mission control, one more of the tunnel's vital systems flashed green.

System	Status
Reactor	Green
Temporal engine	Red
Navigation	Red
Bio	Green
Transponder	Green

Colin yelled to the team leaders of the two outstanding systems, "Temporal engine, navigation, what are your ETAs?"

"Temporal engine, five minutes," replied a voice.

"Navigation, ten minutes."

Colin looked at the clock. Five minutes had passed since his call with Tony.

"Damn!" he said.

Colin weighed his bad and worse options in a split second. He called out to Zhang, "Zhang, can we configure the tunnel to jump without navigation online?"

"Yes," replied Zhang, "though there is no point in doing so. Without navigation, the temponauts' destination would be completely random. They could arrive anywhere at any time."

"We're running out of options," Colin said. "Configure the tunnel to jump without navigation as a fallback."

Zhang nodded and began typing on her keyboard.

An explosion sounded outside the mission control vault door. The attackers had reached the anteroom. Colin looked at the status board. The temporal engine flashed green.

System	Status
Reactor	Green
Temporal engine	Green
Navigation	Red
Bio	Green
Transponder	Green

Zhang called to Colin, "I've enabled you to commit a jump without navigation."

Colin looked on his panel and saw the "COMMIT" light was illuminated. He took a key out his pocket and unlocked a plastic housing over another button, marked "DESTRUCT." DESTRUCT was a system-wide sabotage function that would delete all computer software and damage key Time Tunnel hardware, thoroughly covering Kyle and Padma's tracks through time.

"OK everyone, listen up," Colin shouted. "We're going to fire up the tunnel, but we're going to wait to the last possible second to give navigation time to plot the course, understood?"

"Roger, understood," replied the mission control team.

Mission control shook as another blast rocked its vault door. Computer displays distorted momentarily, then returned to normal.

"Throttle up power to 100 percent," ordered Colin, skipping the usual plateaus at 30 percent and 60 percent.

"Reactor output at 100 percent," replied a voice.

The vault door blew off its hinges, tumbling down the steps of the mission control amphitheater. Smoke blew through the door opening as the first commando dashed into mission control. Colin turned to look at the commando amidst the screams and shouts of the mission control staff. Colin smacked the COMMIT button as two bullets seared through his shoulder blade, knocking him onto his console before he slid to the floor. There was a blinding flash in the Time Tunnel chamber. Kyle and Padma were gone.

"Put your hands on your head and kneel on the floor!" yelled the commando to the mission control staff as fellow soldiers rushed in. "I said, put your hands on your fucking head and kneel on the floor!"

Slouching against his console, Colin reached up from the floor to find the DESTRUCT button. As his fingers fumbled the metal surface of the console, his hand was suddenly smacked away. He was kicked onto the floor. Annika Wise stood over him, her assault rifle trained on Colin's chest.

"Medic!" she shouted. She turned to Colin, who was in shock, bleeding on the floor. "We're definitely going to want *you* alive."

• • •

Kyle and Padma were blinded by the Time Tunnel flash, accompanied by the teeth-rattling hum of the tunnel effect. As the white light faded out, the faint images of people began to fade in. A warm breeze wafted a chorus of surprised gasps over Kyle and Padma.

The images sharpened. Kyle and Padma were standing in a grassy field on a sunny afternoon in the center of an enormous circle of people—hundreds of brown faces framed with long black hair—staring back at them. Some wore feathers in their hair. Most wore buckskin pants and shirts—many with a reddish dye in the form of an inverted triangle. The shocked expressions of the Native Americans mirrored Kyle's and Padma's own faces.

"Please, dear God, tell me this is Frontierland," said Padma.

Time Tunnel Complex
Area 51, NV
December 5, 2008
00:40 hours
Timeline 002

General Craig, Annika Wise, and a platoon of the general's Special Forces soldiers navigated through dead men and debris on the level 1 mezzanine as they made their way to the remnants of the vault door. Flickering lights strobed across the bodies of both Army and Dark Star soldiers as they lay on the ground, along with the rubble blown out of the mezzanine by gunfire and grenades.

When the platoon arrived at the place where the giant vault door once stood, they examined the entrance. Standing outside on the smoking wreckage of the freight elevator pad with their backs to the platoon were Jonah and Joshua Jones. General Craig could see that the Joneses were staring at something laying on the far edge of the elevator pad. The general looked closer. The object on the pad was the torso of a Praetorian guardsman. He had been sliced in two by the Time Tunnel's temporal bubble—the cutting edge of oblivion. Beyond the torso was nothing. Smoke from the ruin of the elevator pad rose into blackness and disappeared into infinity.

"Everything I told you was true," said General Craig.

Startled, the Joneses spun to face the general and his troops.

"But I left out one important detail."

"I am the consul of America," attempted Jones in a hollow voice, shocked by the vision of the vivisected soldier.

"That's true, Consul," replied the general. "But, you see, we're not in America anymore."

The general pulled his pistol from its holster and shot Joshua between his eyes. Jonah Jones screamed.

"Nice shot," noted Annika.

The general aimed his gun at Jonah Jones.

"No! No! *No!*" screamed Jones. He turned and ran from the general, vanishing as he passed through the temporal edge.

"I wonder what's out there," mused Annika.

"There's exactly one fat man out there," replied the general as he holstered his weapon.

Place: unknown
Date: unknown
Time: unknown

Kyle looked around—they had landed in the precise center of a ring of some 200 Native Americans. Some wore fringed deerskin, with beaded belts and feathers. Some wore store-bought clothes—the men in faded cotton shirts and pants, women in prairie dresses. Many wore deerskin shirts with a crimson inverted pyramid stained on the chest.

In the distance, a river flowed. Patches of cottonwood trees bordered the river. While the natives were startled by the sudden appearance of the strange couple, they did not seem fearful. It was as though they had expected the supernatural event.

"Holy shit!" exclaimed Kyle. "I know this! Holy shit!"

Padma went silent as the fantastic enormity of their time travel began to overwhelm her.

"This is a Ghost Dance! Shit! I can't believe it!" Kyle said.

Kyle looked at Padma. Her face was pale. A bolt of fear fired through Kyle as he remembered how the Time Tunnel had taken Annika from him.

"Padma?" he asked, taking her arm. "Are you OK?"

Padma stared forward, motionless. She blinked and shook her head. "Where are we?" she asked.

"This is a Ghost Dance. I recognize this from my West Point studies," Kyle said. "We're in South Dakota."

"*When* are we?" she asked, fearing Kyle's answer.

"1890."

Padma brought her hands to her face as she began to feel the tremendous weight of her crushed dream of life in 1960s San Francisco.

"And why would you know this from West Point?" she asked.

Kyle took a breath.

"Because we studied the Massacre of Wounded Knee," he said, nodding.

Padma shook her head slowly. "Kyle, I love you," she began, "I do. But I gotta tell you, sometimes life with you is no picnic."

Kyle's guilt for bringing Padma into this mess was cut with a boyish excitement over witnessing a moment in history that he had studied in school. He was smack in the middle of an actual *Ghost Dance,* a seminal event in the run-up to one of the most disastrous chapters in American history.

After Colonel George Armstrong Custer's scouting party confirmed a gold strike in the Black Hills of South Dakota in 1874, whites swarmed the Lakota territory, reigniting perennial hostilities between whites and natives. When Custer was eventually killed in the Battle of Little Bighorn in 1876, congress reacted harshly, passing the "Sell or Starve" Act of 1877, forcing the Lakota people off their verdant land in the Black Hills and onto a reservation in the Dakotas—a place guaranteed to be worthless to human beings of any color.

Now vanquished of all hope of the physical earth, the Lakota people looked to the heavens through the lens of the Ghost Dance to rid them of the white menace and return their lands and buffalo to them. The shirts with the inverted crimson pyramids, part of the ritual, were promised to be imbued with supernatural powers, even possessing the ability to shield their wearers from the white's gunfire.

The ghost dancers had begun the dance that summoned the strange couple in the usual way—they began shuffling side to side to a drumbeat. Their pace was slow, and their feet were heavy, as though their ankles were shackled to the worthless dirt they moved upon. As the drum tempo quickened, their feet were lighter. Their bodies were released from the hunger and depression that encumbered them. Their fever rose. Dancers began to leap and spin as the dance crescendoed, building energy into a tempest.

At the dance's zenith, a brilliant light had blinded the dancers, leaving Kyle and Padma in its wake.

The Lakota talked excitedly amongst themselves, pointing at the strange pair that had appeared from lightning. Though the Ghost Dance ritual did not foretell the coming of a mixed race couple, it did appear to be working nonetheless. One man, more ornately attired than his companions, was prodded to investigate the couple. He did so reluctantly.

The man wore fringed pants. A breastplate, assembled of four columns of hair-pipe bones, covered his chest. A matching bone choker wrapped around his neck. Three eagle feathers protruded from a knot of hair at the back of his head. His long hair was tied into two braids that fell on his chest. He wore leather bands on both arms, each adorned with a white feather. He held an ornamental painted leather shield in one hand and an eagle feather in the other.

"Medicine man," Kyle said, watching the man approach. Padma said nothing.

The medicine man began to speak to Kyle in the Lakota language.

"We don't speak your language," Kyle replied.

The medicine man was surprised. Though Kyle was white, he had been conjured by the Ghost Dance and had arrived with what appeared to be a beautiful native woman. The medicine man was disappointed that Kyle did not speak Lakota.

"Takoda!" the medicine man shouted to the crowd.

A young man wearing a ghost shirt with a crimson triangle and buckskin pants ran to join them. He wore an eagle feather in his long braided hair. The medicine man spoke to the younger man while gesturing toward Kyle and Padma.

"My name is Takoda," the young man said. "This is Yellow Bird, our medicine man. He wants to know if you are the Messiah."

Kyle realized that the ghost dancers had confused the time travelers' miraculous entrance with the prophesized summoning of the Messiah.

Kyle began to shake his head. Before he could speak, Padma cut him off.

"Yes. I am the Messiah," she announced.

Kyle looked at Padma, thunderstruck. The medicine man and Takoda looked confused. Though the prophecy did not specify the Messiah's gender, it had been assumed it would come in the form of a man.

"There is a great battle that will happen with the whites in the winter. We are here to defeat the whites. We have brought powerful weapons with us," she said. She turned to Kyle. "Show them, love."

"May I speak with you?" Kyle asked Padma.

"Of course," Padma replied, smiling to the medicine man and Takoda. The two men returned the smile of the gorgeous goddess.

Kyle took Padma gently by the arm and guided her a few feet away.

"Have you lost your mind?" Kyle asked.

"I'm trying to make the best of a *truly* shitty situation," Padma replied. "It's not my fault we landed in a western. If we're not going to be rich hippies in San Francisco tripping on acid, we might as well do some *fucking good!*"

"This is the deal," Kyle said. "Four days after Christmas, 500 US soldiers with repeating rifles and artillery are going to slaughter 300 Lakota men, women, and children."

"I understand there may be challenges," Padma replied.

"I'm one guy with a submachine gun with 1,000 rounds. Those 500 soldiers have nearby reinforcements of nearly 5,000 men. It's the largest single concentration of soldiers since the Civil War. If I hit one soldier with every bullet, that still leaves 4,000 soldiers."

"A thousand rounds? We were supposed to go to Haight-Ashbury, not Vietnam."

"I come prepared," said Kyle, "because you just never know when you're going to be in a gunfight with the fucking US cavalry!

The bottom line is this: We're going to die."

Padma went silent for a moment.

"Do you have a better way to die?" she asked.

"Yeah, actually, I thought I'd die of natural causes after growing old with my wife."

"You seem to forget—I'm not your wife. *Your* wife is dead."

Kyle looked at Padma, astonished. Her words had wounded him with a sucker punch. He collected himself and fired back.

"Fine," said Kyle, "I thought I'd grow old with the other guy's wife."

Padma slapped Kyle's face hard. Kyle glared at her, his eyes wide. He didn't know this woman.

The Lakota gasped. In their patriarchal culture, a wife slapping her husband was almost as shocking as two people appearing out of thin air.

"*Fuck you!* I loved that 'other guy!' You're not that 'other guy.' My Kyle was brave and heroic, and he would have *helped these people!*"

Kyle looked away from Padma and into the puzzled eyes of the people who formed the ring around them. Some faces were old and wrinkled. Even the young faces showed age well beyond their years. All the faces expressed despair, tinged with the longing hope that these two strange people might actually be the answer to their prayers.

Kyle shot Padma a hard look, then angrily took off his backpack and unzipped it, retrieving an MP7 submachine gun. He walked back to the medicine man and Takoda, clicked on the gun's laser target pointer and aimed it at his hand. The two Lakota men pointed at the brilliant red star in the palm of Kyle's hand.

"*Oyuspe sa wichahpi luta mahel nape!*" exclaimed the medicine man. Takoda nodded. He turned to Kyle.

"Our medicine man calls you 'Holds Red Star in Hand,'" Takoda said.

Detention center
Time Tunnel Complex
Area 51, NV
December 10, 2008
09:15 hours
Timeline 002

Colin James stood naked in a 30-by-30 foot gray cement room. His arms were shackled above his head. The room was brightly lit. Hellvetica's teeth-rattling "New Hate" shrieked from a boom box on the floor. Two freshly sutured red scars from excised bullets branded his left shoulder blade.

Colin alternated between standing and resting his weight on his wrist shackles. He had vacillated between standing and hanging for 48 hours, since he was transferred from the Time Tunnel's hospital to the interrogation cell. The 48-hour period was interrupted by a single water-boarding session.

The room had a two-way mirror along one wall. Two Steelcase chairs were parked next to a locked door. The door opened. Annika Wise entered.

"Good morning!" she shouted over the death metal.

She wore black combat pants, black lace boots, and a black tank top. She carried a paper bag, setting it next to the boom box. She turned off the boom box and walked to Colin. She noted that the man was standing in his own waste.

"Yuck," she said. "You're a mess."

She stood close to Colin and looked up at his face. "Shall we continue?" she asked.

"I don't know what you want to know," cried Colin. "I would tell you if I knew!"

Annika appeared compassionate, touching Colin softly on his sweaty chest. "I don't want to hurt you. You believe that, don't you Colin?"

Colin nodded his head desperately. "Yes, yes, I believe you."

"That's good, Colin," Annika replied, "because it's very important that you and I are able to trust each other."

Annika paused, walking a slow circle around Colin. "I only have one question for you, Colin. Answer my question correctly, and you can go to your apartment. You can sleep in your bed. You can eat. You can drink. You can have a hot bath. Doesn't that sound good, Colin?"

"Yes," Colin replied.

"This is my question: Where did Kyle and Padma go?"

Colin began to cry.

"That's all I want to know—nothing else," Annika continued. "Just answer my question and everything is good. Your life is *so good*, Colin.

"Or, if you prefer, we could lie down again, you and I," Annika said, smiling, nodding toward a wet rubber mat in the corner of the room she used to waterboard Colin.

Colin sobbed, "I don't know! I would tell you if I knew. Navigation was offline when they jumped!"

Annika said, "I think navigation was online, and you erased the data."

"No! I'm telling the truth!" he cried.

"OK, I think you've been standing up long enough. Time for you to lie down," Annika said, unlocking his wrist shackles.

"No! No! I don't want to lie down!" Collin screamed. "I want to stand up! I want to stand up!"

Colin reached for Annika like a zombie. She slapped an arm away, stepped behind his leg, grabbed his testicles with one hand, and pushed the hollow of his neck with her thumb. Colin screamed in pain as he tumbled over Annika's leg onto the floor.

She shoved her knee on his sternum.

"You never, ever touch me without my permission," said Annika emphatically. "We've talked about this."

"I'm sorry! I'm sorry! I'm sorry!" cried Colin.

There was a knock at the two-way mirror. Annika got up.

"Don't worry, lover," Annika said, smiling. "I'll be right back."

Annika exited and joined General Craig in the shadowed observation room. They viewed Colin through the two-way mirror.

"He's telling the truth. He doesn't know anything," said Annika.

"A jump without navigation is madness," replied the general. "They could end up anywhere at any time—the bottom of the ocean, in the stratosphere, in molten lava."

"Maybe they thought molten lava was preferable to this," Annika said, nodding toward Colin, now clutching his legs in a fetal position in a corner of the room.

"No one appreciates my loving touch," she said, shaking her head.

"Sometimes I seriously worry about you," said the general.

"If you think I enjoy this, you're wrong," Annika replied. "I just happen to be good at it, which is why I'm telling you you're wasting your time. Everyone's story stacks up, and it's corroborated by the system log files. They jumped without navigation. They're probably dead."

"I won't be satisfied until I see the bodies," replied the general. "Strangelove thinks it may be possible to track the jump trajectory. Theoretical, but it's all we've got."

Standing Rock Reservation
South Dakota
September 11, 1890
14:32 hours
Timeline 003

The medicine man said something to Takoda, then gestured for Kyle and Padma to follow him.

"Our medicine man wants you to meet our chief, Tatanka Iyotake. Come, please."

Kyle's brow wrinkled in thought. The name was familiar to him.

The ring of ghost dancers parted to allow the four to pass through. The hundreds of dancers then closed behind, following them. Yellow Bird and Takoda led the couple east toward a village of buffalo hide tipis. To their right was a river that flowed east, partially obscured by knolls and groves of cottonwood trees. In the distance, beyond patches of trees, the river flowed into a much larger river that ran south.

"This is the Grand River," Kyle said to Padma, gesturing to the right. "That big river in the distance the Grand merges with is the Missouri."

Padma couldn't care less about the local geography. She still clung to hope that she would awaken from the nightmare through which they were strolling.

They entered the tipi village, several hundred yards north of the Grand River. The villagers stared at the strange couple with Yellow Bird and Takoda. Some wore traditional deerskin Lakota clothing, though many wore threadbare store-bought clothes—cotton dresses, trousers, and buttoned shirts.

Kyle and Padma noted the inhabitants were largely idle. Their appearance was gaunt—they were obviously malnourished.

"These people are Sioux?" asked Padma.

"That's what white people call them," said Kyle. "'Sioux' isn't a native word. It's a combination of native Ojibwa and French. It comes from the word *Natowessiwak*, which is what the Ojibwa call these people. It means 'little snakes'—presumably not a term of endearment.

"The French substituted their plural ending on the word and turned it into Nadoues*sioux*. Then the whites shortened it to 'Sioux,' and the name stuck. These people call themselves 'Lakota.'"

Kyle acknowledged the villagers' condition. "White people have hunted the buffalo to near extinction—mostly for sport. They shoot the buffalo and leave the carcasses to rot.

"The Lakota people were forced to live in this wasteland, where there is no food and nothing will grow. They live off government rations, which are at half the level they were promised in the latest broken treaty. The Lakota people are slowly starving to death."

The gathering emerged from the village. Fifty yards away stood a split-wood log cabin near the Grand River. A teenage girl sat in front of the cabin. Upon seeing the approaching crowd, she ran inside. Kyle and Padma watched as a man emerged, followed by two women. The man was in his late fifties, with two long braids resting on his chest. He wore a store-bought striped blue shirt, buckskin pants, and a matching fringed jacket. A beige felt hat with a narrow brim rested on his head. The Lakota women were wearing plain store-bought cotton dresses—ankle length, long sleeved, with modest necklines. The taller of the two wore a crimson dress. The other woman's dress was navy.

The woman in the navy dress carried a rough wooden chair, setting it on the ground in front of the cabin. A white horse stood near the cabin, munching on dry grass. The horse, a trick pony, had been a gift to the cabin's owner from the showman Buffalo Bill Cody.

The man sat in the chair, watching the approaching crowd warily. As they drew closer, Kyle recognized him.

"Holy shit," Kyle said.

"What?" asked Padma.

"It's Sitting Bull," he said. "I can't believe it."

Padma was silent.

Sitting Bull had achieved mythical status within his lifetime. In 1876, he received a vision foretelling the defeat of the white army at the hands of the Lakota. Inspiring his people, the Lakota annihilated General George Armstrong Custer's 7th Cavalry at the resulting Battle of Little Big Horn, leaving Custer and nearly 300 of his soldiers dead.

The public responded to news of the massacre with outrage. Thousands of troops were dispatched to the Dakotas, forcing the

Lakota tribes into unconditional surrender and onto the Standing Rock Reservation. Sitting Bull's tribe evaded the army for years, escaping to Canada. Facing starvation and pressure from the Canadian government, Sitting Bull eventually capitulated. In 1881, he became the last member of his tribe to surrender his rifle to the white army.

Sitting Bull was permitted to leave the reservation in 1885 when he joined Buffalo Bill's Wild West Show. He earned $50 a week to ride around the arena to the jeers of the white audience. During his stint with the show, he became close friends with both Buffalo Bill Cody and sharpshooter Annie Oakley. Cody gave Sitting Bull the white horse that munched grass outside his house.

In 1890, the old chief was a shell of bitterness, resigned that he would live out his remaining days in this wasteland prison, dependent on the whites for what few scraps they might throw. In 1883, he was trotted out to give a speech as the guest of honor at the opening ceremonies for the Northern Pacific Railroad. In his native language he said, "I hate all white people. You are thieves and liars. You have taken away our land and made us outcasts." Takoda, his interpreter, told the crowd the chief was happy to be there and that he looked forward to peace and prosperity with the white people. Sitting Bull received a standing ovation.

When the crowd arrived at the cabin, the medicine man approached Sitting Bull. He gestured at Kyle and Padma as he explained the story of the strange couple's miraculous appearance at the Ghost Dance.

Sitting Bull stared at the couple. His expression was grim.

Padma studied the chief's face—searing eyes atop cheekbones that defied gravity. A powerful aquiline nose hung over a recalcitrant chin. Padma noticed that a monarch butterfly was pinned to the front of Sitting Bull's felt hat. To Padma, the butterfly's vibrant orange and black wings seemed like an accessory that was incompatible with the man's circumstance. Then something occurred to her...

...*the butterfly is dead,* she thought.

As Yellow Bird spoke, the chief eyed Kyle and Padma closely. Their appearance was strange. Both were very tall—indeed, Padma was taller than most men he had ever seen. She was also the most beautiful woman he had ever laid eyes on. Until that moment, he had not believed he would ever see anything so beautiful for the rest of his life.

Yellow Bird gestured emphatically as he spoke, attempting to convey the enormity of the miracle the ghost dancers had witnessed.

Sitting Bull was unmoved. His stare did not leave Kyle and Padma. He had never believed in the magical powers ascribed to the Ghost Dance, though he had nonetheless permitted his tribe to practice the ritual. He rationalized that anything that kept his people distracted from their hopeless situation was probably a good thing.

Sitting Bull suspected the appearance of the strange couple to be yet another one of the white man's tricks. He gestured for Kyle and Padma to come forward. He spoke to them in Lakota.

Takoda translated, "Tatanka Iyotanka says he does not believe you are the Messiah. He believes this is a trick. He says if you are the Messiah, you must prove it."

Kyle looked at Padma. "Go right ahead, Messiah."

Padma shot Kyle a cold look. "My white servant will provide proof."

Kyle returned Padma's hard look. "You and I are going to have a talk later."

Kyle turned to Sitting Bull. "You had a vision a few years ago. You saw a meadowlark land on a hill beside you. It said, 'Your own people, Lakotas, will kill you.' Your vision is true. You will be shot dead by reservation police in a few months. Your son, Crow Foot, will also be killed."

As Takoda translated, Sitting Bull's dour expression did not betray his surprise. He had not shared the vision of his death with anyone.

"After your death," Kyle continued, "your tribe will flee and join with Chief Spotted Elk's tribe. The 7th Cavalry Regiment will intercept them and take them to Wounded Knee Creek. It is very cold. The Lakota people are freezing to death. Spotted Elk is dying from pneumonia.

"On the morning of December 29, the army will attempt to disarm your people."

Kyle pointed to Yellow Bird. "When they do, Yellow Bird will begin the Ghost Dance. He will throw a handful of dirt in the air and say, 'I have lived long enough.' He will tell the warriors not to fear the soldiers' bullets, that the bullets cannot penetrate them.

"Black Coyote, who is deaf, refuses to give up his rifle. When the soldiers try to take it from him, they struggle. A shot is fired.

"The soldiers open fire on Lakota men, women, and children with their rifles and Hotchkiss gun artillery. Over 300 Lakota men, women, and children are slaughtered, including Spotted Elk."

Kyle reached into his backpack and retrieved a laptop computer. Contained in its terabytes of storage was a vast storehouse of information, including history and technology. Kyle and Padma's original plan was to leverage part of that trove to rebuild their fortune.

Kyle typed on the keyboard. He turned the screen to face Sitting Bull. The chief's grim expression broke. His eyes went wide as a gasp emerged from his lips.

On the display was the grizzly image of Sitting Bull's half-brother, Chief Spotted Elk, known as "Big Foot" to the whites, frozen to death at Wounded Knee. In the picture, the frozen corpse's arms reached up from the ground. His head was elevated, as though he was attempting to rise from a fall at the moment he died.

Sitting Bull reached out to touch the screen, then put his hand on his chest.

"Twenty-five of the soldiers will receive the Medal of Honor for acts of valor for their role in the massacre," Kyle said.

Kyle touched a button on the keyboard. An image of an old newspaper article flashed onto the screen. Kyle slapped the laptop shut before Padma could see it.

"We don't need to look at that," he said, stuffing the laptop into his pack.

Sitting Bull looked at Kyle and Padma, shaken by the horror of the image of his brother's frozen body. That a white man had presented the obscenity to him was almost more than he could bear. Sitting Bull reviled the whites. Their easy capacity to lie, cheat, steal, and murder was woven into their pasty flesh. It was as though nature had bleached all the goodness out of men and all that remained were pale specters—the skin of evil.

Sitting Bull tried to regain his composure. He looked at Padma, asking a question while pointing at Kyle. Takoda translated.

"This white man is your servant?"

Padma rolled her eyes. "He is my husband."

"He will betray you," he said.

Padma's eyes locked on Kyle's. "Never!" she said.

Sitting Bull could see that Padma was sincere, though he could not reconcile the union of the beautiful native Messiah with the white demon.

The chief posed a question to the crowd. They answered in unison with a single word.

"*Han!*"

Takoda explained, "Tatanka Iyotanka asks the people if they saw what Yellow Bird saw. They say 'yes.'"

A breeze drifted through the congregation. Sitting Bull sat quietly for a few moments, looked up toward the sun, then let out a long sigh. He turned and spoke to Yellow Bird. The medicine man was surprised, and challenged Sitting Bull. The chief was insistent. Yellow Bird yielded.

Kyle and Padma looked at Takoda.

"What's going on?" asked Kyle.

Sitting Bull stood up, then unbuttoned his shirt and pulled it open for the couple to see his chest. Padma gasped.

On each breast, above the nipple, Sitting Bull's flesh had been mutilated, as though two large claws had ripped holes in his chest. A roar erupted from the crowd.

Sitting Bull gestured to Takoda to explain. Takoda, unsettled, took a few moments to recover.

"Tatanka Iyotanka will seek a vision in the Sun Dance," Takoda explained. "Big medicine. It is dangerous for him. It may kill him. Also, the whites have outlawed the Sun Dance. If he is caught, they will take him."

Sitting Bull spoke again, gesturing to Kyle and Padma. He then turned to one of the tribesmen and gave a command. The brave turned to leave, waving to several other tribesmen to follow him.

"They are preparing the lodge for the Sun Dance," said Takoda. "It is our chief's wish that our tribe provide you with food and shelter. We don't have much. The whites starve us, but what we have is yours."

Standing Rock Reservation
South Dakota
September 11, 1890
14:32 hours
Timeline 003

The orange sun was low in the western sky as Takoda guided Kyle and Padma to a tipi on the outskirts of the village. Several women and girls from the tribe trailed behind the Messiah-apparent and her white husband. They carried food, blankets, and clothing for the strange visitors. A starving yellow dog, ribs outlined through his skin, followed the group.

The tipi was isolated from the village, perched on a knoll of wavy grass near a grove of cottonwood trees that separated it from the Grand River. From the knoll, Kyle and Padma had an excellent view of the village some 50 yards away.

The tipi was large—nearly 20 feet tall with a base 20 feet in diameter. Unlike most of the other village dwellings, this one was painted. A band of red with white circles wrapped around the buffalo skin base. The top quarter of the cone was painted black. Two flaps opened at the top of the tipi, from which the supporting cottonwood poles thrust out of the tan buffalo shell into the blue sky. The image of a man was painted next to the door flap. In one hand, he held a long wooden pipe. In the other hand was a yellow circle, adorned with black and orange feathers.

"We have a saying," Takoda said. "A beautiful tipi is like a good mother: She hugs her children and protects them from heat and cold, snow and rain."

The women stepped forward with gifts. Most were for Padma. Sitting Bull's wives, Seen By Her Nation and Four Robes, were first in line. Seen By Her Nation was in her forties, tall compared to the other Lakota women. Padma estimated her height to be 5'7". Her two long braids framed a large brown face with powerful cheekbones that hollowed long cheeks into a rugged jaw and forward chin. Her braids fell upon her plain crimson cotton dress. Unlike many of her fellow tribeswomen, the hot sun and an excruciating life had not broken the stony expression she wore on her face. The exhausted woman exuded a look of inexhaustible defiance.

Without saying a word, Seen By Her Nation extended a bundle toward Padma. Padma took it—it was light, soft, folded doeskin with exquisite blue, red, and yellow beadwork. Padma unfolded it—it was a dress with a separate yoke, dazzling with thousands of blue glass beads. Geometric patterns of yellow, red, and white beads were set within a sea of blue.

"Oh my God!" Padma exclaimed. "It's beautiful!"

"It is a wedding dress," Takoda explained. "There is no more game to hunt, and no more beads, so it is rare and special."

Seen By Her Nation handed Padma matching beaded moccasins and a leather belt with smooth silver conchos.

Tears began to well in Padma's eyes. "I don't want to take

something so precious from her."

Seen By Her Nation could not understand Padma's words, though she could see how the gift affected her. She clutched Padma's arm affirmatively then turned to leave.

"How do I say 'thank you'?" Padma asked.

"*Pee-lah-mah-yah-yea*," replied Takoda.

"*Pee-lah-mah-yah-yea!*" said Padma, tears streaming down her cheeks.

Seen By Her Nation stopped and turned back to Padma. She placed a leathered hand on Padma's face, smiling as she wiped away a tear. She then turned to walk back to her cabin.

One by one, the others stepped forward with food, blankets, clothing, and supplies. One of Sitting Bull's teenage daughters, Standing Holy, handed Kyle a bundle of clothes—fringed buckskin pants, matching boots, and a cream-colored cotton work shirt. Kyle smiled and thanked the pretty young woman. She gave the handsome white man a shy smile in return.

After the others had left, Takoda turned to Padma and Kyle. "Is there anything else you need?" he asked.

"No—thank you, I mean, *pee-lah-mah-yah-yea*," said Padma, smiling. "Your people have been generous beyond words."

Kyle looked at Padma and Takoda. The handsome young brave concealed his crush for the beautiful Messiah behind serious, dutiful brown eyes. Though overwhelmed by the selflessness of Takoda and his people in the face of their desperation, there was still room in Padma's mind's eye to notice Takoda's chiseled face, dark chocolate eyes, and beautiful brown-skinned physique. Kyle noticed how well matched the pair seemed physically, with their skin and eyes and long black hair. Kyle felt a pang of jealousy, stirred with the awareness that he did not belong in this Lakota village.

"I will see you in the morning," Takoda said as he turned to leave. Kyle watched as Padma's gaze held on to Takoda's wake a moment too long. Suddenly aware of Kyle's eyes on her, Padma turned to him.

"What?" she asked, feigning innocence.

"Uh huh," Kyle replied skeptically.

"Honestly—I'm old enough to be his mother," Padma said. "Almost."

"Cougar," Kyle said.

Padma smacked Kyle's shoulder.

Kyle lifted the flap of the tipi for Padma and motioned for her to enter.

"After you, Messiah," he said.

"That's going to get old in a big hurry," she warned, clutching her dress and moccasins as she ducked into the tipi.

As she crossed the threshold, she was struck by the musky smell of buffalo hides mixed with charred wood. Blankets and buffalo pelts lay on the ground on either side of the tipi. Charred stones surrounded a fire pit in the center. An inner wall of deerskin, an ozan, was tied to the tipi's supporting poles. The ozan extended seven feet up the tipi's walls, then broke into a circular canopy above Kyle's and Padma's heads. An opening in the center of the canopy allowed smoke from the fire pit to escape from the tipi. Brightly colored painted geometric patterns ran vertically up the seams where the ozan was tied to the cottonwood poles—red bars with yellow spots and black accents, red and blue diamonds, red, yellow, and blue circles.

Kyle took off his backpack and set it on the ground, then exited to retrieve their supplies, including a wooden bucket, a charred metal pot, several cloth bags, a few ears of corn, and several wrapped paper bundles. He grabbed the food just before the skinny yellow dog that had been following them snatched away one of the parcels. Kyle opened one of the wrappers—inside was a one-pound cut of dried beef. He looked around to see if anyone was watching, then tore off a piece and tossed it to the dog. The yellow dog scarfed it down and wagged his tail for more. Kyle realized he had created a new problem.

The stillness inside the tipi contrasted with the noisy energy of the crowds that had greeted Kyle and Padma. For the first time since their arrival, the couple was alone.

Padma watched Kyle as he knelt on one of the buffalo hides to inventory their food rations. She clutched the wedding dress in her hands. Her heart began to race, and her breathing ran increasingly shallow as the impossibility of their situation landed on her. She gripped the dress tighter as she began to panic.

Kyle looked up from what he was doing to see Padma in distress, gasping for air. He leapt up from the buffalo skin and snatched the wedding dress and its wrapper from her hands. He tossed the dress aside and quickly fashioned the wrapper into a makeshift paper bag.

"Love, hold this," Kyle instructed. "Breathe into the bag."

Padma's eyes were wide with panic. She nodded and took the

bag, breathing into it as Kyle stroked her back.

"That's it," Kyle said. "You're doing great, love."

As Padma recovered the carbon dioxide she had exhaled into the bag, her respiratory alkalosis abated, and her breathing gradually calmed to normal.

"Sit down, love," Kyle said.

Kyle took her arm with one hand, his other on her back as he gently sat her on one of the buffalo hides. He sat beside her, stoking her back as she recovered.

"Deep breaths, love," said Kyle. "Nice, relaxed, deep breaths. You're doing great."

Padma inhaled fully and exhaled.

"It just hit me," Padma said. "I can't believe this."

"I know," Kyle said.

"This seems real," she said. "This doesn't seem like a dream. But this can't be real."

Kyle had not fully embraced their new reality either, though his mind was too fully immersed in their survival to reality-check their circumstances.

"Love," he said, "I think this is real."

Padma tried to summon herself.

"I'm OK now," she said, nodding. "What are we going to do?"

Kyle nodded at the foodstuff parcels on the other buffalo skin.

"We've got a pound of dried beef, a pound of dried bacon, a few ears of dried corn, a couple cups of beans, and a cup of sugar. If we ration it, it's only enough for a day—maybe two. If this is the best these people can do for their messiah, I don't want to think about what they're trying to live on.

"Survival is the first order of business. After that, I can figure out how to defeat the world's largest army. I have to get food and supplies."

"How does that work, exactly?" asked Padma. "It's not like there's a corner bodega."

"No, there isn't. I'm going to need to go to the nearest store."

"Which is where, exactly?"

Kyle made a blade with his hand, slicing the air to the left of the orange of the setting sun glowing through their tipi wall.

"About 200 miles," he said. "That way."

Padma raised her eyebrows. "And how, exactly, are we going to make a 400-mile round trip?"

Kyle took a deep breath. "*We* are not going to make a 400-mile round trip. I am."

Padma looked at him, stunned. "Don't even *think* about leaving me here alone!"

Kyle held Padma's shoulders and looked into her eyes. "To the whites, you'd be an Indian squaw who's off the reservation. You'd attract a lot of attention—a lot of *bad* attention."

"You would protect me. You always protect me."

"The place where I'm going, everybody's got a gun," Kyle said. "Maybe I could protect you, but that's what I'd be spending most of my time doing. Our best-case scenario is that we don't get killed and you don't get raped, but we're going to have a tough time getting the supplies we need while I'm in a gunfight with the entire town."

Padma looked down, trying to reconcile her fear with Kyle's logic.

"Seven years ago, you promised you would never leave me," she said.

"Technically, I'm not going to make that promise for another 111 years," replied Kyle.

Padma allowed a laugh to break the moment.

"Asshole," she said. "How long will you be?"

"Four days to get there, one day to supply, five or six days to return—I'll be driving at least one loaded wagon, and I'll be moving slower."

"Why does it take so long?" asked Padma. "Can't you take a train?"

"The trains don't cross the Lakota territory from east to west," explained Kyle. "Technically, it's illegal to lay tracks on Lakota territory, though the reality is that the railroads are worried about the financial downside of native attacks.

"The only train in South Dakota runs north-south along the southwest edge of the state, from Deadwood to Rapid City to Nebraska."

Padma marveled at how the former Delta operator had already thought through the logistics.

"You're in your element here," observed Padma. "All my MBA skills are completely useless. Crunching a spreadsheet or running a Bloomberg terminal won't do a fucking thing to keep us alive."

Kyle took his wife's hand.

"You're a leader. You made an executive decision to save

these people," said Kyle. "Your 'white servant' is just following your orders."

"Sorry about that," she said.

Kyle kissed her hand. "I'll make sure you're set before I go."

"I can manage," Padma said. "You do what you need to do."

Kyle watched Padma's face as she struggled to summon bravery in the face of unimaginable circumstance. Kyle pulled her close.

"Beloved, if there was another way..." Kyle said.

"I know," she nodded. "I'll be fine."

Padma was silent for a moment, thinking.

"Kyle?"

"What?"

"What was that article on your computer?"

Kyle looked at Padma, then pulled his computer out of his pack. He turned it on and handed it to her.

Padma read the article and gasped.

> Sitting Bull, most renowned Sioux of modern history, is dead. He was not a Chief, but without Kingly lineage he arose from a lowly position to the greatest Medicine Man of his time, by virtue of his shrewdness and daring.
>
> He was an Indian with a white man's spirit of hatred and revenge for those who had wronged him and his. In his day he saw his son and his tribe gradually driven from their possessions: forced to give up their old hunting grounds and espouse the hard working and uncongenial avocations of the whites. And these, his conquerors, were marked in their dealings with his

> people by selfishness, falsehood and treachery. What wonder that his wild nature, untamed by years of subjection, should still revolt? What wonder that a fiery rage still burned within his breast and that he should seek every opportunity of obtaining vengeance upon his natural enemies.
>
> The proud spirit of the original owners of these vast prairies inherited through centuries of fierce and bloody wars for their possession, lingered last in the bosom of Sitting Bull. With his fall the nobility of the Redskin is extinguished, and what few are left are a pack of whining curs who lick the hand that smites them. The Whites, by law of conquest, by justice of civilization, are masters of the American continent, and the best safety of the frontier settlements will be secured by the total annihilation of the few remaining Indians. Why not annihilation? Their glory has fled, their spirit broken, their manhood effaced; better that they die than live the miserable wretches that they are. History would forget these latter despicable beings, and speak, in later ages of the glory of these grand Kings of forest and plain that Cooper loved to heroism.
>
> We cannot honestly regret their extermination, but we at least do justice to the manly characteristics possessed, according to their lights and education, by the early Redskins of America.
>
> —L. Frank Baum

"This is the Frank Baum that wrote *The Wonderful World of Oz*?" asked Padma.

'Yup. He'll write the book in about 10 years. Right now, in 1890, he's the editor of *The Black Hills Pioneer*. He'll write this article in a few months after Sitting Bull is murdered by reservation police. The fact that he advocated genocide doesn't get much play."

"We're not exactly over the rainbow, are we?"

"No," Kyle said, shaking his head. "This is not the place where dreams come true."

Standing Rock Reservation
South Dakota
September 12, 1890
08:39 hours
Timeline 003

Padma opened her eyes. A shaft of morning light pierced the center of the ozan, making the center fire pit an oasis of light in the shadows. She felt for Kyle next to her in their buffalo bed—the space was vacant. She tried to sit up. Pain wracked her back from a fitful sleep on the ground. She reached for her backpack next to the bed, unzipped it, and retrieved a bright orange Hermès toiletry bag. She examined her face in a compact mirror.

"Oh God!" she exclaimed. "I look like shit."

The dirty face in the tiny mirror had puffy eyes and tangled hair.

She noticed that the wooden bucket the tribeswomen had provided was sitting next to the fire pit. It was full of water. A scrap of cloth intended to pass for a washcloth was draped on the side.

Kyle must have fetched water, she thought.

Padma heaved off the heavy buffalo pelt and crouched naked in front of the bucket. She dipped into the water with her cupped hands and drank, then splashed water on her face. She soaked the washcloth and gave herself a cursory sponge bath. Water ran down her legs and onto her feet, crusting them with mud on the dirt floor.

"Goddammit!" she said.

She knocked the mud off her feet as best she could and sat down on her buffalo bed. Reaching for her Hermès bag, she pulled out some makeup.

"If I'm going to be a messiah, I might as well look the part," she said.

She applied a light base, brushed a whiff of rouge and enhanced her eyes with liner, shadow, and mascara. Satisfied that she had salvaged her face as best she could, she set to work combing the tangles out of her long black hair.

Her clothes lay on the fur bed on the opposite side of the tipi. She walked to her frontier dressing room and reached for her jeans, then stopped. The beautiful doeskin dress, beaded yoke, and concho belt lay next to her jeans and blouse. She pulled the dress over her head, followed by the yoke. She then tied the leather belt with its smooth silver conchos. The belt's excess strap ran down her left thigh to her ankle. For extra measure, she decided to pull her hair into two long braids. She instinctively looked for a full-length mirror, then settled for her compact. She nodded at the results.

*I look **good**,* she thought.

Ready to greet the day, Padma swung open the door flap of the tipi and gasped with surprise.

Over 100 Lakota men and women were sitting in front of the tipi. They began to murmur excitedly at the sight of the beautiful Messiah in traditional dress.

"Good morning," said Takoda.

Startled, Padma whipped her head to her right to see the sentry guarding her door.

"Who are these people? Why are they here?" she asked.

"They have come from neighboring tribes to see the Messiah," explained Takoda. "Word of your arrival is spreading quickly."

"Does the Messiah require anything?" asked Takoda.

"Yes," Padma replied. "The Messiah needs to pee."

A smile broke Takoda's stoic face. He pointed to the grove of cottonwood trees behind the tipi.

"That is a good place," he said.

"Thank you," she said.

As Padma began to walk toward the trees, the others rose to their feet and began to follow her. Takoda raised his hands and ordered them to halt. Padma walked into the grove, finding a place that was out of sight of her paparazzi. She hiked up her dress and squatted.

When she returned to Takoda and her throng, she asked him if he had seen Kyle.

"Yes, I will take you to him," he said.

Padma and Takoda, followed by the multitude, walked to the opposite side of the village. There, she saw Kyle and several tribesmen with horses. Kyle was wearing his gifted fringed frontier pants, boots, and cotton pullover work shirt with band collar, pleated front, and puffed sleeves. When Kyle saw Padma, a broad smile broke onto his face.

"You look gorgeous!" he said.

"I like your new look too," she said, mirroring his grand smile. "What are you doing?"

"Arranging a ride," he said. "I'm thinking this one."

He patted the neck of a white mustang stallion. The stallion was tall compared to the other small horses—a little over 15 hands. The tribesman held the horse with a simple leather strap that served quadruple duty as bit, bridle, halter, and reins. Kyle nodded to the tribesman, who handed the reins to Kyle. He led the mustang a few feet away from the other horses.

"What do you think you're doing?" asked Padma. "You're not getting on that!"

Kyle peeled off his frontier shirt, exposing a superhero torso erupting out of his buckskin pants. He handed his shirt to Padma.

"It's a little warm this morning. Can you hold this for me, love?" he said.

Padma took his shirt with an exasperated gasp. Before she could protest, Kyle took the horse's reins and swung them over its neck. He walked to the horse's left side and prepared to mount, then changed his mind and walked to the horse's right side. He mounted the mustang from the ground, scissor kicking his leg up and over the horse's back.

The tribesmen nodded at each other. They had never seen a white man ground mount a bareback horse before. They didn't think the whites could ride a horse without a saddle. Kyle knew he had scored bonus points by mounting on the horse's right side—whites always mounted on the left.

Kyle applied leg pressure to bring the horse to a trot. He trotted a few circles around the group, then asked the horse for more. The mustang broke into a gallop to the yips of the tribesmen impressed with Kyle's riding skill. Kyle rode out of the village at high speed, wind blowing through his hair and the horse's mane. Kyle laughed as he galloped the grassy plain, thrusting his pelvis in time with the mustang's powerful rolling gait. He then turned and rode back to the group, sliding to a stop.

"I told you I'd look good on a white horse," he said to Padma, flashing a brilliant smile.

"I am so hot for you right now," she said.

Kyle swung his right leg over the horse's head and slid off in front of Padma. He grabbed her by the waist and gave her big kiss. Padma swooned.

He turned to the horse's owner. "That was fun—*pee-lah-mah-yah-yea*," Kyle said.

He offered the owner a spare combat knife he had brought with him as compensation for the horse. The owner took the knife, admiring its shiny blade. The owner made a horizontal slicing motion with his hand, signifying that the two men had made a deal. Kyle echoed the hand motion.

"I've known you for two lifetimes, and I still had no idea you could do that," Padma said.

"When I went to high school in Palo Alto, I used to hang with the Stanford polo team after school. They taught me how to ride. At the time, I never knew I'd have a practical application for polo."

"Pegasus!" Padma said.

"What?"

"Pegasus—he's going to help Bellerophon kill the fire-breathing Chimera," Padma said. "Bellerophon—that would be you," she added as she poked Kyle in his bare chest with her finger.

Kyle grinned. "Indeed I am."

• • •

An hour later, Kyle, Padma, and Takoda stood in front of their tipi. Kyle wore his MP7 submachine gun strapped to a holster on his right thigh. His combat knife was fixed in its sheath on his belt. He held Padma's smaller black backpack, which was stuffed with essentials he needed for his journey.

"You'll protect my wife while I am away?" Kyle asked Takoda for the umpteenth time.

"Nothing is more important than the Messiah," Takoda replied. "I will protect her with my life."

Kyle turned to Padma. She took his face in her hands and kissed him hard. It felt like the goodbye kiss Kyle '01 had given her seven years earlier in their honeymoon suite at the Soho Grand, before he went to his death.

Padma tried to summon strength in the face of her fear. She feared for Kyle's life, as she had during his mission to the other Time Tunnel, though this was worse. Kyle was going to be gone much longer, leaving Padma alone—an alien in the Lakota world, entirely dependent on strangers for survival. All her skills as Empress of America amounted to nothing in this place. She didn't know how to get food or build a fire. She was helpless.

She felt a panic ascend from her core. It felt like a child's raw fear. She tried to fight it. She began to cry.

She could not stop the tears. Part of her, the Empress of America, criticized the part of her that was overwhelmed by a wellspring of feeling—mourning the loss of her first Kyle all over again and preemptively mourning the second Kyle, all the while fearing for her own life.

"I can't lose you again," she sobbed.

Kyle took her hands and kissed them. "You won't. I promise I'm coming back, beloved."

The empress reminded her that the Messiah needed to put on a good show for her flock. Her feeling side told the empress to fuck herself.

Padma wrapped her arms around his neck and held on tight.

"You swear?" she asked.

"I swear," Kyle said. "Please don't worry, love."

She slowly pulled away from him, trying her best to put on a brave face, not for the Empress of America or for the Messiah's multitudes. Instead, she tried to be brave for her courageous warrior, for whom the distraction of a heartbroken wife could spell the difference between life and death.

Kyle handed his backpack to Takoda, then leapt onto his horse. Takoda handed the pack to Kyle. He slung it on his shoulders and waved goodbye as Pegasus trotted southwest toward the town of Deadwood.

Standing Rock Reservation
South Dakota
September 13, 1890
12:29 hours
Timeline 003

Sitting Bull drew a knife across his forearm for the hundredth time. His arms were red with blood, which flowed onto his legs, bent akimbo on the floor in the lotus position. He sat on a bed of sage in a sweat lodge in total darkness. The heat in the dome-shaped lodge was sweltering. Sweat mixed with the holy man's blood, soaking his loincloth, his only stitch of clothing. Sitting Bull breathed in scents of sage and cedar, intermingled with his own blood and sweat. Outside the lodge, Sitting Bull could hear a steady drumbeat. Yellow Bird sang.

The purpose of the sweat lodge rite of Inipi was to purify Sitting Bull and prepare him for his vision quest in the Sun Dance. Outside the door of the sweat lodge, facing east, a fire pit represented the sun. A crescent mound partially encircling the lodge represented the moon. These symbols represented the outer world, or cosmos, which held the inner world Inipi lodge like the womb of the universe. Inipi would rebirth Sitting Bull's soul, leaving his impurities within the lodge when he made his eventual exit.

Three times over the course of hours, Yellow Bird had thrown open the lodge door to signify three of the four ages described in lore. Sitting Bull awaited the fourth age and his exit from the lodge.

The chief felt a stirring he had not known in years. Until the arrival of the strange visitors, he had been living a slow death on the white man's reservation. The life of the Lakota people was over. They had been driven off their sacred green land in the Black Hills and deprived of their buffalo, around which their lives revolved. The Lakota people did not depend on the buffalo merely for food and shelter. They also relied on the herd to set the rhythm of their lives. Unlike the whites, the Lakota people were not stationary. They were nomads, flowing with the currents and eddies of the buffalo herd.

The buffalo were now all but extinct, as were the Lakota people.

Now in this wasteland, the Lakota people were forced to become farmers on land that could not be farmed. They were required to change their nature instantly to something completely foreign, as though a fish was suddenly required to be a tree.

With every draw of the knife blade against his skin, the pain awakened a part of Sitting Bull that he had thought dead. His pain, blood, and sweat pooled in the Inipi into a spiritual maelstrom.

The lodge flap was flung open, sending a shaft of blinding yellow sun onto Sitting Bull. He rose from his sage bed and emerged from the lodge. Hundreds of Lakota tribespeople surrounded the lodge, watching in reverence as the legendary holy man was reborn. They prayed that his rebirth would also be their own.

The drum continued to beat as Yellow Bird sang. Sitting Bull followed Yellow Bird from the sweat lodge to the Sun Dance pole, a large cottonwood tree trimmed of its branches and sunk vertically into the ground. Two leather straps were tied to the pole. Buffalo skulls created a circular perimeter around the pole at a radius of 20 feet. Yellow Bird stopped in front of the pole and brushed it with sage. He then turned to face Sitting Bull. Sitting Bull nodded for Yellow Bird to continue.

Yellow Bird held a piece of sharpened bone approximately five inches long. He placed the sharpened tip to Sitting Bull's left breast, beneath the scarred flesh from his previous Sun Dance, and pushed the bone into the skin and muscle behind the nipple. Sitting Bull's expression did not flinch as the bone was driven through the flesh, the tip emerging on the opposite side.

Yellow Bird repeated the process on the opposite breast. He then returned to the cottonwood pole and retrieved the leather straps. Loops were tied in the ends of the straps, which Yellow Bird fitted over the two bones protruding from Sitting Bull's chest.

As Yellow Bird began to sing, a dozen drummers began pounding their drums in unison. Sitting Bull pulled hard against the leather straps, pulling his flesh away from his chest in twin cones. Blood seeped from the tears in his skin, flowing down his torso and into his loincloth.

Over the next two hours, Sitting Bull heaved against the straps as the drums pounded and Yellow Bird sang. Others from the tribe joined in the singing, swept up in their chief's odyssey.

Sitting Bull gazed at the straps that connected his chest to the cottonwood pole. The old chief was exhausted from the sweat lodge, the blood loss, the excruciating pain. He questioned whether he had the strength to complete the ritual.

Sitting Bull gritted his teeth and roared as he summoned his remaining strength to heave against the strap. One of the bones ripped away from his chest. The strap hung with the bone and shreds of his flesh. The crowd went silent as they watched their chief, barely able to stand, his chest tethered to the pole by a single leather strap.

Sitting Bull paused for a moment, then gave another heave, ripping the second bone from his chest. He fell to the ground on his back, looking directly into the sun.

Though the sun was blindingly bright, he did not avert his gaze from it. He began to see small fuzzy dark patches float leisurely across the sun's face. The patches began to descend slowly to earth, settling on the ground around him. They were feathers. At first there were only a handful of feathers. More feathers fell to the ground—dozens, then hundreds. Sitting Bull picked up one of the feathers to examine it. It was old and dry. The feather's smooth vane was cracked and splayed. He looked around. The feathers now numbered in the thousands. A gentle wind began to blow from the east. The feathers began to tumble across the dried grass plains toward the hills to the west. Sitting Bull followed them. Millions of feathers now began to drift and tumble toward the Black Hills. Sitting Bull noticed that the hills seemed gray in color, as though the trees and vegetation were covered in dust. The feathers began to ascend, rising with the hills. Sitting Bull snatched one from midair. It was young again, flawlessly formed into a supple blade. The feathers began to converge toward a single mountaintop. A shape began to take form—a giant golden eagle! The eagle was female. The eagle gave Sitting Bull a hard look. Sitting Bull saw that the eagle was missing one flight feather from her wing. He reached behind his head, pulling his sole feather from his hair. He inserted it into the eagle's wing, completing her plumage.

The eagle's beak opened wide. A deafening screech quaked the mountain, shaking the gray dust off the trees and restoring the verdant green to the hills. Sitting Bull then watched as the eagle spread her wings and ascended into the blinding sun.

Sitting Bull opened his eyes. He saw Yellow Bird's concerned face hovering over him.

"The woman," Sitting Bull gasped, "she is the Messiah."

South Dakota
September 13, 1890
21:10 hours
Timeline 003

Kyle watched the flames leap and flicker from his campfire. The sound of water flowing over stones in a nearby stream intertwined with the crackling wood of his fire. He pulled a piece of rabbit flesh from the bone. He had shot the animal that afternoon when it darted across his path.

Pegasus stood nearby. Full from munching grass and tired from the day's ride, his eyelids grew heavy. He began to doze.

The Milky Way arced brilliantly across the sky, interrupted only by a crescent moon. Kyle now lived in a time when humans lacked the capacity to diminish the lights of the cosmos as they could in the twenty-first century. He wondered what else humans had lost in his time as they had bleached out the stars.

Kyle heard rustling in the brush. He pulled his MP7 from its holster. Its laser sight lit between the eyes of the yellow dog he had fed the previous day.

"I guess I'm stuck with you," he sighed, holstering his weapon.

He picked up the remains of the rabbit and tossed them to the dog. The hungry dog downed the rabbit carcass, complete with bones, in seconds. He wagged his tail. The dog resembled a small yellow Labrador retriever.

"We'll find more for you to eat tomorrow," Kyle said. "In the meantime, what shall I call you?"

The dog looked at Kyle, wagging his tail. Kyle thought about the speed with which the dog had vacuumed the rabbit.

"Hoover," Kyle said.

Kyle lay on the soft ground next to the fire.

"C'mon, boy," Kyle said, patting the ground. "It's OK."

Hoover stepped cautiously to Kyle and lay down next to him. Kyle stroked Hoover's head and back. After a few moments, Hoover let out a long sigh, relaxing his guard with his new human friend. Within minutes, they were both fast asleep.

Standing Rock Reservation
South Dakota
September 14, 1890
13:50 hours
Timeline 003

Daniel Royer held the reins of two horses pulling a buckboard wagon across the Standing Rock Reservation prairie. Bouncing next to him in the leaf-spring wooden bench seat was his nephew, Lewis McIlvaine, whom he had recruited to teach the Lakota people baseball.

Lewis was dressed for the occasion, wearing an Edwardian club collar shirt tucked into brown and white plaid knickers with calf-length socks. Leather suspenders were hiked over his strapping shoulders. A newsboy cap sat on his head. He held a leather baseball mitt in his hand, folded over a ball. A wooden bat bounced on the floorboard next to Royer's Henry rifle.

Royer's attire was inappropriately formal for the frontier. He wore a charcoal frock coat with matching waistcoat, a white shirt with a high-stand collar, and a black silk tie with a brass tie tack. A black derby hat sat atop a prematurely balding head of blond hair. Wire-rim spectacles perched on a beak-like nose. His full moustache was bordered by ample sideburns.

Royer had been named Indian agent at Pine Rock a few weeks earlier, the result of political misfortune. Newly elected President Benjamin Harrison had decided to make the office of Indian agent a political patronage post. Described as a man "destitute of those qualities by which he could justly lay claim to the position—experience, force of character, courage, and sound judgment," the inexperienced Royer was the worst possible choice for constructive reconciliation with the Lakota people.

In his 39 years, Royer had already proven himself a failure in a variety of professions, including medicine, pharmacology, teaching, and newspaper editing. He was terrified of the Native Americans in his charge, so much so that the Lakota had named him "Young Man Afraid of Indians." He always kept a loaded rifle in his buckboard, and had already shocked his nephew by firing it in panic at a band of blowing tumbleweeds he mistook for marauding warriors. Lewis had been brainstorming excuses to return to his native Huron, South Dakota, when Royer asked him to accompany him on a tour of the fringe of Sitting Bull's village. At the top of his lengthy list of Lakota phobias was their new religion, the so-called "Ghost Dance," which Royer mistook for a war dance. Royer was convinced that it was only a matter of time before the Lakota rose up and wiped out the neighboring whites. From the moment he landed in his post, he issued telegram after telegram to Washington, warning of the Ghost Dance threat and anxiously requesting troops to disarm the Lakota people before the massacre that was sure to happen.

Leveraging connections from his newspaper days, Royer fanned the flames of hysteria through the media. Some publicly argued for the complete extermination of all Native Americans.

Ostensibly, Royer's excuse for the buckboard excursion was to introduce Lewis to the tribespeople for their indoctrination into America's favorite pastime. In reality, Royer had no plans to go anywhere near the Lakota people. His intention was to use his looking glass to spy on the Lakota from a safe distance in order to gather additional evidence of their Ghost Dance and impending massacre of the whites. His buff companion Lewis was onboard purely for protection.

Royer fretted about the increasingly bizarre stories coming out of Sitting Bull's village. It was said that Sitting Bull had broken the law by participating in a Sun Dance. Another rumor was that the ghost dancers were impervious to bullets. Stranger still was gossip that the ghost dancers had actually succeeded in summoning their messiah—a breathtakingly beautiful native woman who spoke perfect English.

Royer and Lewis drove south toward the creek that bordered the north edge of Sitting Bull's village. As they approached, Lewis pointed toward a band of tribespeople—perhaps 30 men and women. They had crossed the creek and were approximately one mile north of the village.

"Shall we teach them the game?" asked Lewis.

Royer frowned. He had not anticipated encountering natives this far from the village. He felt his heart race, though he also felt the expectant eyes of his nephew on him. After the embarrassing shooting match with the tumbleweeds, he did not want to appear the cowardly paranoid that Lewis had already sized him down to be.

"We shall," declared Royer, steering the buckboard toward the group.

Padma eyed the buckboard warily as it approached. Tired of being followed everywhere by the growing multitudes—now numbering well into the hundreds—she'd told Takoda that she needed a break. Takoda had reluctantly agreed to a walk outside the village, though he insisted that the party be accompanied by armed escort. A small army of two dozen warriors with rifles joined Padma, Takoda, and Sitting Bull's wives, Four Robes and Seen By Her Nation, as well as his daughters, Lodge In Sight and Standing Holy.

"Young Man Afraid of Indians," said Takoda, as he watched the buckboard approach.

"What?" exclaimed Padma.

Takoda explained Royer to Padma.

"He is only dangerous if he spooks," explained Takoda. "Though he is very spooky."

Royer's buckboard rolled up to Padma's entourage. Royer was instantly struck by the beautiful squaw, nearly half a foot taller than the others in her party. He eyed the warriors' rifles with fear. Lewis looked at Royer, waiting for him to say something. Royer stood up from his seat, clutching his rifle.

"We have come to teach you the game of baseball," announced Royer.

Takoda translated. The tribespeople looked at each other, confused. Padma burst out laughing. Heaping baseball atop the pile of surreality—time travel, starving Native Americans, the pending massacre at Wounded Knee—was simply insane. Padma gripped her stomach, laughing so hard that it hurt. Takoda and the others hadn't the faintest idea what Padma found funny, though her laughing was infectious. In moments, the entire group was cackling. Lewis covered his mouth with his hand, fighting back a chuckle.

Humiliated by the hysterically laughing squaw, Royer attempted to regain control.

"Before we begin, you will all disarm. You will give your rifles to this man," Royer commanded, pointing to Lewis.

The laughter died down as Takoda translated. The tribesmen grumbled and pulled the hammers on their rifles.

Panicked, Royer raised his rifle and pointed it frantically at the tribespeople, shifting his aim manically from warrior to warrior.

Padma raised her hands and stepped forward. "No, wait!" she shouted.

Royer fired, hitting Padma in the chest, knocking her flat on the ground. Takoda and the others were stunned. Royer had killed the Messiah! Through the clearing gun smoke, Takoda and the others looked at Padma's still body on the ground, then instantly snapped up their rifles to kill Royer.

"Stop!"

They turned. To their astonishment, Padma was sitting up. Smoke wafted from the charred bullet hole in the heart of her doeskin dress.

She stood up and walked defiantly to Royer. Royer's rifle was pointed directly at her. The rifle barrel was shaking.

"You may leave now, or you may die," Padma told Royer grimly. "You have five seconds to decide which you prefer."

Royer was frozen in terror. He had shot the squaw through the heart, and yet she was now standing and speaking to him in perfect English. Were these people really bulletproof, as their Ghost Dance religion claimed? Was this their messiah?

Lewis looked at the petrified Royer, then snatched the rifle out of his hands, grabbed the reins and cued the horses to gallop away. Unprepared for the jackrabbit departure, Royer flipped backwards over the wooden bench seat, face-planting on the buckboard bed. His derby hat bounced on the ground in the buckboard's dusty wake.

Takoda and the others stared at Padma, stunned. They dropped to their knees. Padma was truly the Messiah.

"I want to return to the village now," said Padma. "Please get up."

Royer's derby hat rolled up to Padma's feet. She reached down and picked it up, handing it to Takoda.

"Do you want this?" she asked.

Takoda took the hat with the reverence with which a nun would have received the Shroud of Turin. Had Padma handed him a buffalo turd at that moment, he would have treated it as a sacred relic.

"Yes! Yes!" Takoda replied. "Thank you, Messiah!"

Takoda pulled the hat on his head. The others envied the special treatment afforded Takoda by the Messiah.

No one said a word during the walk back to the village. Takoda and the others stole glances at Padma. Her eyes never met theirs.

Her forward stare and severe expression never budged.

When they arrived, Padma immediately disappeared into her tipi as the others ran to tell their fellow tribespeople of the latest miracle they had witnessed.

Inside her tipi, Padma clapped her hands over her mouth to muffle her gasp of pain. The long walk back to the village had strained every last fiber of fortitude. Every breath she took fired shrieks of searing pain through her chest. She removed her dress, revealing her Kevlar vest beneath. The flattened remnant of a spent bullet was impacted in the center of the vest. Kyle had made Padma swear that she would wear the vest in his absence.

Padma carefully removed the vest, examining the fresh purple welt on her sternum where the bullet had impacted. She touched the mark between her breasts. The pain from her cracked sternum was excruciating. Outside the tipi, she heard a growing chorus, crackling with excitement as word of the Messiah's latest wonder spread through the camp like a prairie wildfire.

Standing Rock Reservation
South Dakota
September 15, 1890
08:15 hours
Timeline 003

Sitting Bull opened his eyes to see the rough-hewn boards of the ceiling of his log cabin. His chest and arms were wrapped with torn cloth, stained with two tones of crimson from dried and fresh blood.

He struggled to sit up in a bed made from several layers of old blankets piled on the floor. He raised his back against the wall and scanned the cabin. His wives, Seen By Her Nation and Four Robes, worked at the opposite side of the cabin preparing rations on a wooden table. When they saw that Sitting Bull was conscious, they came to him and knelt at his bed. Seen By Her Nation felt one of his wounds. He winced.

"You're a fool," she said.

"I had to know," he said. "I needed proof."

"People appearing out of lightning isn't proof enough for you?"

"I didn't see them appear."

They heard someone step into the doorway of the cabin. Sitting Bull's wives turned to see a barrel-chested Lakota man, about 50 years old, dressed in a threadbare suit. The man had a wide face, high cheekbones, and a cleft chin. They recognized the man. His name was Gall—formerly Chief Gall.

Gall had commanded the Lakota counter-attack on General Custer's troops at the Battle of Little Big Horn, annihilating the general's army. After years on the run pursued by federal troops, Gall eventually gave up and surrendered, renouncing Sitting Bull and his hatred of white people. Gall took up farming, curried favor with Daniel Royer's predecessor, and was appointed as a judge of the Court of Indian Affairs. He enjoyed a rare prestige among the whites, along with double the rations his people received. Sitting Bull and Gall had not spoken in years.

Sitting Bull noticed that Gall had gained weight since he had last seen him.

Sitting Bull's wives rose from the floor and exited the cabin, giving Gall a hard stare on their way out the door.

"So it's true," Gall said, observing Sitting Bull's bloodstained bandages. "You performed the Sun Dance."

Sitting Bull was silent. Gall walked to the table, picked up a rickety wooden chair and set it at the foot of Sitting Bull's bed. He sat in the chair.

"The Sun Dance is illegal," said Gall. "I could have you arrested."

"Do what you need to do to serve your white masters," replied Sitting Bull scornfully.

"They are *not* my masters!" shouted Gall. "I am a judge! I have honor!"

The two men stared at each other. Sitting Bull broke the silence.

"What do you want?"

Gall folded his arms. "Agent Royer says he shot a woman through the heart and she lived. The people say she appeared from lightning. They say she is the Messiah of the Ghost Dance prophecy. Are these stories true?"

Sitting Bull was quiet. He felt growing fatigue as the pain of his wounds siphoned his strength.

"If Young Man Afraid of Indians says he shot a woman through the heart and she lived, why do you need to ask me?" asked Sitting Bull. "I wasn't there. I didn't see it."

Sitting Bull could see that Gall was uneasy.

"Why did you perform the Sun Dance?" demanded Gall. "You know it's illegal. You know you could go to prison. You could die. Why would you take such a risk?"

"I did not witness the woman's arrival," answered Sitting Bull. "I had to know whether what my people said was true."

"Did you have a vision?" asked Gall anxiously.

"Yes," replied Sitting Bull.

Gall waited for Sitting Bull to render a verdict. Sitting Bull enjoyed the moment, tormenting his former mentee.

"And?" persisted Gall.

"She is the Messiah," answered Sitting Bull.

"She is *not* the Messiah!" shouted Gall rising from his chair and kicking it over. "There *is* no messiah! The prophecy is false—it was concocted by a charlatan."

"I did not believe in the Ghost Dance," Sitting Bull said. "I permitted the dance because it gave my tribe hope, but I did not believe in it. I was wrong. The woman is the Messiah."

Gall put his hands on his hips and paced, agitated, across the cabin floor.

"Years ago, I told you of my vision of our victory at the Little Big Horn," Sitting Bull said. "You know that vision was true. Since that time, I have had only two visions, this one about the Messiah… and another about my death."

Gall turned, surprised.

"Your death? How?"

"Later this year. I will be killed by Indian police."

Gall was distressed. The thought of his mentor's death sliced through the years of bitterness that divided the two men. Gall did not take Sitting Bull's visions lightly.

"Have you met the Messiah?" asked Sitting Bull.

"Stop calling her that," replied Gall.

"Have you met her?"

"No," Gall replied.

"You should," advised Sitting Bull.

Gall turned and looked out one of the cabin windows.

"Why did you come here?" asked Sitting Bull.

"I came to ask about the woman," replied Gall.

"No," said Sitting Bull. "You came for much more."

Gall was silent.

"Your white clothes are at war with your Lakota blood," said Sitting Bull, divining the conflict within Gall. "This story of the Messiah—it has awakened your Lakota heart. You thought it was dead. You wanted it to be dead."

"I have given up hope," conceded Gall.

"I have too," said Sitting Bull. "My hope has not been restored. I am too old and tired for hope. I simply know what is true. I don't know where the truth goes. I only know the truth carries me now, downstream, wherever it goes."

"I don't dare to hope," said Gall. "Hope holds too much pain." Gall put his hand on the left side of his abdomen, over a scar where he had been bayonetted and left for dead by soldiers years earlier.

"It is futile to fight the whites. We tried to avenge our Cheyenne brothers and sisters after the whites slaughtered them at Sand Creek. Our brothers and sisters asked for peace with the whites. They raised the white's flag over their village at Sand Creek. The whites killed women and children. They took scalps. They cut babies out of the bellies of their mothers.

"Chief Red Cloud tried to avenge them. We won many battles… but we lost the war. They starved us out of the Black Hills. We ended up here. This is where we wait to die. The armies of the whites are too powerful, and we are now too weak. We can refuse our circumstances and die now, or we accept our defeat and die later. Those are our only choices."

Sitting Bull raised his hands to his chest wounds. "It doesn't matter whether you hope or not. What will happen will happen whether you have hope or you don't."

"I wish she had not come," Gall said bitterly. "I was resigned to this life. She tempts me to remember my old life—the life I have tried to forget."

Sitting Bull stared at Gall. "White clothes do not change the warrior's color."

Gall turned to leave. "Whatever she is, she is dangerous," he said as he exited the cabin.

Mount Moriah Cemetery
Deadwood, SD
September 16, 1890
08:50 hours
Timeline 003

Kyle sat astride Pegasus on a plateau overlooking the town of Deadwood, South Dakota. The sprawling town was cradled in the arms of hills that had been largely denuded of their evergreen trees by the town's citizens. As Kyle beheld the nineteenth-century town below him, one thought was center in his mind.

God, my ass hurts.

Kyle had alternated between riding and walking the four days to Deadwood, carrying a heavy backpack the entire way. Pegasus had been a trooper on the journey—remarkably steady for a wild horse, particularly a stallion. In the course of their time together, Pegasus had accepted Kyle as a trustworthy companion, someone who would keep him out of danger. The trust was reciprocal—the more Kyle rode his horse, the greater his confidence that Pegasus would not spook or bolt with his bareback passenger. Over four days, the two had become a team.

The plateau on which Kyle and Pegasus stood was Mount Moriah, home to Deadwood's cemetery. Kyle walked his horse to the only gravesite he wanted to visit. A simple wooden marker stood behind a wrought iron fence. Black letters were painted on the tall, white, narrow wooden marker—a painful farewell from one dear friend to another.

Kyle dismounted his horse and stood for a few moments before the monument. He had missed the murder of the legendary Wild Bill Hickok by 14 years. Jack McCall shot Hickok in the back of the head the day after Wild Bill won all of McCall's money in a poker game at Deadwood's Number 10 Saloon. Hickok was holding two pairs at the time, aces and eights, forever since known as the "dead man's hand."

McCall was acquitted of the charge of murder, claiming revenge for his brother's slaying by Hickok—a brother McCall never had. Commenting on the verdict, the town's newspaper, the *Black Hills Pioneer*, reported, "Should it ever be our misfortune to kill a man, we would simply ask that our trial may take place in some of the mining camps of these hills."

Unbeknownst to McCall, his trial had no legal basis, as Deadwood was on Indian Territory in 1876. Fearing for his life in Deadwood, McCall fled to Wyoming, where his non-stop bragging about shooting Wild Bill Hickok earned him a second trial, followed by a swift hanging in 1877. He was buried with the noose around his neck.

Hoover looked up at Kyle inquisitively.

"OK, boy," Kyle said. "Let's go."

Kyle set his heavy backpack on a headstone, then remounted his horse. After remounting, he heaved the pack off the headstone and strapped it on his back.

Kyle guided Pegasus down the hill along a narrow dirt path to Deadwood's Main Street. Hoover followed Pegasus closely, just out of the horse's kick range. Standing in the center of the thoroughfare, Kyle shook his head at the sight, unable to fully believe he was actually in nineteenth-century Deadwood.

The Deadwood of 1890 was very different from the one where Wild Bill Hickok played his last poker hand. A fire in 1879 decimated the miners' ramshackle wooden camp. What rose from those ashes was a Gilded Age city of stone and brick buildings bordering a wide central thoroughfare. Gold from George Hearst's Homestead mine and other strikes had transformed Deadwood into a prosperous modern town that even included South Dakota's first telephone exchange.

As Kyle rode Pegasus down Main Street, he tried to avoid staring at the people walking along the thoroughfare. Though exhausted from the long journey, he was thrilled to step into a day in the historic town while its history was still being written.

Filthy from the journey, Kyle expected to be inconspicuous in the legendary mining town. Instead, he found himself a ruffian compared to Deadwood's well-heeled citizens. Though many of the Caucasian men still wore the rough-and-tumble frontier wear of cowboys or mine laborers, many wore business suits, long frock coats with high-collared excelsior shirts, silk ties, and top hats or derbies. Women's clothing left everything to the imagination, covering every inch of skin with the exception of the hands and face. Many women wore jersey bodices over long draped skirts with modest bustles. Chinese men wearing traditional long Changchun shirts walked to and from Chinatown in the northern part of Deadwood. Black Xiao Mao skullcaps covered their heads, which were shaved in the front and on the sides, with hair in the back braided into long queues. The hairstyle was mandated by the Manchus, and cutting one's queue was an open act of rebellion, punishable by death. Their long queues tethered them to a homeland thousands of miles across the ocean.

Kyle walked his horse up Main Street, past all the obvious stores where he could purchase essentials—food, clothing, and supplies. Instead, he drove Pegasus to the very first place Padma insisted that Kyle visit upon his arrival in Deadwood. He stopped his horse in front of a narrow three-story red brick building. The gold letters on the building's windows read "First National Bank of Deadwood."

Kyle slid off Pegasus' back, tied his reins to the hitching post in front of the bank, and walked in. Hoover followed him.

Inside, he faced a carved wooden wall at the opposite side of a large room. Three small rectangular teller windows guarded with iron bars were inset to the wall. Wooden signs with gold paint letters reading "Teller" were mounted above each window. Only one of the three teller windows was open—the other two were shuttered. Kyle looked to his left. A man sat at a desk, scribbling into a ledger with a fountain pen. The man was in his thirties, with a mustache, long sideburns, and brown hair combed tightly across his head. He wore a high-collared white shirt, with a navy silk tie inserted into a charcoal vest. Daylight from the bank's large front window lit the man's ledger. An armed guard wearing a navy uniform stood to Kyle's right.

"Dogs are not permitted in this establishment," said the guard.

"They are today," replied Kyle.

Peering behind the teller window was another man in his early thirties, with wire-rim spectacles and brown hair in a tight combover. His clothing was virtually identical to the man behind the desk.

The man at the desk looked up. His eyes widened. Standing before him was a very tall man—physically imposing, disgustingly filthy—with a yellow dog. Kyle's shirt was stained with sweat and dirt. His hair was greasy, and he had a four-day growth of beard. The man noticed that Kyle had a strange weapon holstered on his thigh. He had never seen anything like it—it was larger than a pistol, though much smaller than a rifle.

The man rose from his desk and called out to Kyle, "How may I be of service, sir?"

"You may introduce me to your bank president," Kyle replied.

The banker looked at Kyle, incredulous. "I am quite sure that I can assist you with whatever services you require, sir."

Kyle walked to the desk and looked the banker in the eye. "I am quite sure, sir, that you cannot."

As Kyle slid his pack off his back, the banker said, "Sir, I am going to need to ask you and your dog to vacate the premises immediately." The banker motioned for the guard.

Kyle dropped the black nylon pack on the desk with a loud "clunk" and unzipped it. The banker looked at the backpack. He had never seen the material from which it was made. At that moment, the guard put his hand on Kyle's left shoulder.

"Let's go," he said.

Kyle ignored the guard. He reached into the pack, retrieved a 25-pound gold bar, and set it on the banker's desk. The banker gasped. He picked up the bar. He observed the Swiss *Produits Artistiques Métaux Précieux* stamp on its smooth contours. He had never seen gold so exquisitely refined. In 2008 dollars, at 1890 gold prices, the bar was worth nearly a quarter of a million dollars.

"Do you have more?" asked the banker.

Kyle pulled a second bar from the pack and set it on the desk next to the first.

"Many more," replied Kyle. "That is not the right question."

"May I ask, what *is* the right question?" asked the banker.

"The right question," said Kyle, "is into whose bank will these be deposited?"

"Ah, yes," the banker said, laughing nervously, "I am terribly sorry for the misunderstanding. I am happy to be of service."

The banker turned to the guard. "Thank you Mr. Johnson," he said, dismissing him. "That will be all."

To Kyle, he said, "Please permit me to introduce myself. My

name is Daniel Dickinson."

Dickinson extended his hand to Kyle. Kyle took it with a firm grip.

"Colonel Kyle Mason," replied Kyle. "United States Army. Retired."

"Please have a seat, Colonel," Dickinson said, gesturing toward the polished wooden chair in front of his desk.

"Colonel, regrettably, our bank president, Mr. Salisbury, is, at present, in Salt Lake City, Utah. I am the bank's vice president. Perhaps I can be of service?

"I hope you can, Mr. Dickinson," said Kyle. "I am guiding a team of Swiss assayers to a location I am not at liberty to disclose. I've been sent here to establish a banking relationship and procure provisions. I am visiting the banks of Deadwood in order to evaluate services and make a recommendation to my clients.

"I am authorized to inform you that my clients will make an initial deposit of 100 bars of gold bullion—2,500 pounds. I have brought two of these bars to open an account."

Dickinson's eyes widened. Twenty-five hundred pounds of gold had an equivalent 2008 value of $25 million. He knew that there could be only one possible reason a former US Army colonel would be leading a team of assayers to a secret location.

"Can I assume your clients are associated with a gold strike?" fished Dickinson.

"I am sorry, Mr. Dickinson. I am not at liberty to discuss it."

"Of course," said Dickinson. "Please be assured that our transactions will be handled in the strictest of confidence. Have you visited other banks in our town?"

"Yours is the first," said Kyle. "I just arrived in town."

"Colonel Mason, if I may," Dickinson said, "perhaps it will not be necessary to visit the town's other banks. I have full confidence that the First National Bank of Deadwood can meet all of your clients' banking needs."

"Well, I don't know," Kyle said. "I have a fiduciary duty to my clients to be thorough in my evaluation."

"Please," Dickinson said, "I can see you've had a long journey. Allow me and my staff to attend to your needs. May I offer you coffee?"

・・・

Within the hour, Kyle had managed to leverage 50 pounds of gold plus a cock-and-bull story into a $2 million line of credit. Mr. Dickinson personally introduced Kyle to Deadwood's Main Street shop owners, as well as to a first-class foreman who could organize a wagon train to Kyle's secret destination. Word spread rapidly of the town's latest high roller. The residents of Deadwood stole glances and pointed discretely at "Colonel Mason." Gentlemen made wide detours across the thoroughfare to introduce themselves. Women whispered behind gloved hands, with longing looks at the wealthy Adonis.

The gold Kyle placed on deposit was half of his and Padma's nest egg to begin rebuilding their fortune in 1966. All that remained of their trillion-dollar treasure were two additional gold bars stashed in their tipi.

The foreman, Pete Webb, was an exuberant man in his fifties,

5'6", with a chaos of white hair firing in all directions from beneath a brown felt western hat with the front brim turned up. A long gray beard and mustache covered most of his ruddy skin, save for a bulbous nose and bulging, excited eyes. He wore brown canvas pants with leather suspenders hoisted over a tan and cream striped cotton shirt that ballooned over his pants. His trousers were stuffed into leather boots.

Between assignments, Pete was thankful for good-paying work to fall in his lap. Kyle found him knowledgeable and overly eager to please.

Kyle asked Pete to organize a train of a dozen horse-drawn wagons with drivers, packed with food, supplies, clothing, and weapons. He also asked Pete to purchase 500 head of cattle and arrange for wranglers to drive the herd.

"Don't you worry about a darn thing, Colonel!" said Pete. "I'll get it squared away. You go get yourself cleaned up."

Deadwood, SD
September 16, 1890
13:15 hours
Timeline 003

Damp heat from a hot towel melted the stress from Kyle's face as he reclined in a barber's chair. He heard the clunk of a shaving soap puck being dropped into a mug, followed by the alternating swishing and clinking of a shaving brush as the barber worked the soap into a lather. The mug was set on a stand by the chair. Kyle heard the slapping sound of a straight razor being sharpened against a leather strap hanging from the chair.

The towel was lifted from Kyle's face. The barber hovered over Kyle. He was in his early forties, with a round face, handlebar moustache, and combed-over salt-and-pepper hair. He wore a white tunic with silver buttons.

Kyle lifted his head to observe Pete's progress through the barber's large glass storefront window. In the three hours since Kyle shook hands with Pete, the foreman had moved at a miraculous pace. On the opposite side of the street from the barbershop, a train of 12 wagons hitched to draft horse teams was now parked on Main Street. Shop workers hustled to load their inventories into the wagons for the big spender who paid double the asking price for their wares. Pete hollered commands to the shop workers in a cracking high-octave voice while making outsized motions with his hands.

Kyle had used the time to clean up, getting a bath and a fresh shirt. After a steak lunch for himself and Hoover, he was now indulging himself with the closest thing to spa treatment a nineteenth-century man could ask for.

Kyle noticed Hoover, curled up asleep in a corner of the shop. Though dogs were not allowed in Deadwood's businesses, shop owners had learned quickly that if they wanted Kyle's business, they needed to make an exception for Hoover.

Kyle laid his head back on the chair's headrest, staring at the surprisingly ornate tin ceiling tiles behind the barber's face. Gathered leaves in the corners of each tile were connected with curves and swirls, encompassing medallions in the center. Beneath the ceiling was a floor of black and white checkered ceramic tiles.

The barber tilted Kyle's head away from him, held the straight razor to his cheek, and scraped the blade against his skin. Kyle felt the pull of his beard as the blade sheared it away.

"Been travelin' long, Colonel?" asked the barber.

"About four days."

"I hope you don't mind my askin', but I've never seen a sidearm like that," the barber said. "What is it?"

"It's German," Kyle said. "It's a rapid-fire pistol."

"Like a Gatling gun?" asked the barber.

"Yes," said Kyle, "except you don't have to crank it."

"What a remarkable modern age we live in," said the barber.

"And was is that device on your wrist?" the barber asked, pointing at Kyle's Breitling chronometer.

"It's a timepiece," Kyle said. "It's from Switzerland."

"You sure do get around, Colonel."

"Indeed I do."

• • •

Kyle stepped out of the barbershop onto the boardwalk, rubbing his clean-shaven face.

He noticed the freestanding red and white striped wooden barber pole standing next to the door. The pole was an icon from medieval times, when barbers performed medical services, like leaching. The red and white stripes represented the patient's bloody bandages. The cap represented a leach bowl, while the basin at the base of the pole represented the receptacle into which the patient's blood drained.

Pete moved exuberantly up and down the length of the wagon train, calling out orders to the store workers queued up to load their goods into the wagons. He saw Kyle standing outside the barbershop with a clean shirt and a fresh shave.

"You clean up good, Colonel!" Pete yelled, cackling.

Kyle smiled and waved.

"We'll have you ready to roll in a jiffy," said Pete, returning to his work.

At that moment. Someone grabbed Kyle's hand, startling him. Kyle saw a tiny woman sitting in a rocking chair, wearing a faded blue calico dress. A quilt lay across her lap, covering her legs. Her white hair was worn in bangs with a ponytail down her back. Milky blue white covered her blind eyes. Kyle estimated that she was at least 100 years old.

"You'd best get home to your wife," said the woman.

"How do you know I'm married?" asked Kyle.

The woman tapped Kyle's wedding ring with a bony finger. Kyle could see blood vessels beneath her fragile skin. The woman released his hand.

"Go on now," she said. "Go on home."

Kyle backed away, shaken. He stepped into a general store next door to the barbershop. Hoover trotted in behind him.

Kyle was struck at the front door by a rich blend of smells—coffee, saddle soap, lamp oil, spices, and tobacco.

The walls of the store were lined with wooden shelves crowded with colorful tins, boxes, jars, bottles, and tools. Dry goods, clothing, tools, and bolts of cloth stood on tables. Sacks of coffee beans were piled on the floor. Sacks of flour, salt, and sugar were piled on a nearby table. A dozen bright red kerosene lanterns sat on the floor next to a stack of tin buckets. Shovels leaned nearby against the wall. Hatchets, saws, rope, and other tools completed the store's hardware section.

A pot-bellied stove stood in the center of the store. A cracker barrel was parked next to the stove with two wooden chairs. A checkerboard sat atop the barrel.

To Kyle's left was a long glass display case topped with a wooden counter. A red iron coffee grinder sat on the counter. Next to it was a scale. An open box of Cuban cigars sat on the counter next to two large glass jars, one with hard red candy and the other with yellow. A small pile of the *Black Hills Pioneer* was stacked neatly next to the candy.

A walk space divided the display case from the shelving on the wall behind it. Tins and bottles of toiletries and apothecary items stood on the shelves.

At the far end of the display case was a bright brass cash register. The shopkeeper sat behind the register. On the wall next to him was a gun rack with rifles and shotguns. Boxes of ammunition sat on shelves beneath the rifles.

The shopkeeper was a plump man in his forties with dark balding hair, a bushy mustache, and sideburns. He wore a white shirt with a band collar, dark trousers with suspenders, and a black vest with silver pinstripes. When Kyle entered the store, he noticed the shopkeeper was reading a red book.

When he saw Kyle in the doorway, the shopkeeper leapt from his seat, placed the book on the counter next to the cash register, and hustled to greet his new favorite customer.

"Colonel! What can I do for you?" he asked.

"That woman outside," Kyle said. "Who is she?"

"Oh, Grandma Annie?" the shopkeeper said. "Don't pay her any mind. She's not long for this world and sometimes says the darndest things. I hope she didn't disturb you."

"No," Kyle said, "it was just…" His voice trailed off.

"Colonel, my name is Mr. Richards, and I am pleased to assist you in any way I can. Your man Pete has already purchased many of our wares, though we still have quite a few for your consideration."

"Well, perhaps I could see if there is something my wife might like."

"Of course, of course," Mr. Richards replied. "Come this way."

Mr. Richards guided Kyle to a table with neatly folded clothing—mostly trousers and cotton work shirts. Some boots were parked nearby on the floor. One item on the table stood out from the rest—a parcel wrapped in tissue paper. It smelled of sandalwood. Mr. Richards unwrapped the contents and unfolded a gold robe with bronze embroidery.

"It's pure silk," Mr. Richards said. "From the Orient. One of the Chinamen brings these to me from time to time. A cousin of his gets them off the boat in San Francisco."

"It's beautiful," Kyle said, touching the fine silk. He smelled the faint scent of sandalwood infused with the silk. He knew Padma would love it.

"I'll take it," Kyle said.

"Excellent choice, sir."

Mr. Richards carefully refolded the robe in its tissue paper, then took it to the display case, setting it on the counter next to the cash register. Kyle admired the register, brand new with beautiful floral brass metalwork.

Kyle noticed a set of silver brushes and combs in the display case.

"May I have these as well?" Kyle asked.

"Of course, sir."

Mr. Richards rung up the purchase on the big brass cash register. The mechanical cogs beneath its buttons crunched as the metal tabs signaling the total due popped up in the register's glass window as its bell announced the sale.

"That will be eight dollars and thirty-two cents, Colonel," said Mr. Richards. "Shall I wrap these for you?"

"Please," replied Kyle.

Kyle picked up a copy of *The Black Hills Pioneer* from the small stack on the glass counter. He gasped when he saw the title of a front-page article:

The Indian Messiah

Tales of the supernatural appearance of an Indian "Messiah" are sweeping the plains with the hellish ferocity of a prairie wildfire. The Redskin Messiah, the alleged product of a savage ritual "Ghost Dance," is said to bring with her a new day, cleansing the Whites from former Indian lands and restoring the majestic buffalo that once roamed upon them. That the Messiah is claimed to be a woman is simply another cruel twist in the corrupt bargain the Indians have struck with delusion, a pathetic hope beyond hope that their former world, long ago destroyed by the Whites in the natural course of progress, will spring new and eternal in the desolate wilderness remains of Standing Rock Reservation.

The proud spirit of the original owners of these vast prairies inherited through centuries of fierce and bloody wars for their possession, lingered last in the bosom of a few remaining warrior chiefs. With their fall the nobility of the Redskin is extinguished, and what few are left are a pack of whining curs who lick the hand that smites them. The Whites, by law of conquest, by justice of civilization, are masters of the American continent, and the best safety of the frontier settlements will be

> secured by the total annihilation of the few remaining Indians. Why not annihilation? Their glory has fled, their spirits broken, their manhood effaced; better that they die than live the miserable wretches that they are. History would forget these later despicable beings, and speak, in later ages of the glory of these grand Kings of forest and plain that Cooper loved to heroism.
>
> We cannot honestly regret their extermination, but we at least do justice to the manly characteristics possessed, according to their lights and education, by the early Redskins of America.
>
> —L. Frank Baum

Kyle was stunned.

History has already changed! he thought.

Word of Padma's appearance had caused Baum to write an editorial virtually identical to the one he was to write about Sitting Bull's murder.

In only five days, without Internet or broadcast media, word of Padma's arrival had already spread via telegraph to journalists hundreds of miles from Standing Rock. If news had spread to Deadwood, Kyle knew it was also sure to be in Washington DC. The telegraph wires would be burning with orders to the army's commander at Fort Yates, North Dakota—General Nelson Miles.

The image of the bloodthirsty mob of 70,000 at Jonah Jones' 2008 hate rally flashed into Kyle's mind. Padma was now hunted in both the nineteenth and twenty-first centuries.

A bolt of terror fired through Kyle. He heard Grandma Annie's voice in his head.

You'd best get home to your wife.

Padma was in mortal danger. Kyle had left her unprotected, hundreds of miles away.

I must abandon the wagon train, he thought. *I must ride back and rescue Padma—**now**!*

He realized the thought of waging war against the United States Army was completely insane. He would convince Padma or, if necessary, deliver her out of harm's way against her will. Either way, they weren't sticking around for the extermination.

Kyle dropped the newspaper. Mr. Richards looked up from his parcels.

Instinctively, the Special Forces operator scanned his surroundings for weapons—anything that might be useful to protect his wife.

Kyle noticed the rifles on the wall behind the display case. One in particular caught his attention.

"May I have a look at that rifle?" he asked. "The one with the scope."

Mr. Richards took down the rifle and handed it to Kyle. The repeating rifle was the only one with a scope—a rare find in 1890. Unlike compact modern scopes, this one was long and narrow, running nearly the entire length of the rifle barrel.

"This is a…" Mr. Richards began.

"… a Marlin 1881 with a Slotterbek scope," Kyle finished. "It fires 45-70 government cartridges."

"Of course, you would know your weapons, Colonel," said the shopkeeper.

Kyle admired the beautiful specimen, with its polished wood and engraved silver receiver. He checked the rifle to ensure it was not loaded, then aimed it at the storefront window, spying on Pete through the scope crosshairs.

"I just received it a few days ago," said the shopkeeper. "Fellow used it for buffalo hunting. All the buffalo are gone though, so he gave up his rifle. Shame."

Kyle knew he was holding one of the most powerful rifles in the world in the year 1890, provided it had the right ammunition. With the proper ammo, and in the hands of a skilled marksman, the Marlin 1881 was one of the world's best sniper's rifles in that time, capable of hitting a target at over 1,000 yards. However, 45-70 government cartridges were as uncommon as the scoped rifle he was holding.

"You wouldn't happen to have 45-70 cartridges, would you?" asked Kyle.

"Indeed I would," beamed the shopkeeper. "The gun's former owner sold me 10 boxes of ammunition along with this fine rifle."

"I'll take them all," said Kyle.

Kyle looked at his watch, anxious to be on his way. As Mr. Richards finished wrapping up Padma's robe and brushes, Kyle noticed the shopkeeper's red book sitting on the display case next to the cash register. He picked it up. The illustration on the book's cover was of a knight in armor riding a flying dragon. The book was titled *A Yankee at the Court of King Arthur*—one of the early titles of Mark Twain's *A Connecticut Yankee in King Arthur's Court*. The book had been published a year earlier. Kyle smiled as he realized that he was living in the same time as Mark Twain. He thought about the irony of holding an original of one of the first time-travel books.

"Do you read Twain?" asked Mr. Richards.

"I do," replied Kyle.

"I just received this book. I am thoroughly enjoying it," the shopkeeper said.

Kyle began to set the book down, then hesitated. He thought about the Connecticut Yankee, Hank Morgan, who used his knowledge of nineteenth-century technology to defeat a medieval army that vastly outnumbered his own.

Mr. Richards saw a thought flash across Kyle's face as he held the book. He assumed Kyle coveted the book. A troubled look momentarily crossed the shopkeeper's own face as he pondered whether to offer up the unfinished book to his new best customer.

"Colonel, I'm happy for you to have the book, gratis, to thank you for your patronage," offered Mr. Richards.

Kyle snapped out of his thoughts. "That is very generous of you, Mr. Richards, but I've already read it."

Kyle set the book on the counter. Mr. Richards smiled, relieved.

"Mr. Richards, do you have paper and a pencil?" asked Kyle.

"Coming right up!"

Kyle hastily scribbled on the paper, then bolted for the door. Hoover, busy sniffing a sack of coffee beans, snapped up his head and ran after him.

"Colonel!" the shopkeeper called after Kyle.

"I'll be right back!" Kyle shouted over his shoulder as he flew out the door crashing into two women walking the boardwalk.

"Colonel!" the ladies exclaimed.

"I am so very sorry, ladies," Kyle said as he turned to run toward Pete. Hoover charged out the door and between the two women.

"I declare!" exclaimed one of the women.

"Pete!" Kyle yelled down the street. Pete came running.

"Yessir, Colonel," said Pete, out of breath.

"I need you to go to the Homestake Mine and buy as much of this as you can get your hands on," said Kyle.

Pete read the note, then raised one leg, slapping his knee with his hand.

"Dang, Colonel! You struck gold! I knew it!"

"I can't talk about it," said Kyle. "Hurry!"

Pete gave a high-pitched cackle as he scrambled away.

Deadwood, SD
September 16, 1890
14:45 hours
Timeline 003

Pegasus, tied to a hitching post at the head of the wagon train, munched on an apple Kyle had given him. The big draft horses hitched to the lead wagon nickered covetously as they watched the mustang eat his apple.

Kyle glanced at his watch. Pete saw that his client was anxious to get the wagon train underway.

"Thirty minutes, Colonel," Pete said, "and we'll be ready to roll."

Kyle had aborted his knee-jerk plan to abandon the wagon train and ride Pegasus solo back to Standing Rock. He surmised that the express return in advance of the wagons might buy him a day, though he would risk a fortune in merchandise left in the hands of the complete strangers driving the wagons. When they eventually realized they were driving into Lakota territory, the chances were excellent that, without Kyle's motivation, they would never arrive.

Kyle deduced it would take time for the massive army stationed at Fort Yates, North Dakota, to move on Sitting Bull's village. It would easily take dithering lawmakers in Washington a week or more to issue orders. From the point General Miles received his marching orders, it would take days to formulate a battle plan, muster troops, and make the 40-mile trek to Sitting Bull's village. Even if scouting parties arrived in advance of the army, Kyle knew Takoda and the tribe would protect their messiah with their lives.

Kyle eyed the last two wagons in the train. The materials Pete had procured from the Homestake Mine offered the faint glimmer of a defense against the coming storm. Though the odds of a successful outcome were very long, it was the only hope Kyle had to make good on his promise to Padma to protect the Lakota people.

Pete had made arrangements for the wagon train to rendezvous with a cattle drive outside of Sturgis, 14 miles to the east. From there, they would continue east. Despite Pete's persistent questioning, Kyle would not disclose the destination, only that the crew should plan for a week on the trail.

Kyle was frustrated. The wagon train was already 30 minutes behind schedule.

"Colonel, this wagon train ain't gonna move any faster than it's movin'," said Pete. "You go on in to the Gem and get yourself a drink. We'll be ready by the time you're done."

Kyle glanced at the infamous Gem Variety Theater, a few doors down from the lead wagon. The Gem of 1890 was a sprawling entertainment palace compared with its original mining camp ancestor. The original Gem burned in the fire that had consumed most of the town in 1879. The new Gem was a large two-story building with a long upstairs balcony from which patrons could watch Main Street parades.

The notion of downing a drink in one of the Old West's most

famous saloons tempted Kyle. He conceded that there was nothing he could do to make the wagon train move sooner. He had 30 minutes to kill.

"All right," said Kyle, resigned.

Kyle pushed through the swinging bar doors. The saloon smelled of sweat, whiskey, and noxiously sweet perfume.

To Kyle's right, several men stood at a long wooden bar. Two of the men were chatting with women, haggling over the price of a trip to one of the upstairs bedrooms. Men huddled around three round tables, playing poker. To his left, at the far end of the large room, was a vacant stage. A pianist churned "Little Annie Rooney" out of an upright piano.

The sights, sounds, and smells exhilarated Kyle's senses. He sidled up to the bar.

"What'll ya' have?" asked the bartender.

"Whiskey," replied Kyle, slapping a silver dollar on the counter.

The bartender uncorked a bottle and poured a shot glass, leaving the bottle on the bar before walking away.

One of the women at the bar eyed the silver dollar and abruptly ended her conversation to join Kyle.

"Howdy, stranger," the woman said with a grand smile. "You wouldn't be Colonel Mason, would you?"

Kyle estimated the woman to be in her late twenties. She was an attractive redhead with porcelain skin, blue eyes, and dimples that bookended full smiling lips. Her long hair was pulled up into a Gibson Girl pompadour, capped by a bun on top of her head. She wore a threadbare cranberry and black striped dress with an ample neckline that generously displayed her cleavage. A corset tightly constricted her waist, until her shape was liberated to flow into full hips.

"You have me at a disadvantage," replied Kyle, returning the young woman's smile.

"My name's Margaret. I am *very* pleased to make your acquaintance, Colonel. How long will you be in town?" she asked.

Kyle glanced at his watch. "Twenty-seven minutes."

Margaret looked at Kyle incredulously and laughed.

"Sakes alive! I've never before heard anyone speak about the time with such…exactitude."

Kyle smiled in return. "I'm anxious to get home…counting the minutes. Meanwhile, may I buy you a drink?"

"I thought you'd never ask," said Margaret, motioning to the bartender for a second glass. Kyle poured Margaret's drink.

"What shall we drink to, Colonel?" asked Margaret, holding up her shot glass.

"To seizing the day," Kyle replied.

"To seizing the day," Margaret echoed with a delicious smile as they clinked their glasses.

The final manic bars of "Little Annie Rooney" ricocheted off the saloon walls as the song drew to a close. The three-quarter strains of "Clementine" began to pour from the piano. The pianist hammered the song at a hectically cheerful tempo, crowding out its sadness.

"Would you like to dance with me, Colonel?" asked Margaret.

"Call me Kyle."

"Would you like to dance with me, Kyle?"

"It would be my pleasure," Kyle said.

She called out to the pianist, "Slow it down, Billy!"

The pianist nodded. He was a young man with curly brown hair and a striped vest over a white band-collared shirt. The tempo of "Clementine" slowed, transforming its mood from coerced happiness into nostalgia.

Margaret took Kyle's hand and guided him to the vacant floor between the bar and the poker tables. Kyle took Margaret's waist and hand as she placed her other hand on his shoulder. She felt the powerful body beneath his soft cotton shirt. She looked up into the handsome man's face, smiling as Kyle led her into the waltz. Margaret began to laugh as they swirled around the floor.

Conversations in the bar died down as men and working girls paused to watch the only couple on the floor. Something about the moment touched the spectators—the attractive couple, the dance, the song longing for a time that was gone and would never return. Perhaps it was something different about Margaret that captivated them. Though they thought they knew her well, they had never seen this particular shade of smile on her face before.

"You are a *very* good dancer, Kyle!" Margaret said.

"I have a feeling you tell everyone they're a good dancer," said Kyle.

"I do," she conceded. "Though sometimes I mean it."

"Where do you come from, Margaret?" asked Kyle, detecting the trace of an accent.

"Massachusetts."

"You're a long way from home," Kyle observed.

"Yes, I am, Kyle," she said, adding a sad edge to her smile.

"What brought you to Deadwood?"

"A newspaper advertisement," said Margaret. "For actresses for the Gem Variety Saloon. That and a one-way ticket was what got most of the girls out here. When we arrived, we found out that it wasn't our acting skills that the establishment was interested in."

"I am so sorry, Kyle. I don't know why I told you that," she said. "I'm spoiling the ball."

"I'm glad you told me."

Kyle looked into Margaret's eyes. It suddenly dawned on him that Margaret was dead. She had been dead for at least half a century.

Margaret saw the thought flash across Kyle's face.

"What are you thinking, Kyle?" she asked.

Kyle shook his head. "You wouldn't believe me."

She looked into his eyes. Her expression turned serious. "I just might believe anything you tell me, Kyle."

"Clementine" slowly wound to a close. Kyle and Margaret remained in their waltz embrace, looking into each other's eyes. Margaret reached up to kiss Kyle on the cheek. She whispered into his ear, "Would you like to come upstairs with me, Kyle?"

"I would love to, Margaret, but I'm married."

Margaret looked at Kyle with disbelief, then tossed her head back and laughed.

"Kyle, can I tell you a secret?"

"Yes."

She reached up to whisper into his ear again, "You would not be the first married man I'd ever been with."

Kyle laughed.

"Anyway, I only have 17 minutes," he said.

"Most of my clients don't take half that long," she riposted.

Margaret glanced up. Kyle saw her smile turn to worry. He turned to look. On the upstairs balcony, a man with a mustache and combed-over, greasy black hair glared at the couple with menacing eyes. Kyle knew it was the Gem's infamous owner, Al Sweringen.

"Kyle, it would be better for me if you came upstairs," Margaret said, fearful of what Sweringen might do if she failed to turn an expensive trick.

Kyle didn't take his eyes off Sweringen. "I think it would be better for you if you came with me instead."

Kyle turned back to Margaret. Her jaw dropped in stunned surprise. Minutes earlier, her best case scenario was sex for money with a more-handsome-than-usual client. The possibility of freedom was beyond her imagination.

Margaret's expression turned to confusion and hurt as she permitted a rogue hope to escape that Kyle might actually be serious. She had crushed those dreams long ago.

"Kyle, it would be cruel to play a trick on me," she said, trying to stuff her feelings back where they belonged.

"I'm dead serious," Kyle said, looking Margaret in the eye.

"Mr. Sweringen…he has a terrible temper," Margaret said.

"Let me worry about that."

"I just met you," said Margaret.

"Right."

Margaret stared at Kyle in disbelief. She was given an impossible choice —whether to remain in the hell she knew versus taking a gamble with her life, placing it in the hands of a complete stranger. She had nothing to guide her decision but the look in the stranger's eye.

"All right," said Margaret, taking a deep breath. "Let's go."

Kyle took Margaret by the arm and headed for the door. She darted to the bar to grab her handbag then rejoined Kyle.

"Just where the fuck do you think you're going?" asked Sweringen.

"To a better life," Margaret tossed over her shoulder.

Kyle could feel Margaret shaking. Before they reached the swinging doors, a large man stepped in front of them. He had long, greasy brown hair and an unkempt beard. Suspenders held up brown pants, into which a blue and white striped shirt was tucked. He wore a Colt revolver on his thigh.

"This life is as good as it gets for you, Margaret," said Sweringen's lieutenant, Dan Doherty.

"Step aside," ordered Kyle.

"Fuck you!" shouted Doherty, reaching for his Colt.

In the blink of an eye, Kyle punched the hollow of Doherty's neck, crushing his windpipe. Doherty clutched his throat, gagging. He fell to the floor. His eyes bulged with terror as he struggled to breath.

A man in a black western hat appeared outside the swinging

saloon doors. He pulled his revolver before Kyle could react.

"Get down!" the man shouted.

Kyle pushed Margaret to the floor as the man fired over the top of the saloon doors, hitting the bartender in the chest. The bartender dropped a shotgun as the force of the blast knocked him against the wall, shattering glasses stacked neatly on shelves.

The stranger pushed through the saloon doors, holding his pistol and carefully eying Sweringen and the others in the saloon. He glanced at the upstairs balcony to ensure he wouldn't be bushwhacked by one of Sweringen's men. The stranger had a dark brown mustache that spilled over his upper lip. Bushy eyebrows hung over dark eyes. He wore a charcoal-colored frock coat over a black and silver striped vest, a white band-collared shirt, and black pants.

Gun smoke wafted out of the barrel of the man's Colt 45 pistol as he scanned the room.

"We gonna have any more trouble, Sweringen?" he asked.

Sweringen glared at the man for a moment, then spat on the floor below the balcony. "No trouble here, Sheriff."

The man reached to help Margaret off the floor, keeping his pistol and eyes raised.

"Miss," he said, taking Margaret's hand.

"Sheriff Seth Bullock," the man said, introducing himself to Kyle while keeping a close eye on the interior of the Gem. "I recommend you find yourself another drinking hole, Colonel."

Kyle and Margaret exited the Gem. Bullock followed them, backing out of the saloon doors before holstering his pistol.

Kyle extended his hand. Bullock shook it. "Much obliged, Sheriff," he said.

"Just doin' my job, Colonel," said Bullock.

Pete saw the commotion at the Gem, arriving at the door just as Kyle, Margaret, and Sheriff Bullock were exiting.

"You all right, Colonel?"

"I'm fine," said Kyle. "Thanks to the sheriff."

Pete grinned at Margaret and tipped his hat. "Howdy, Miss Margaret!"

"Pete," Margaret said curtly, reluctantly acknowledging their professional relationship.

Pete turned to Kyle. "We're all hitched up and ready to skedaddle!"

Kyle turned to the sheriff. "Sheriff, there's a train from Deadwood south to Rapid City, right?"

"Yes sir," the sheriff replied. He pulled a pocket watch out of his vest. "The 3:30 leaves in 15 minutes."

"Can I trust you to get Margaret safely on that train?"

"It would be my privilege," said the sheriff.

"Wait!" said Margaret to Kyle. "I'm coming with you!"

Kyle unzipped his pack and pulled out a stack of bills—$10,000—a small portion of his bank line of credit. In 2008 dollars, the currency was worth nearly a quarter of a million dollars.

"Put this in your bag," Kyle told Margaret.

"No!" said Margaret. "Don't leave without me!"

"It's not safe where I'm going."

"It's not safe *here!* Al will kill me!"

"No one's going to hurt you, ma'am," said the sheriff.

"Listen to me," Kyle said. "Your life only gets better from here. You take this money, get on that train, and don't look back. Put a thousand miles between you and this place. Buy yourself the life you deserve."

Margaret gasped. She struggled to grasp her world as it turned inside out with incomprehensible speed. A chance meeting. A waltz. A new life. It was as though a hand had been placed on the Earth, stopping its rotation and giving it a swift spin in the opposite direction. She was flying off her planet, hurdling toward another.

"We need to hurry if we're gonna catch that train," said the sheriff.

Kyle and Margaret stared at each other, anxious, wishing there was more time.

Margaret began to cry.

"Thank you," she said, "for saving my life."

"May I ask one favor?" asked Kyle.

"Anything," Margaret said.

"When you settle, wherever that place is, use a little of that money and take out an advertisement in the local newspaper to let me know that you're OK," he said.

"I don't understand," said Margaret. "You won't know where I'll be. How will you see the advertisement?"

"You remember you said you might believe anything I told you?"

"Yes."

"Believe me when I tell you that I will see it."

Margaret looked into Kyle's eyes. She could see he knew something—some enchantment that would permit him to watch over her. It comforted her.

"I believe you," Margaret said, wiping tears from her face with her hands. "Does this mean that I'll see you again someday?"

Kyle shook his head. "Probably not."

Margaret put her hands on Kyle's cheeks, then kissed him. Her soft lips warmed his. He returned her kiss, pulling her close.

"Goodbye, Margaret," he said, pulling away.

Sheriff Bullock took Margaret's arm and began to escort her away. "You have my love—always," she said as they hurried away to the train station.

Kyle knew that if he ever made it back to the Time Tunnel, every word of every newspaper ever printed would be accessible via the tunnel's nexus to the databases in this timeline. All that would remain of Margaret—her advertisement, as well as her obituary—would be rendered to a few sentences in a digital warehouse.

Pete led Pegasus to Kyle. Hoover trailed behind. Kyle took the reins and mounted his horse. He looked once more at Margaret and the sheriff as they sped down Main Street.

"Let's go," he said to Pete as he turned Pegasus to leave.

Grand River
Standing Rock Reservation
South Dakota
September 23, 1890
08:15 hours
Timeline 003

Padma walked along the grassy bank of the Grand River. She headed upstream, away from the village, to find a private spot to bathe. The morning sun was at her back, casting her shadow in her path. The stiff grass and brush crunched under her moccasins. In one hand was her orange Hermès toiletry bag. She shook her head at the absurdity of her situation, wearing a beaded Lakota doeskin dress while clutching a haute couture bag on her way to a cold bath in a frontier river.

In her other hand, she held an unopened bar of Ivory soap in its blue and white paper wrapper. Takoda had caused the soap to magically appear after Padma complained about being forced to bathe without it. The soap had been included among some of the rations meted out by the government.

Padma looked at Procter & Gamble's logo on the wrapper—the man in the crescent moon gazing at a midnight blue sky of 13 stars. Padma hadn't seen the old logo in years. Religious fundamentalists had forced Procter & Gamble to remove the logo in 1985, claiming that it was a satanic symbol. The company cowed to the extremists, replacing the beautiful classic art with a simple "P&G"—guaranteed not to offend anyone, with the possible exception of those who had grown up with the majestic man in the moon.

A nineteenth-century manufacturing accident had resulted in an abnormally high air-to-soap ratio, causing Ivory soap to float. The defect was instantly recognized as a feature, and "It Floats!" became an Ivory trademark. Floating soap would come in handy for a bath in a murky river.

Padma worried about Kyle. He had been gone for a week and a half.

A few weeks earlier, in 2008, Padma could have instantly spoken with almost anyone, anywhere on the planet. She had instinctively reached for her iPhone more than once since arriving in the past. It was strange and uncomfortable for her that the scope of her world was now restricted to those within earshot. It pained her that Kyle's voice was disconnected.

Though Padma did not look forward to her river bath, she relished the time alone. Since her miraculous resurrection, the crowds following her had grown to over 1,000 people. Members of neighboring tribes on the 3,600 square mile reservation poured into Sitting Bull's village, swelling its ranks to nearly 3,000. Over Takoda's vehement objections, Padma ordered him to misdirect the multitudes so that she could take her bath in privacy.

"I swore an oath to Red Star to protect you!" he said. "I cannot allow any harm to come to you."

Padma saw the pained concern in Takoda's face. It was plain to Padma that his worry was driven by more than duty to Kyle. She placed her hand on his cheek.

"Please," she said. "I can't bathe with a thousand people watching me. I'll just go up river a little ways. I'll be OK."

"Anyway," she added as she inserted a finger into the charred bullet hole in her dress, "I'm bulletproof, remember?"

Takoda looked away.

"What's wrong?" asked Padma.

"I cannot look at it," Takoda replied.

"Why not?"

"It is a fearsome magic," said Takoda.

Padma placed her hand on Takoda's cheek, "I'm not fearsome." Takoda smiled and walked away.

• • •

Padma thought about Takoda as she walked upstream to her bathing spot. She could not deny her growing feelings for the handsome and devoted Lakota brave. It was difficult for her to parse her feelings. The fact that she found the young man physically attractive was beyond doubt. She did not know whether what she felt was affection for an unconditionally caring man, or something else—a chamber of her heart reserved exclusively for Kyle.

Is it possible to have two soul mates? she thought.

She instantly chased the thought out of her head, feeling a pang of guilt for entertaining it, even for a second.

I am Kyle Mason's wife...or, rather, I am the wife of one Kyle Mason and the widow of the other.

She shook her head at the complete madness of the situation—walking to take a bath in a river in 1890, clutching her twenty-first-century Hermès toiletry bag, and thinking about her living and dead husbands who were the same person.

I am completely mental, she thought. *I am not wearing a Lakota dress in nineteenth-century South Dakota—I am wearing a straitjacket in a twenty-first-century psych ward at Bellevue.*

She looked apprehensively at the cool dark water.

"If I'm in a psych ward, I sure wish they'd give me better drugs," she sighed.

Hundreds of little conveniences she'd taken for granted in her former life were now impossibilities. There were no toilets or toilet paper. There were no corner groceries with food and coffee. There were no paper towels. There was no toothpaste. There were no tampons. Water, something that formerly came from ubiquitous plastic bottles, now came from a river, a bucket, or a buffalo bladder.

For years, she had slept in an ample bed, made every day with crisp, fresh sheets. Now, she didn't have a bed—ample or otherwise. Even with blankets for padding, sleeping on the ground was uncomfortable, yielding a fitful sleep. She awoke in the morning sore and exhausted, her eyes puffy.

While dozens of amenities of twenty-first-century life competed for the title of most missed, Padma would have traded most for a hot bath. Hiking to her bath in the bracing waters of the Grand River was a march toward an unjust punishment. The only thing worse than the frontier bath was skipping a day and allowing the prairie dirt and grime to cling to her face and body and hair. Though she'd never required most of the trappings of the "Empress of America," she had never expected that she would be deprived a hot shower, a comfy bed, food, and toilet paper. If she ever got out of this mess, she swore she would never take those things for granted again.

Padma paused at a sandy bank in a narrow stretch of the river, split in two by a sand bar. She set her Hermès bag down on a rock and looked around to make sure she was alone. She then removed the blue beaded yoke, untied her Concho belt, and pulled her doeskin dress over her head, draping it on a boulder. She pulled apart the Velcro fasteners that held her Kevlar vest in place and pulled it off, then tipped off her moccasins next to the boulder. She unbraided her long black hair, then unwrapped the bar of Ivory soap. She walked to the edge of the water and stepped in up to her knees. She felt the sandy river bottom on the soles of her feet. The sand mixed between her toes. She stood for a moment, bracing herself as she watched the gradual eddies of the slow river current.

She gingerly touched the purple and black welt between her breasts. It fired pain through her chest, forcing a gasp. She thought about the irony of Kyle leaving her behind for her protection.

I hate this part, she thought.

Padma took a breath and sank beneath the surface, clutching her soap. The weight of the cold water pressed against her cracked sternum, firing pain from the center of her chest.

She surfaced, gasping.

Padma stood in the shallow water and lathered quickly. Covered in soap, she immersed herself in the water to rinse. She surfaced a second time and walked to the bank to dress. Another essential she was missing in 1890 was a bath towel. She stood on the bank, dripping on the sand, trying her best to squeegee her wet skin with her hands.

As she picked her dress off the rock, she startled. On the bank, 100 feet downstream, a man sat on the riverbank, watching her. He was a young man in his twenties, wearing a navy cavalry shirt with cadet blue pants held up by suspenders. Dark riding boots ascended to his knees. He wore a gray hat with the rim turned up at the forehead. Around his waist was a cartridge belt, with a butt-forward revolver holster on his left hip and a knife sheath on the right. The man had a long blond mustache.

Padma and the man eyed each other. After a few moments, the man stood up and began to walk toward her. Padma clutched her dress to her chest. She began walking backwards, preparing to turn and run.

She bumped into something behind her. She turned—it was another man, a cavalry scout in his forties, with a bushy brown beard and a grotesque smile of yellow teeth.

"Mornin'!" the scout said.

A third cavalry soldier, in his thirties with black wavy hair and a mustache, approached from behind.

A bolt of terror shot through Padma. She ran toward the river, attempting to dive in. The scout caught her left arm. As she struggled to break free, the blond soldier grabbed her right arm. As they struggled in the shallows, Padma's dress was stripped loose. As the men dragged her out of the water, she watched her beautiful dress and the Ivory soap bar drift away in the current.

The men dragged her to the riverbank and threw her on her back. Padma rolled over and scrambled on all fours to get away. The blond soldier tackled her. The impact drove lightning pain through her chest. She screamed.

The soldier wrapped his arm around Padma's neck and turned her over, holding her tight against him on the ground. He drew his knife with the other hand, holding the blade against her throat.

"Where ya' goin', purdy injun lady?" the soldier asked. "This ball's just gettin' started!"

The soldier let out a whoop.

Padma's mind tried to speak to her terror. She knew she was about to be raped. Her best possible outcome was that she would not be shot or stabbed to death in the process.

The scout approached Padma, looking down at her. Unlike the

other two soldiers, the scout was wearing fringed buckskin pants in place of the standard Army-issued trousers.

The scout tucked his gloved thumbs in his trousers, examining the naked native woman on the ground before him. "I ain't never seen a squaw like this before," he said. "They're all so short and wrinkled and ugly. I never seen one so tall and purdy."

"Me neither!" said the blond soldier. "Hurry up and poke her so we can have our turn!"

The blond soldier holding Padma noticed the purple and black mark between her breasts.

"What'd you do?" he asked. "Didja hurt yourself?"

The soldier grabbed Padma's long hair and wrapped it tight around his left fist. With his knife hand, he pressed on Padma's sternum with the butt of his knife. She screamed in pain. The soldier laughed.

"Hey! Lookee what I can do!" he said as he ground the knife butt down on her sternum again. Padma let out another bloodcurdling scream.

"Darlin', this is nothin'," he said. "Just you wait—you'll see!"

The other soldier grabbed Padma's left arm. The glint of her diamond ring caught his eye.

"Lookee!" he said excitedly, holding up her hand. "Where'd you steal this, squaw?"

He began pulling her wedding ring off her finger as Padma clenched her fist. The blond soldier smacked her in the sternum with his knife butt. The pain caused Padma's eyes to bulge as her mouth gaped wide, gasping with unbearable pain. She opened her hand, allowing the soldier to pull her wedding ring from her finger. It was the first time it had left her hand. The soldier stuffed it in his shirt pocket. Padma gasped for breath and sobbed.

The scout at Padma's feet began pulling off his boots, hopping on one foot as he hurriedly undressed. He slipped the suspenders off his shoulders, then pulled off his pants. The other two men laughed nervously.

The scout was now clad only in dirty long johns that buttoned from his crotch to his neck. He unbuttoned his two crotch buttons and pulled out his erect penis. The man standing before her, in long johns with his upright penis, looked unbelievably absurd to Padma. Everything about the situation was unbelievable. It was not possible that she was in the nineteenth century, about to be raped by soldiers of the US cavalry.

"Your johnson's standin' at attention!" said the blond soldier. "We better salute!"

The three soldiers guffawed as the two men holding Padma saluted.

"She don't talk much," observed the scout.

"She's a ig'rant injun!" said the blond soldier. "She don't speak American. Go on and fuck her!"

The scout knelt at Padma's feet. She snapped up her knees and pressed them close together. The scout put his hands on her knees and struggled to pry her legs apart.

"Fuckin' cunt!" he shouted.

The blond soldier tapped her sternum with the butt of his knife. "You want more of this, squaw?"

Padma cried as she opened her legs, sickened to cooperate in any way in her own rape. She could not withstand another blow to her cracked chest.

The scout crawled between Padma's legs. Her heart pounded as the reality of what was about to happen overwhelmed her denial. In her mind, she shouted back at the terror. She had lost control over her body. Her mind was the only part of her she still governed.

You're going to be raped. You're going to be raped. She repeated in her mind, acknowledging the reality, trying to prepare.

Survive. You must survive. You must survive. She repeated the mantra in her head as the scout knelt between her legs.

The two other men tightened their grip on Padma as she felt the scout's weight on top of her. He tried to kiss her on her lips as she turned her head. His breath was foul. Padma forced back the retch of her vomit. The scout grabbed her breast and began to suck. Padma felt his coarse, dirty fingers fumbling between her legs.

"He can't find the hole!" taunted the blond soldier.

"Shut up!" yelled the scout.

"He can't find the hole!" the blond soldier repeated, laughing.

The scout ignored the taunting soldier. "You don't know what I'm sayin', but I'm gonna repay you in kind for what you savages did to us at the Little Bighorn!" the scout said.

"I know precisely what you're saying, you stupid, pathetic waste of skin!" shouted Padma. "This is going to be the most expensive fuck of your life, because my husband is going to kill you for it, and when he does, I'm going to enjoy watching you die, you ignorant pile of lilywhite dog shit!"

Padma's perfect English struck the men like an electric shock. The two men holding her jumped back. The scout sprang to his feet.

At that instant, the two soldiers watched in stunned amazement as the scout suddenly spun on his feet like a twirling top. He then fell to the ground atop Padma's legs. The scout howled like a braying donkey as he frantically reached for his right shoulder blade, where blood pumped from a fresh wound, staining his long johns crimson. The scout's cries masked the soft report of a rifle shot, arriving seconds after the bullet hit its target.

Precious seconds passed before the two soldiers realized they were under attack. They drew their Colt revolvers. They couldn't see who had fired on them. They scanned the landscape. Padma got up on her elbows and pulled away from the scout on her legs.

"You're going to die now," Padma said to the blond soldier with a vengeful smile on her face.

"Shut up!" the soldier yelled, panicked.

"Listen to me," she said. "It's very important that you listen to me, because these are going to be the last words you hear."

"Shut up, you fucking bitch!" the soldier shouted.

"I want you to know that I'm enjoying this," said Padma. "I'm loving every moment of watching you die."

"Shut up! Shut up!" the soldier screamed, pointing his revolver at Padma's face.

At that instant, the soldier's head split open. His body landed on its side in the dirt next to Padma, then rolled slowly onto its back. As before, the soft report of a distant rifle shot landed seconds after the bullet passed through the soldier's head. The time gap between the bullet's impact and the latent sound of the rifle shot meant the assassin was over 1,000 yards away.

The remaining soldier with the black hair made out the faint figure of a man far downstream on the riverbank. The man was calmly walking toward the soldier and Padma. He appeared to be reloading his rifle.

The soldier fired all six shots of his revolver toward the figure. The assassin, well beyond the pistol's effective range, did not bother to take cover. He continued walking deliberately upstream.

"Your turn," said Padma. "Time to die."

The soldier looked at Padma, terrified. He threw his spent pistol on the ground and began to run upstream. Padma watched as the distant figure knelt on the ground.

• • •

Kyle watched the solder through his riflescope. He raised the cross hairs above the soldier, estimating the bullet's arc trajectory for the long-distance kill shot. The former Delta marksman exhaled softly as he pulled the trigger.

The Marlin rifle bucked hard against Kyle's shoulder. He watched the soldier through the scope as the bullet knocked him face down. The soldier slid to a halt in the sand and lay motionless on the riverbank.

Kyle rose to his feet and began to run toward Padma. On the riverbank, he saw Padma's dress washed ashore. He collected it and ran to her. When he arrived, he found her sitting on the ground, her arms around her legs, studying the wounded scout as he writhed and groaned in pain a few feet away.

Padma looked up at Kyle, then turned to continue watching the dying scout, as though she were engrossed in a TV show. The scout had turned onto his back, staining the sand around him crimson with his blood. He groaned with excruciating pain from the bullet wound that had smashed his shoulder blade. His flaccid penis, encrusted with sand, hung from his long johns.

After a few moments, Padma stood up and faced Kyle. She did not embrace him. To Kyle, her expression seemed flat—he saw no relief in her eyes. Peeking through the numbing shock of her attack was her realization that this event was simply another horrible episode in a dreadful place and time. Resignation washed over her. Grim survival was the very best one could hope for in this brutal frontier life.

The scout groaned again. Padma and Kyle glanced at him, then locked eyes with each other.

"I'm surprised you missed," Padma said without emotion, noting the fact that one of Kyle's three shots was not a kill shot.

"I didn't miss," Kyle replied.

Padma looked into his eyes, momentarily puzzled. She then realized that Kyle had intentionally saved her attacker for her. Without unlocking her eyes from his, she reached for his belt and pulled his combat knife from its sheath. She then turned toward the scout. Nearly spent from blood loss, only minutes of his life remained. Padma knelt beside him.

"You fuckin' cunt!" the scout said in a hoarse whisper.

Padma reached into the scout's underwear and took the man's testicles and penis in her hand. She then looked into his face.

"This is going to hurt," she said, nodding in slow affirmation.

Padma did not take her eyes off the scout's face as she began to slice off his genitals. She was patient, taking her time as the dying scout screamed and writhed in unbearable pain.

"Hold still," she said. "You're just making this worse."

Warm blood gushed over her hands. As she cut away the remaining flesh that tethered the scout's manhood, the now genderless person watched, horrified, as Padma dropped the bloody organs on his chest with a splat. His eyes bulged, and his mouth opened wide in a silent, terrified scream. Moments later, he lost consciousness as his last ounce of lifeblood flowed onto the riverbank.

Padma rose and walked to the body of the last soldier to die, the black-haired one who had stolen her ring. He lay face down in the sand, his arms stretched in front of him as though he was offering his surrender. She rolled him onto his back. The soldier's eyes were open. His expression of terror was frozen on his dead face. Padma set the knife on the soldier's chest as she fished in his shirt pocket for her ring. Upon retrieving it, she slid it back onto her ring finger, squishing blood. She held up her bloody ring hand, examining it as though she were shopping at Tiffany's.

Padma picked up the knife, rose, and turned to Kyle, her hands dripping with blood. Kyle pulled off his shirt for her. She ignored it and brushed past him in a daze, walking downstream along the riverbank.

"Beloved," he called after her.

Padma said nothing. She dropped the knife in the sand and continued to walk downstream.

Place: unknown
Date: unknown
Time: unknown

Padma opened her eyes into darkness. Her head swirled, disoriented, heavy.

Swaddled in blankets in bed, she slowly sat up.

I need to use the bathroom, but I can't see the way. The apartment is dark.

She reached for the lamp on her end table. She couldn't feel either the lamp or the table. She felt around her bed. It didn't feel like her bed.

Where is the lamp?

She heard sounds—voices singing, pounding boom box bass drums—sounds of celebration.

Is there a party next door?

Padma felt a pang of fear. She didn't know where she was. Her chest blazed with pain. She touched her sternum. The shooting pain made reality surface through her haze.

I'm not in my apartment.

The realization that she had not awoken from her 1890 nightmare landed hard in her stomach. She raised her hands to her face and began to cry.

Fragments of memory returned, swirling with groggy

disorientation.

She remembered Kyle's arm around her shoulders, a hand on her arm guiding her back to the village after the attack. Hundreds of tribespeople had swarmed around them. Horrified expressions reflected the sight of Padma, clothed only in Kyle's bloodstained shirt, her hands and face stained with blood. She remembered the roar of the mob. They'd crowded the couple, putting their hands on Padma. Kyle shouted at the mob to back off. When they didn't, he pulled his MP7 and fired into the air, then aimed it at the crowd. Takoda pushed through the mob to join the couple. He stood in front of them, wearing his bowler hat and an anguished expression. Kyle smacked Takoda across the cheek with his gun.

"You swore to protect her," he shouted in Takoda's face. "You *swore!*"

The hundreds of tribespeople huddled outside the tipi gasped, outraged that a white man had so brazenly disrespected one of their braves. Takoda raised a hand to silence them. He looked at the ground. "He is right," Takoda said to the multitudes. "I failed the Messiah. I was entrusted to protect the one who is most important. I failed. The shame is mine."

Padma remembered images of horse-drawn wagons in the village, brimming with supplies and equipment. Tribespeople swarmed all the wagons but two. Those two wagons were parked on the outskirts of the village, far away from the tipis.

She remembered Kyle removing her bloodied shirt and washing the blood off her hands and face with a damp cloth. She could still smell the scout's blood.

After bathing her, Kyle had tucked Padma into her buffalo bed. He stroked her hair as he looked into her eyes. Her beautiful brown eyes were flat with shock, transitioning to depression. She remembered Kyle saying something about promising to check on her as he left.

Padma turned on her side, staring at her right hand, the one that had wielded the knife, until she fell unconscious.

• • •

Padma felt as though she had slept for days.

She still needed to pee. She wrapped herself in a blanket and felt the tipi walls for the exit flap.

She pushed the flap open into a nighttime celebration. Fires burned, and people sang and danced to beating drums. She smelled something—it was steak.

"Love?" said Kyle.

Padma was startled. Kyle was seated at her feet to the side of the tipi flap, his Marlin rifle in his lap. Hoover lay beside him, looking up at Padma. Performing sentry duty for hours, Kyle had shooed away the Messiah's multitudes. He stood to embrace her. He wrapped his arms around her blanket-wrapped body. Her attempt to return his embrace was perfunctory. She placed her hands on his waist.

"How do you feel?" he asked

"I need to pee," she replied, dazed, deflecting the question.

Padma walked several yards away from their tipi, lifted her blanket and squatted to urinate. She ignored the warm excess that ran down her leg as she stood up. When she returned, she began to re-enter the tipi. Kyle took her hand.

"I need to show you something," he said.

"I don't feel well," she said. Padma badly wanted to return to her buffalo bed and go back to sleep. She wanted to sleep for the rest of her life.

"I know, love," Kyle said. "I think this will make you feel better."

Kyle guided her by her hand through the darkness. Padma followed, resigned, as though walking to her execution.

Thirty yards away from their tipi stood two tents. The larger of the two, some 60 feet long by 30 feet wide, was illuminated from within by lamplight. Kyle opened the door flap for Padma.

As she stepped into the tent, Padma held her hands to her face. In the large lamp-lit room, she stood on an enormous Persian rug. Directly in front of her stood a wooden table with four chairs. The table was set with Staffordshire China—white porcelain plates, bowls, and serving ware accented with blue toile designs. Blue and yellow wildflowers sprang from a glass vase.

Behind the table was an iron wood-burning stove, its chimney pipe rising through the tent's 15-foot ceiling. Pans, bowls, knives, and kitchen utensils sat on a utility table next to the stove. Two raw steaks sat on the table, along with greens.

Padma turned to her right. In the far corner stood a brass bed with two pillows, fresh linens and a blue and white quilt with diamond patterns. A lamp burned on the nightstand next to the bed. Opposite the bed was a wooden vanity and chair with a large porcelain water bowl and mirror. The silver brushes and combs Kyle had bought in Mr. Richards' store sat on the vanity. An armoire stood next to the vanity, with clothes for Padma.

On the left side of the tent, steam rose from a clawfoot tub. Crimson rose petals simmered on the surface of the hot water.

Padma's hands rose to her face. She was overwhelmed. Her mind challenged the reality of what her eyes beheld. Just when she thought her rabbit hole could not possibly go any deeper, she had emerged into yet another impossible scene. This one was different from the others—it was beautiful, with lost comforts that beckoned to her like temptress sirens.

She didn't dare to trust them.

The monsters that attacked her had succeeded in breaking her spirit. She was reconciled to her miserable reality. Daring to hope for better was not only futile—it was dangerous. After being shot and violently assaulted, her vessel was fragile. Yielding to the powerful illusion of comfort risked wrecking what little remained of Padma on the sirens' rocky shores.

Padma turned to leave. Kyle gently stopped her, holding her shoulders. He hugged her. Padma did not return the embrace. She sensed danger.

The woman Kyle held felt unfamiliar to him. The former Empress of America, the strongest person he knew, felt delicate in his arms, as though the slightest pressure would crumble her to dust.

Kyle felt the sickening pit of guilt. His worst fear had come to pass. He had left Padma unprotected, and she had been attacked. He had brought his wife back to life with the Time Tunnel, only to subject her to a life of misery in this nineteenth-century hell.

"Love, it's OK," Kyle said.

"I don't know," she replied.

"Would you like a hot bath?" Kyle asked.

Padma was silent.

Kyle guided her to the bath. He picked up a steaming kettle from the potbelly stove and topped off the bathwater, testing the temperature with his hand. Padma watched the rose petals glide on the surface of the steaming water.

Kyle took Padma's blankets and helped her into the tub. She sank into the hot, sweet rosewater. The sirens were powerful, flowing into her body, seducing her. She closed her eyes and let out a long sigh.

Padma sat motionless in the tub. After a while, Kyle spoke.

"You should eat something," he said. "I'll make you some dinner."

Padma shook her head. "I want to go to bed."

Kyle nodded and helped her out of the tub, handing her a fresh towel. Padma held the white terrycloth towel in her hands as she dripped on the Persian rug.

"Let me help you, love," Kyle said, gently taking the towel from her.

Her dried her with the towel, then took another towel to dry her hair. He went to the armoire to retrieve the gold silk robe he had bought for her in Deadwood. He gently helped her into the robe and tied the sash around her waist. Kyle then guided her to her vanity.

"I'm going to brush your hair, then tuck you in, OK?"

Padma was mute.

She looked at the reflection in the vanity mirror as Kyle brushed out her long hair. It was the first time she had seen her face's full reflection since their arrival weeks before. It was even worse than she'd expected. Dark patches had formed under her eyes. Her cheeks had hollowed. Fine wrinkles had widened into fissures. To Padma, it was as though she had aged ten years in only two weeks.

She suddenly reached toward the mirror and slapped it, flipping it over. Its wooden back faced her. She did not want to see the other Padma's face ever again.

"You're still gorgeous, love," Kyle said.

"No, I'm not," replied Padma, resigned to her destruction.

Kyle pulled back the bedcovers. He untied her robe sash. She clutched the robe shut.

"I want this on," she said.

Kyle helped his wife into bed and tucked the covers around her. She conceded that the fresh cotton sheets and goose down pillows felt wonderful. The sirens were irresistible.

Kyle reached for the oil lamp on the nightstand to extinguish the flame.

"Don't," Padma said.

"I'm going to make a quick check outside, then I'll be back," Kyle said, picking up his MP7.

Before he exited the tent, he turned to Padma. "Nothing's getting in here tonight," Kyle promised. "Nothing's ever going to hurt you again."

Padma nodded. "I know…"

...but you're too late... she thought.

...I'm already broken.

Padma felt that something about her was now irreparably damaged, like the fouled inner workings of a child's wind-up toy. The gears and wound springs were mangled, unable to perform properly. She still appeared to be Padma, but she no longer functioned as Padma.

After Kyle left, Padma turned on her side, facing the lamp. She extended her right hand in front of the lamp. In the distance, she heard the drums and songs of the Lakota people, singing praises to their messiah. She turned her hand over to examine her palm, then turned it again to scrutinize the back of her hand in the dim light. Her hand eclipsed the flame. An orange corona glowed between the shadowed fingertips of her knife hand.

Now I can kill too, she thought.

Standing Rock Reservation
South Dakota
September 24, 1890
07:30 hours
Timeline 003

Padma opened her eyes. Morning light illuminated the tent's canvas walls. The lamp on the nightstand had been extinguished.

Padma heard crackling and popping. She smelled bacon cooking. She looked up. Kyle was hovering over a cast iron skillet on the potbelly stove. Hoover sat next to him, looking up hopefully at the stove.

"Mornin'!" he said cheerfully.

An ice bolt of terror jolted Padma as she heard the echo of the dead scout's voice in her head.

Mornin'!

Padma clenched the sheets close to her chest as Kyle scrambled eggs with bacon in the skillet, oblivious to Padma's post-attack trauma.

Padma's breathing became shallow, ramping in frequency as fear ascended in her chest. The pain from her wound seared her chest with every breath, compounding her panic.

The bacon popped, spraying Kyle with hot grease.

"Shit!"

He dumped the eggs and bacon jumble onto two plates.

Two parts of Padma's mind wrestled with each other. One voice tried to inform her that the white man cooking in her tent was her husband. The other voice shrieked with fright.

Kyle opened the stove door with a potholder and extracted an iron toaster with two slices of unevenly burnt toast. He plucked out the toast slices, put them on the plates, then set the plates on the table.

"I'm still trying to get the hang of this," he said.

Padma looked around the tent.

"Where is my dress?" she asked, attempting to maintain an appearance of calm as she hurled an escape plan together in her head.

"You can get dressed later. There's no hurry. Have some breakfast."

"I need to dress *now*," she replied.

"You need to eat," Kyle said.

"I know what I need!" Padma screamed. "I need to dress and I need to go—*now!*"

Kyle was stunned. After a moment, he yielded. "Your dress is hanging in the armoire."

Padma got out of bed, swung open the armoire and pulled her dress from a wooden hanger. She began to remove her robe, then stopped, gasping when she realized Kyle was watching her.

"Sorry," Kyle said, surprised. In the years they had known each other, Padma had never before been modest in his presence. He averted his eyes as Padma quickly tossed the robe and pulled on her dress. She walked to the tent flap. Kyle rushed to her, taking her arm.

"Padma!"

"Leave me alone!" she snapped as she squirmed away from him.

Kyle watched the tent flap fall shut in his face, stunned. He felt lead in his stomach as he turned to look at the two expectant toile breakfast plates on the checkerboard tablecloth, sitting before two empty wooden chairs. Hoover looked up at Kyle with a worried whimper.

• • •

Padma emerged from the tent into the morning sunlight. She closed her eyes, exhaling a deep sigh of relief. She took a deep breath and exhaled. The panic abated. She opened her eyes.

Hundreds of her followers stood in front of her. Standing to her right beside the tent door was Takoda. She noticed something was different about him. He was no longer wearing his Ghost Dance shirt with its inverted red triangle. His chest was bare, save for a fringed leather vest and a diamond-shaped black and yellow beaded medallion that hung around his neck.

Padma's eyes met Takoda's. Her anxious face warmed into a loving smile. Takoda returned her smile. She took his medallion in her hand. The center of the diamond was made of yellow beads and surrounded by a perimeter of black beads. Padma glanced at her followers. They wore the same yellow and black diamond symbol. Some, like Takoda, wore medallions. Others had painted the symbol on their shirts and dresses. The diamond was painted in the center of their chests, directly over their hearts.

"What is this?" asked Padma, holding the diamond.

"It is the symbol of the Messiah," replied Takoda, pointing toward the bullet hole in her dress.

Padma nodded, smiling. She lay Takoda's medallion back against his chest, allowing her fingertips to linger a moment against his muscled brown chest.

Standing Rock Reservation
South Dakota
September 24, 1890
16:45 hours
Timeline 003

Kyle walked through the grove of trees that separated the tent from the Grand River. He carried two empty wooden water buckets—one in each hand. His MP7 was holstered on his thigh. His combat knife was strapped to his belt. Hoover trailed behind him.

He had kept himself very busy during the day, doing anything to distract his mind from his wife and her new infatuation. Kyle saw Padma's adoring eyes on Takoda—a loving gaze that had previously been reserved exclusively for Kyle. Takoda was smitten as well. Kyle's mind burned—a jealous rage made heavy by depression.

Kyle translated his pain into productivity, spending most of the day building a wooden water tank for the tent. He used tools brought from Deadwood to cannibalize one of the wagons for the materials. The tank fed into a pipe with a crude spigot that entered the tent through a small hole—the reservation's first indoor plumbing.

Having completed the tank, he was now making sorties to the river to fill it with water. The tank was nearly full. He headed to the river to fill the water buckets for the last time.

It was late afternoon, and the trees cast long shadows on the dry prairie grass. As Kyle made his way through the cottonwood grove, he saw glints of afternoon sunlight shimmer off the river through a gap in the trees.

The shimmering light grew brighter. Hoover growled and gnashed his teeth. Kyle squinted against the light as it became blinding. A teeth-rattling hum accompanied the light. In the instant Kyle recognized the phenomenon, the light faded, leaving Annika Wise in its place, standing directly in front of him. She was dressed in black, with commando pants and a long-sleeved black shirt, fingerless black gloves, a utility vest, a web belt with a knife, and a large backpack. An MP7 submachine gun was holstered on her thigh.

She reached for her gun. Kyle swung one bucket into her gun hand, knocking the gun away as Annika grunted in pain. Kyle backhanded the bucket, smacking her on the side of her head. Annika staggered, stunned by the blow. The bucket opened a gash in her right temple. Kyle could see that her backpack was heavy, slowing her down.

As Kyle stepped toward Annika, she flipped her backpack over her head toward him. It hit him in the face, obscuring his vision for a moment. As the bag fell away, he saw the sole of Annika's boot take its place, a nanosecond before it smacked him in the cheek. He spun, swinging his buckets as Annika ducked beneath them. Crouched on the ground, she swept her leg behind Kyle's feet, knocking him onto his back.

Hoover leapt at Annika, clamping his jaws onto her left forearm. She punched his face with her free hand. Hoover held tight, growling fiercely. Annika pulled her knife to stab Hoover when Kyle side-kicked her in the gut, doubling her over. He raised his leg for a follow-up kick to her face. Annika slid to the side and out of harm's way. She clubbed Kyle over the head with Hoover—the jolt knocked the dog free of Annika's arm. He rolled on the ground, then lay motionless.

Kyle glanced at his dog. The distraction cost him, as Annika whacked him in the gut with a roundhouse kick, then leapt in the air, knocking him on the back of the head with a scissor kick. Kyle face-planted on the ground.

Kyle had never been a match for Annika, even when they trained together for their mission. Now seven years older, Kyle felt as though he moved in slow motion compared to his bantamweight ninja opponent.

Annika drew her knife and lunged for Kyle. He rolled away, and Annika's knife struck dirt. She drove her knee onto his sternum, grabbing a handful of his hair with one hand, preparing to thrust her knife with the other.

"Annika!" screamed Padma.

At the sound of her name, Annika's focus lapsed momentarily. She instinctively turned her head. In a millisecond, she turned back to Kyle for the kill, just in time to see a rock in Kyle's hand a moment before it smacked the right side of her head, bringing instant darkness.

Standing Rock Reservation
South Dakota
September 24, 1890
19:15 hours
Timeline 003

Annika heard shuffling. Blurry dark and burnt orange shadows intertwined with images and sounds from her subconscious. She heard her father's voice asking her something. She tried to respond to him, but her thoughts could not translate into words. She uttered unintelligible sounds.

She felt the heaviness of her head. It was hanging down. She tried to lift her head—it swayed under its weight. She felt an intense throbbing pain from her right temple.

A fragment of lucid thought peeked through the chaos. She struggled to open her eyes. They seemed impossibly heavy. She slowly lifted her head. She was in a tent. It was night. A single oil lamp, sitting on the floor in front of her, illuminated the tent, casting orange and black shapes against the tent walls. She tried to move. She was seated on the ground. Her hands were bound behind her to a tent pole. Her legs were stretched in front of her, bound at the ankles with one of the plastic zip strips she had brought to bind Kyle and Padma if she captured them.

Beneath her was a large rug that covered most of the floor area of the 20-by-30-foot tent—Kyle's "war room" in which to plan the campaign against the US Army. A simple wooden table surrounded by four chairs stood to Annika's right.

On the opposite side of the tent, Kyle was unpacking Annika's pack and vest, taking inventory as he stacked the contents on the floor.

Padma sat nearby on the floor, her legs pulled up, her eyes locked on Annika. Hoover lay next to Padma, his head resting on his front paws. Padma was unaware that she was petting the injured dog. When she noticed what her hand was doing, she jerked it away from Hoover and held it up to examine it, vexed that it seemed to have a mind of its own.

Kyle saw that Annika was coming to. Dried blood caked an open gash on a swollen purple mound on her right temple.

"Welcome back," said Kyle.

"Fuck you," said Annika.

Kyle smiled and continued unpacking Annika's bag.

"Let's see—one MP7A1 submachine gun, 3,000 rounds, one Glock 17mm pistol, 500 rounds, 20 pounds of C4 with wireless detonators, knives, and night vision goggles," said Kyle. "I'm flattered—all this to kill little ol' me?"

"I could kill you with a teaspoon, old man," snapped Annika.

Kyle smiled and continued, "Mil spec laptop computer with extra batteries, binoculars, $10,000 in period currency, first-aid kit, flashlight, MREs, glow sticks, plus some personal effects. Toilet paper—that'll definitely come in handy."

Kyle tossed the roll to Padma. She caught it without taking her eyes off Annika.

"You came prepared," he said.

Annika was silent. She looked around the tent, studying her environment. Padma observed Annika's behavior with contempt, as though she were watching a captured scorpion.

"There's one thing that's missing," Kyle said. "Care to guess what it is?"

Annika scanned the pile of arms, cash, and accessories. She felt a pang of fear.

"The transponder," she replied. "Where is it?"

"Actually, I have no idea," Kyle answered. "I gave it to a tribesman, with instructions to give it to another tribesman, and so on. One of them buried it somewhere. While they were at it, I had them bury mine too.

"It's insurance—life insurance for my wife and me, as well as insurance that you're going to help us with our mission."

"And what mission would that be?"

"We're going to win the Battle of Wounded Knee."

Annika's eyes went wide.

"You are outside your mind," said Annika. "Even with these weapons, we're hopelessly outnumbered and outgunned."

"I have to say, I'm a little disappointed," said Kyle. "I guess I overestimated you."

"I'm from DC, not Planet Krypton," she replied.

"Still, if we don't succeed, one thing you can be sure of is that you'll never see home again. You can't torture the transponder out of us, because we don't know where it is."

Kyle watched Annika as she considered her situation. He saw the glimmer of a thought flash across her eyes. He knew she was intrigued with the challenge, though he had no illusions about Annika's allegiance. If she could find a way to kill Kyle and return to 2008, she would do it in a heartbeat.

Annika considered the dual challenge of changing the outcome of the Wounded Knee Massacre while still realizing her original kill-or-capture mission. Her gaze wandered with her mind as she began to delve into the problem. She snapped out of her deep thought and looked up, meeting Padma's stare.

"The fuck you looking at?" Annika said.

Without saying a word, Padma rose and exited the tent. Kyle watched her leave.

"Touchy, isn't she?" Annika said, enjoying the moment.

Kyle squelched an angry impulse. He got up and stepped over the pile of weapons and ammo. He picked up the oil lamp on the floor and set it down beside him as he crouched at Annika's feet. He folded his hands in front, resting his elbows on his knees. He looked down, took a breath, and exhaled.

Annika watched Kyle, trying to divine what he was up to. The flickering lamp flame threw moving light against his face and burnt shadows against the tent wall.

Annika understood both sides of prisoner-of-war dynamics. She knew how to coerce, and she was trained to resist. She knew Kyle would know that. She steeled herself for what was about to happen.

Kyle looked up, staring Annika squarely in her eyes.

"Let me ask you something," Kyle began. "Did you ever learn to fly?"

The question seemed harmless to Annika. "Of course," she said. "I flew Blackhawks and Apaches in Desert Storm."

"No," Kyle said, "did you ever learn to *fly?*"

"I don't understand,"

"Like a shadow warrior."

Annika's face went white. She had never shared that childhood dream with anyone, including her ex-husband. Kyle had fired a lightning bolt into her core, shattering its citadel with a single stroke.

She tried to regain her composure. "Look, I don't know what you think you know about me, but..."

"I know everything about you, Annika. Everything. I know about your childhood—I know the first Bruce Lee movie you ever saw with your father. I know you met his teacher, Ip Man, before he died. I know how you met your husband...and I know how your husband died."

"You're confused. My *ex*-husband is alive," replied Annika.

"In one timeline, yes," said Kyle. "In another, both of our spouses are dead."

Annika was stunned. "We knew each other."

"Yes."

They paused, eyes locked. Annika was momentarily disarmed. She studied Kyle's face, searching for evidence that this might truly be the one person she had dared to trust. She could see the sadness in his eyes. She had never known a depth of love that could have surfaced her most intimate secrets. She had not dared to hope that was a possibility for her. She wondered if the eddies and currents of time had reunited them, washing them onto the same shore.

An epiphany flashed onto Annika's face. "Anderson Wild," she said. "A.W.—you took my initials."

"Yes."

The fact that Kyle had inscribed her initials onto his identity gave her guarded heartstrings a powerful tug. She gasped.

"She knows?" Annika asked.

"Yes."

"Awkward."

"Yes."

Kyle pulled his knife from his belt and sliced off the zip strip binding Annika's ankles. He walked behind her and cut her wrist strip. Annika rubbed her wrists. She propped up her knees and rested her wrists on them. Kyle returned to his crouched position, facing her.

"I'm supposed to kill you," she said.

"I think I already figured that out."

They sat silently as Annika attempted to process the staggering epiphany and reconcile it with her mission.

"Well," she said, "I suppose we can fight this crazy stupid battle first. There's no way we'll both survive, but if by some miracle we do…"

Kyle nodded.

"…we can figure it out then."

"All right," Kyle said. He rose to his feet and extended a hand to help Annika up. She took it.

"There are some blankets," he said, pointing to a couple of folded blankets in the corner. "I'll bring you some food and water. That wound is going to need attention. I'll help you with it."

Kyle turned toward to leave.

"I never learned to fly," Annika said.

Kyle turned and gave a sad smile.

"I've never seen anyone fly higher," he said.

Kyle opened the tent flap and exited. Annika watched the man and his burnt shadow leave the tent.

Standing Rock Reservation
South Dakota
September 24, 1890
19:40 hours
Timeline 003

Kyle scanned the moonlit landscape for Padma. Campfires near tipis dotted the nighttime scene. Blended with the sounds of crickets, Kyle could hear conversations as families talked about their day, including the news of the latest strange arrival. Who was the tiny woman in black? She brought with her the same magic weapon as Red Star. The Messiah was obviously displeased with her presence. Were they enemies? Was the white woman in black a demon intent on defeating the Messiah?

Families debated about whether the strangers were indeed sent by the Great Spirit, and, even if they were, if anyone was truly capable of defeating the massive army of the whites.

Kyle saw that their tent was dark. He walked through the cottonwood trees toward the river. When he reached the high bank, he scanned the landscape for Padma. To his right, a few dozen yards away, he saw the orange glow of a cigarette. Padma was seated on the bank, watching the moon and starlight ripple off the slow-motion current.

The stars brilliantly pierced the night sky. The electric dust of the Milky Way stretched across the vista. A cool breeze wafted off the river.

Padma held her knife hand up to the moon, eclipsing it. The blue-white corona glowed between her fingertips.

Kyle sat down next to her.

"It's breathtaking," Padma said.

"Almost as breathtaking as my wife," Kyle said.

Padma nodded. "So that was the perfect thing to say to me right now."

Kyle knew his wife needed to talk. He waited patiently.

Padma took a draw from her cigarette and exhaled. The moonlight illuminated the smoke from her lips.

"I want you to kill her," Padma said flatly.

Kyle swung his head to face Padma, stunned. Padma's stare did not shift from the river. Kyle wasn't sure whether his wife was joking.

"Excuse me?"

"She will kill us both in a heartbeat. We're going to war against the United States Army. We can't fight an army at the same time we're wondering when our assassin is going to kill us in our sleep."

"She can't kill us and return to her time," Kyle said. "I've seen to that. She doesn't want to be here anymore than you do. She's an asset in the war that is coming."

"Convenient that your lover has a nice asset," Padma snarked.

Kyle was wounded. "That woman is not my lover! The woman you're referring to is dead and decomposed at the bottom of a river in Connecticut. In case you hadn't noticed, this version tried to kill me a few hours ago."

"All the more reason to kill her now," said Padma. "If you won't do it, I'll have my people take care of it."

"*Your* people?" Kyle asked, incredulous. "I beg your pardon?"

"In case *you* hadn't noticed, I'm the fucking Messiah," Padma said. "There are 3,000 people in this village—*my* people. And more are on the way."

Padma snapped her fingers. "I do this, and she's gone."

Kyle didn't recognize this vengeful woman, intoxicated by power.

"It's a mistake," Kyle said. "She's the only shot we have at getting back to our time and our lives. We can't show up at the front door of the Time Tunnel and expect a warm welcome. We'll be locked up the moment we do."

Padma was silent as she took another draw on her cigarette.

"That's your time," she said. "Not mine. You want to go back with her? Feel free to leave anytime."

Padma put out her cigarette on the bank, got up, and walked away, leaving Kyle alone.

Standing Rock Reservation
South Dakota
September 25, 1890
07:15 hours
Timeline 003

Annika followed Kyle toward the two covered wagons on the outskirts of the village. The tribespeople had been warned by the Messiah to stay well away from them. The morning was overcast. A cool breeze hinted of fall.

A train of sutures ran along Annika's right temple. Kyle had performed the field procedure the previous night using supplies from Annika's medical kit. Though her head throbbed with pain, Annika refused painkillers, preferring to stay sharp in her dangerous new world.

Kyle unlatched the back panel of the wagon, swinging it down. Annika surveyed the wooden crates and barrels. Kyle jumped in the wagon and lowered a crate to Annika. He hopped to the ground, picked up a crowbar in the rear of the wagon, and pried open the crate.

Annika looked at the contents—dozens of sticks of dynamite to be used for mining.

"How much have you got?" she asked.

"A thousand sticks," Kyle said.

"Not bad," Annika said. "Not enough."

"There's something else," Kyle said.

Kyle hiked up the cover on the side of the wagon. Packed in the wagon with the dynamite crates were wooden barrels. Annika read the words stenciled on the barrels: "Sulfuric Acid."

"Used to process gold ore at the Homestake Mine," Kyle explained.

"So what?" she asked. "Is your plan to dissolve the army?"

"Not exactly," Kyle said, walking to the other wagon. He pulled up the cover. Annika read the stenciling on the crates inside. Her eyes went wide.

"Whoa—now *that* is interesting," she said. "You know you're smarter than you look. One problem—how do you deliver the weapon?"

"I'm still fuzzy on that part," Kyle said.

• • •

A few hours later, Kyle and Annika pored over a map of the territory in their makeshift command center. Black stones with numbers represented Army regiments. White stones represented various Lakota tribes.

Annika took a sip of coffee from a blue enamel tin cup, set it on the table, and sighed.

"If you know me as well as you claim to, you know that I like a challenge," Annika said. "So you should know that it's a big deal when I tell you that something is impossible.

"This is impossible. We're up against 5,000 battle-ready cavalry and infantry soldiers with repeating rifles and light artillery. Their artillery can fire grapeshot canisters from well over 1,000 yards out and shred every living person in this village to bits without even bothering their cavalry to mount a horse or asking their infantrymen to ready their rifles.

"We have similar numbers, but a fraction of the arms, no artillery, no natural defenses, no training. Add to that the fact that our troops have no unified command, with the possible exception of your wife.

"We have your dynamite and my C4 and wireless detonators, though I don't see how that makes a dent, even if we know where to put it. We have your secret weapon, but no way to deliver it. Have I missed anything?"

Kyle shook his head grimly. "No. I think that's an excellent battle assessment."

"The bottom line is this: We're all going to be slaughtered," Annika concluded. "Everyone here is going to die, just as they did in December 1890. The only difference is that a few extras are going to die with them."

Annika's head snapped up as she heard the rumble of horses in the distance.

"You hear that?" she asked.

Their eyes met for an instant, then they scrambled for their guns. They heard shouts and yips from the Lakota tribespeople as they exited the tent.

From their perch on the knoll, 50 yards from the village, Kyle and Annika watched as a company of some 70 cavalry soldiers trotted their horses into the village center. A flag bearer carried the company flag at the front of the column. The flag, the United States Stars and Stripes with a pie-wedge cutout from its trailing edge, fluttered in the breeze. In the rear of the column, a soldier drove a wagon pulled by two bay horses.

Annika marveled at the sight of a company of nineteenth-century Army cavalry wearing their navy-colored uniforms and sitting astride their bay quarter horses.

"I still can't quite believe this," she said.

As the soldiers entered the village, women gathered their children and disappeared into their tipis. The men grabbed their rifles. To Kyle and Annika's astonishment, Padma walked calmly into the soldiers' path and raised her arms, motioning the soldiers to halt. In moments, over 1,000 Lakota warriors had joined her. Takoda stood at Padma's side.

"Exactly what the fuck is she doing?" asked Annika.

The company commander, a captain, raised a gloved hand for the riders to halt. The captain was in his late thirties, pale with a freckled face, bushy red mustache, and sideburns.

The captain eyed the tribespeople nervously. He had expected light resistance—perhaps several dozen half-starved warriors. Instead, he found his company outnumbered 15 to 1. He stared at the breathtakingly beautiful squaw standing before him. Her fearless eyes were locked on his. A supreme confidence turned the corners of her full lips into a daring smile. He had never seen a woman like her before—at once irresistible and deadly. Everything about the situation unnerved him—the strange sorceress leading an army of Lakota warriors with much greater numbers and armament than expected.

The captain looked closer at the woman's dress. A charred hole pierced the dress over her heart. Icy terror jetted through his veins. He had heard Daniel Royer's wild tale of a tall, beautiful, English-speaking squaw who rose from the dead after being shot through the heart. The captain had dismissed the absurd story. Yet here she was—a woman precisely matching Royer's description, right down to the bullet hole. Was this truly the Messiah of Lakota prophecy?

The men of the company looked to their captain for guidance. Though a wiser commander might have exercised the better part of valor and retreated, the captain, feeling the eyes and expectations of his soldiers upon him, opted instead to allow his pride to dictate the next move.

The captain cleared his throat, collecting his composure. "By order of the United States government, I hereby order you to disarm. You will deposit your weapons on the wagon at the rear forthwith."

Takoda translated the captain's order. Angry murmurs rose from the Lakota army.

Padma replied in a loud defiant voice, "The Lakota Nation does not recognize the United States government's authority. Accordingly, we have no intention of relinquishing our weapons."

The captain's jaw dropped. The siren squaw's English was better than his.

Before he could respond, Padma continued, "However, I will make you a counter-offer. If you and your soldiers disarm and leave peacefully, we will agree not to kill each and every one of you right here, *right now!*"

Padma punctuated the time and place of the soldiers' fate with a strict finger, pointed toward the earth.

As Takoda translated, a roar erupted from the Lakota army. The anxious cavalry soldiers pulled their rifles from their saddles.

"You are ordered to lower your weapons, or we will open fire!" shouted the captain.

The war yells from the hundreds of Lakota warriors combined into the roar of a ferocious mob.

"Company: ready!" shouted the captain over the din.

The soldiers raised their rifles.

"What are we doing?" asked Annika.

Kyle set his Marlin rifle on the ground and unholstered his MP7 machine gun, targeting the soldiers at the front of the column. "Looks like we're going to war."

"Aim!"

"Fuck!" Annika said. She ran toward the soldiers.

"What the fuck are you doing?" shouted Kyle.

"Hold on, wait a minute! Wait a minute!" shouted Annika, approaching the soldiers, waving her arms. "Everybody settle down."

The cavalry soldiers eyed the petite woman running toward them. She was strangely dressed in black, wearing a man's clothes with a large sidearm holstered at her thigh. Kyle picked up his Marlin rifle and trailed behind her, wondering what on earth she was thinking. Padma motioned her arms down to quiet her army.

When Annika reached the crowd, she stepped between the captain's horse and Padma. She put her hand on the horse's nose. The horse pinned his ears.

"Step away from my horse, madam!" commanded the captain.

"I am so sorry, Captain," replied Annika. "Please forgive me. I am only trying to prevent bloodshed."

She turned to Padma. "No one wants bloodshed, right?" Padma glared at Annika.

Annika turned back to the captain and smiled, batting her eyes. "Captain, sir, I believe I have a solution."

Before the captain could speak, Annika jerked his horse's left rein, scissor-kicking into the air as the horse and the captain tilted to the left. Annika smacked the captain on the side of the head as he pitched off his saddle. She flipped backwards, reaching for her MP7. By the time her feet touched the ground, bullets blazed from her submachine gun at a rate of 950 rounds per minute. Before any of the soldiers could react, a quarter of the company's soldiers had already fallen dead or wounded from their horses.

Horses spooked and bucked amidst the screams and shouts of panicked and wounded soldiers and the whoops of the Lakota tribesmen. The Lakota warriors opened fire, cutting down dozens of soldiers. Four soldiers at the rear of the column spun their horses and galloped away.

"If they get away, they'll be back with help!" Annika shouted to Kyle.

Kyle ran through the chaos, dodging horses and soldiers to find a clear line of sight. He knelt on one knee and raised his Marlin rifle, peering through the scope. He squeezed the trigger. The first soldier fell. He rapidly worked the rifle's lever to chamber another round. He aimed and fired—the second soldier hit the ground. He fired again—three down.

Kyle chambered a fourth round. The last soldier was well over 1,000 yards away. Kyle pulled the trigger.

Kyle and Annika watched as the soldier galloped out of sight.

"You missed," said Annika.

Kyle ducked his head, incensed. "There's only so much of your mess I can clean up! You could have dialed me in on your plan."

"So you think there was a plan?" asked Annika, incredulous. "That was pure improvisation for your wife's crazy stunt! Anyway, you could have been a better shot."

"I hit three rapidly moving targets with an ancient rifle at 1,000 yards. You think you could have done better?"

"Possibly not," Annika conceded, secretly impressed with Kyle's crack shooting.

Kyle and Annika turned as a roar erupted from the tribesmen, celebrating their victory. They crowded around their beloved Messiah. She raised her arms in the air, beaming in response to the adulation.

"Y'know, I'd like to think that we had a little something to do with the outcome," complained Annika.

"It's going to be a short party," said Kyle, grimly. "They're going to be back, and they're going to be back *strong*."

The tribesmen turned to the remains of the battle. Dead and wounded soldiers lay scattered on the ground. Their frightened horses, snorting, eyes wide, trotted nervously through camp without their riders. The tribesmen began rounding them up.

Kyle and Annika watched horrified as other tribesmen began shooting wounded soldiers, then stripping them of their clothes and weapons. They moved to intervene.

Annika ran to a tribesman, standing over a young soldier, his rifle pointed at the soldier's chest. The soldier, with blond hair and a moustache, looked at the tribesman with terror at the realization that his life was about to end.

Annika grabbed the warrior's rifle barrel and kicked him in the gut, doubling him over. Snatching the gun away by the barrel, she smacked another tribesman who tried to stop her on the side of the head with the rifle butt.

The tribesmen ran to stop Annika. Kyle ran to her side, pointing his MP7 at the warriors, its brilliant red laser star skipping across the warriors' chests. Incensed, the warriors raised their rifles.

"Stop!" shouted Padma.

She walked to Kyle. Her expression was grim.

"What are you doing?" she asked.

"The battle's over," Kyle said. "We're not going to butcher the wounded."

Padma took a step forward. "I'm confused…whose side are you on? Because it sounds like you're on the side of the white people who shot me and tried to rape me."

Kyle shook his head. "Does shooting the wounded make everything all right, Messiah?"

"Fuck you!" screamed Padma. "You know they would do worse to us!"

"Yeah, they would!" shouted Kyle. "Is that the best your

people can be?"

Padma stared at Kyle, shaking with rage, her fists clenched. The warriors awaited her order to execute Kyle and Annika. After a few moments, she unlocked eyes from Kyle and turned to Takoda.

"We are going to treat these fallen warriors with dignity," she said. "We are going to treat them in a better way than they would treat us. We are going to be the better people."

Takoda translated to the tribesmen. They grumbled as they lowered their weapons. Padma gave Kyle a final hard stare, then turned and walked away, escorted by Takoda.

"Wow. She's a handful," said Annika.

Kyle's sad gaze lingered in Padma's wake. He secretly wished that his wife had given her warriors the order to kill him.

The moans of the wounded turned Kyle and Annika's heads. Dozens of men, dead and wounded, lay before them.

Kyle turned to Annika. "We'll triage the wounded as best we can."

"We can't treat them here," said Annika. "They need a field hospital."

"Well, the good news is that one will be on the way here soon," Kyle said dryly. "The bad news is that five thousand troops will be coming with it."

"How long do you think we have?" asked Annika.

"To deploy a dozen regiments from Fort Yates and kill us all? Three days."

Annika saw an epiphany flash across Kyle's face.

"What?" she asked.

"Our battle plan just changed," Kyle replied.

Standing Rock Reservation
South Dakota
September 25, 1890
12:00 hours
Timeline 003

Kyle and Annika triaged the wounded men, then loaded the dead and wounded into two wagons. The dead were stacked like corkwood in one wagon. Improvising, they nailed a platform of flat boards to the rear benches of the second wagon, creating a mezzanine to enable more wounded to fit without laying them on top of each other. The grizzly work was exhausting. None of the thousands of Lakota tribespeople in the village offered to help. They watched with scorn as Kyle and Annika tended to their fellow white soldiers. Some spat at the ground as the pair gently loaded the wounded into their transport.

Before riding out, Kyle looked for Padma to let her know that he was leaving to return the fallen soldiers to their comrades. He found her alone on the bank of the Grand River, smoking a cigarette in the same spot they had sat the night before. Kyle sat beside her. Padma exhaled smoke into the fall breeze.

"This is my last cigarette," Padma said.

"You quitting?" asked Kyle hopefully.

"No, goddammit, I'm out of cigarettes," she said.

"I brought you some tobacco and rolling papers from Deadwood. Pretty gnarly, but better than nothing."

"I guess it's come to that," Padma said. "I'm a frontier messiah."

They sat silently, watching the river slowly pass.

"Kyle, there's something I need to tell you," Padma said.

"What's wrong?" Kyle asked, knowing well that good news never followed "there's something I need to tell you."

Padma paused, preparing herself. She took another draw on her cigarette.

"I still see that man's blood on my hands," she said. "The one who tried to rape me. I see it."

Padma held her palms in front of her face. Smoke wafted from her last American Spirit cigarette, pinched between two fingers on her right hand. Sunlight glinted off the diamond ring on her left hand.

"I can see it right now…his blood…dripping off my hands," she said.

Kyle wrapped his arm around Padma's shoulders. She did not respond to his comforting touch.

"I understand, love," said Kyle.

"I don't think that you do," said Padma coldly, pulling away.

"What do you mean?"

"I mean that, now that I've killed, I want to kill again," she said. "I mean that I want more blood on my hands. I mean that I like killing.

"I want to kill them all."

Padma extinguished her last cigarette on the riverbank and got up.

"If you manage to make it back alive this time, I think you should move out of the tent," she said coldly. "You can stay in the tipi until this is over."

She turned and walked away.

Fort Yates, ND
September 25, 1890
20:30 hours
Timeline 003

Kyle and Annika drove their two makeshift ambulance wagons across the prairie in the dark. More than two dozen wounded soldiers lay in the double-decker bed of Kyle's wagon. Annika's wagon contained the flag-draped remains of an additional 40 soldiers.

They drove their wagons east across a land bridge that connected mainland North Dakota to the demi-island in the Missouri River where Fort Yates stood. They could see lantern lights burning in the windows of the Fort Yates buildings. Fort Yates lacked the fortress walls of a traditional nineteenth-century fort. It was a collection of one-story buildings with barracks, offices, and armories.

In recent weeks, thousands of tents had been pitched on the grounds of the fort to house a massive influx of soldiers. The largest army since the Civil War had been mustered at the fort to end the Indian problem once and for all.

Pegasus was ponied behind Kyle's wagon. Hoover walked alongside.

Groans rose from the bed of Kyle's wagon as a wheel hit a gopher hole.

Kyle and Annika drew closer to the fort. They approached a small building that appeared to be a guardhouse. Two soldiers stood outside.

"Halt! Who goes there?" shouted a guard.

Kyle raised a makeshift white flag made from a sheet tied to a cottonwood pole.

"My name is Kyle Mason. My colleague and I are returning dead and wounded soldiers from Standing Rock Reservation," shouted Kyle. "The wounded require medical attention."

Kyle and Annika could see the two guards talking to each other. One mounted a horse tied at the guardhouse and galloped to another building.

"You will stay where you are," shouted the guard.

Kyle and Annika looked at each other.

Minutes later, Kyle saw torches bouncing in the darkness—riders were approaching. Kyle and Annika made out five soldiers on horseback. They cantered their horses to within 30 feet of Kyle and halted—a captain, a lieutenant, and three privates. They rode bay quarter horses with black leather tack. Five brass hearts gleamed from the Y-junctions of the horses' breast collars.

The captain, in his thirties with brown hair and a well-manicured mustache, wore an officer's cavalry hat with a brass crossed-sword insignia and gold cord, capped with traditional ornamental acorns. Captain's boards rode the shoulders of his navy uniform. In one gauntleted hand, he held his horse's reins, in the other, a fiery torch.

They stared at each other—Kyle waited for the captain to speak first.

"I am Captain Montgomery," he said in a confident voice. "State your business."

"My name is Kyle Mason. We are bringing wounded and fallen soldiers to you," Kyle said. "The wounded are in need of medical attention."

"I thank you for returning our comrades to us," said the captain. "Our general wishes to speak with you. You will accompany us."

The request surprised Kyle. He had expected one of two outcomes—either a hasty retreat after returning the men or a swift hanging.

"A minute, please," said Kyle.

He pulled the brake on his wagon, jumped out and walked to Annika's wagon. The soldiers eyed him closely.

"What?" asked Annika

"You should wait here," Kyle said.

"Why?"

"It isn't safe."

"Holy shit!" Annika exclaimed. "You're kidding! It's not safe to return a company of soldiers that we shot and killed back to the army where they came from? Why the hell didn't you tell me?"

The image of Padma, naked on the riverbank with the dying scout, replayed in Kyle's mind.

"I mean, it isn't safe for *you*," he said.

In the torchlight, Annika could see the worry on Kyle's face. She refereed conflicting feelings—the insult of Kyle's sexism against the warmth of his genuine concern for her.

She leaned over and put her hand on his shoulder.

"Look," she said. "Does it make you feel any better to hear that if we get into trouble, I won't let them take me alive?"

"Whew!" Kyle said. "That's a relief. The thought of you dead makes me feel so much better."

Annika flashed a smile. "C'mon—let's go."

Kyle climbed back aboard his wagon and released the brake.

"After you, Captain," he said.

The soldiers turned their horses toward a row of buildings in the distance. The torchlight illuminated hundreds of rows of tents they passed along the way. Dozens, then hundreds of soldiers climbed out of their tents to watch the procession. Many carried lanterns. Some carried torches. By the time they reached the long, narrow, single-story wooden building, Kyle and Annika gazed upon a sea of nearly 1,000 flickering lights mobbed around the wagons. Grumbling sounds ascended from the light brigade.

"The only good Indians I ever saw were dead!" shouted one of the men.

A roar erupted from the mob. Kyle and Annika pulled their wagons to a halt.

The captain shouted, "You men, stand at attention! Doctors! Attend to the wounded." He turned to Kyle and Annika. "You two get out of the wagons."

Kyle and Annika climbed out and stood next to each other between the wagons.

"Still think this was a good idea?" asked Annika.

Kyle shook his head. "Not so much, no."

An alternating series of doors and single windows ran the

length of the long, narrow building in front of them. To Kyle, it appeared to be an administrative building. The door directly in front of them opened, and a large man stepped out. A young African American man followed the general out the door, carrying an oil lantern. The general's valet wore a private's uniform.

"General Nelson Miles," Kyle said.

"I think I must have slept through the General Nelson Miles chapter in history class at West Point," replied Annika.

"Civil War hero," Kyle said. "He went from lieutenant to brigadier general in only six years, and eventually became commanding general of the United States Army. He won the Medal of Honor for gallantry at the Battle of Chancellorsville. He was shot twice in that battle—in the neck and chest."

The cavalrymen dismounted their horses and tied them to a hitching post in front of the building.

Captain Montgomery saluted the general. The general returned his salute. The captain turned to Annika.

"Madam, what is your name?" he asked.

"Annika Wise," she replied.

"General Miles," announced Captain Montgomery, "I present Mr. Kyle Mason and Miss Annika Wise."

"Mr. Mason, Madam, you will disarm," the captain ordered.

A soldier approached Annika from behind and reached for her MP7, holstered to her thigh. She grabbed the soldier's hand and spun to face him, twisting his hand and arm in the process. The soldier suddenly found himself facing the palm of his hand. Annika pressed on the back of his hand. The simple action crashed him to his knees. Another soldier approached, pulling his Colt revolver. While still holding the first soldier's wrist, Annika snatched the second soldier's revolver and smacked him on his temple with the butt of the gun, knocking him unconscious. Annika snapped the kneeling soldier's wrist as a third soldier, standing next to Kyle, stepped toward her. Kyle doubled him over with a roundhouse kick, then leapt in the air, smacking him on the back of the head with a scissor kick. Kyle cracked another soldier's nose with his elbow.

Hoover growled and gnashed his teeth at an approaching soldier who cocked his leg to kick the dog. Kyle pulled his knife and hurled it. The blade plunged into the earth an inch in front of the soldier's boot. Kyle pulled his MP7 and snapped its laser sight on the soldier's chest.

"Don't hurt my dog," Kyle advised.

Annika pulled her MP7 and flicked on her laser sight, standing back to back with Kyle. The targeted soldiers moved their hands over the strange, brilliant red pinpoint light on their chests.

Dozens of soldiers raised their rifles and revolvers to fire.

"You are at a disadvantage, sir," boomed General Miles. "We will have your weapons, one way or another."

"Maybe so," replied Kyle. "Though your army will be a few hundred soldiers lighter by the time you do."

The general eyed the strange weapons Kyle and Annika were holding. The sole survivor of the 6th Regiment's B Company had told him of bizarre weapons, compact but far more lethal than a Gatling gun, cutting down dozens of soldiers in mere seconds. These appeared to be the weapons the soldier described.

"Stand down," ordered the general. The soldiers lowered their weapons.

The general gestured for Kyle and Annika to enter his office. They cautiously holstered their submachine guns as they climbed the short steps to the porch and entered the office.

The office was some 30 by 30 feet. A large wooden desk with a blotter, telegrams, and other documents sat at the far end of the room. An oil lamp sat on the desk, casting yellow light. A journal was open on the blotter, with handwritten notes in blue ink. A Waterman fountain pen bridged the open book.

A small round table with four chairs sat on a hooked rug with a depiction of a bald eagle against a blue sky. A garland of olive branches surrounded the eagle along the perimeter of the rug.

The general gestured toward the table. "Please, sit."

"I prefer to stand," Annika said, keeping an eye on the door.

The general stood, uncomfortable.

Annika realized that decorum would not allow the general to sit while a woman was standing in his presence.

"General, please sit," she said. "I've been riding all day and I would prefer to stand for a while."

"Very well," the general said, taking a seat. Kyle sat as well.

The general's valet entered the office carrying a tray with a whiskey bottle and three glasses. The valet stood at the general's side.

"May I offer you a drink?" asked the general.

"Very kind. Thank you," replied Kyle.

"Don't mind if I do," said Annika.

The valet poured the three shot glasses, placed the bottle on the sideboard, and exited the office. The three downed their drinks. Kyle waited for the general to speak.

"Mr. Mason, I am hearing the strangest stories from Sitting Bull's camp," began the general. "I hear stories of a messiah appearing out of thin air at a Ghost Dance. I hear the apparition is an Indian woman, and that she was accompanied by a white man—you?"

Kyle was silent.

The general continued, "The Indian agent, Mr. Royer, says the woman is bulletproof. Says he fired his Henry rifle straight into her heart at point-blank range and she survived. His nephew corroborated the account.

"And now, I hear that a company of my mounted cavalry was slaughtered by another woman that fits the description of Miss Wise, with a weapon that sounds very much like the ones you both are carrying.

"What I want to know, Mr. Mason, Miss Wise, is who you are, and what are you doing on the reservation?" asked the general.

"That will be difficult to explain," replied Kyle.

"It will be necessary for you to try, Mr. Mason."

Kyle considered the general's request for a moment. "OK, why not?" said Kyle. "I'm a colonel in the United States Army. So is 'Miss' Wise."

Annika rolled her eyes.

"We're from the future—the year 2008, to be precise. These weapons are MP7A1 submachine guns. They fire 950 rounds per minute—enough to kill you and all your men in under five minutes…"

...Assuming we're in close range, we have at least 5,000 rounds of ammunition, and no one kills us while we're reloading, Kyle thought.

General Miles struggled to parse which part of Kyle's explanation was the most bizarre—that he and Annika were from the future, that their compact sidearms were more powerful than Gatling guns, or that a woman could be an officer in the Army.

"Mr. Mason, you will find that I have little patience for insolence..."

"And I have no patience at all," interrupted Annika.

She snapped up her MP7 and fired at the wooden sideboard, shredding it to splinters in seconds.

"Good God!" exclaimed the general.

"Subtle, as always," Kyle critiqued Annika.

"The general needed help suspending his disbelief," replied Annika.

Three soldiers burst through the office door with their Colt pistols drawn. Kyle and Annika trained the brilliant red laser sights of their MP7s on the chests of two of the soldiers.

"Order your men to lower their weapons, General, or we will kill them all," Kyle said.

"Stand down," the general ordered.

"General?" asked the lieutenant who led the charge.

"You heard me, Lieutenant!" said the general.

"Sir, yes sir," replied the lieutenant, saluting and exiting with the men.

"Did the whiskey survive?" asked Annika. "I wouldn't mind another round."

Kyle looked for the whiskey bottle on the floor. It had miraculously survived the sideboard's obliteration. He picked it up and uncorked it. Annika extended her glass for him to pour.

"General?" he asked, motioning the bottle toward his glass.

"Please," replied the general, attempting to regain his composure. Kyle noticed the general's glass was shaking in his hand.

"So it's 'Colonel,' is it?" asked the general.

"Yes sir," replied Kyle.

"I outrank you, soldier," said the general.

"Yes sir, though I'm afraid my wife outranks us both," said Kyle.

The general looked at Kyle, then burst out laughing. "As do all wives," he said.

Then the general looked at Annika with confusion. "Colonel Wise is your wife?"

"No," Kyle said, "my wife is the Indian woman Mr. Royer shot."

Kyle was comfortable with his politically correct use of "Indian" to describe Padma, as she was probably the only authentic Indian-American in the state of South Dakota.

The general continued, "I cannot say that I believe your story, though I am, as yet, unable to explain your impressive parlor tricks. Assuming for the moment that I am willing to accept your explanation, will you tell me why you are here?"

"The honest answer, General, is that I don't know," Kyle said. "There was an accident. We were not supposed to be in this time. We appeared in the middle of a Ghost Dance. The Lakota people took that as a sign of prophesy, as did my wife."

"And your wife is bulletproof, as Mr. Royer claims?"

"We have technology that makes her so," replied Kyle.

"I see," replied the general.

The general pulled at one end of his long salt-and-pepper mustache, eyeing Kyle carefully. He didn't know what to make of the strange man and his bizarre story. Kyle did not strike the general as either belligerent or lunatic—indeed, he found him instantly agreeable. The general acknowledged that Kyle had not brought the fight to the army, though if Kyle's advanced weapons and bullet shields were real, they posed a fearsome threat to the military. Allied with the Indians, Kyle and his Messiah wife could instantly tip the balance of power on the frontier plains.

"Colonel, I have been proven a capable judge of character in my career," began the general. "Though your story stretches the bounds of imagination, your evidence, combined with the accounts of Mr. Royer, his nephew, and my own soldier eyewitness, give me cause to maintain an open mind.

"For this reason, I will speak plainly with you. Your presence here complicates an already difficult situation. Prior to your arrival, Mr. Royer had inflamed passions regarding the Indians, both in South Dakota as well as in Washington. With the aid of newspapermen, he has convinced many that the Indians are on the verge of war.

"I do not hold with Mr. Royer's view. In point of fact, I consider the man to be a stupendous half-wit who has invented a crisis that will soon become a tragedy. The Indians were coerced into signing a treaty that ceded the Black Hills. They understood that ample provision would be made for their support; instead, their supplies have been reduced, and much of the time they have been living on half rations. They are starving. They are wholly unprepared to commit to war against the whites. I opposed a military solution. I believed the answer was simply for Congress to honor its treaty obligations and feed the Indians.

"However, stories of bulletproof messiahs with magical weapons have aroused imaginations. With thousands of Indians massing in Sitting Bull's village, fear has grown into terror. Though I am a major general, my voice has provided no resistance to the dreadnaught that will inevitably crush the Indians. Thanks to Mr. Royer's fear mongering, combined with news of your miracles, it is no longer sufficient to disarm them.

"The public demands a final solution to the Indian problem."

The general placed his shot glass on the table with a clack.

"And now that you both have killed my men," the general said, "I can tell you with conviction that my lonely voice of reason has died along with them."

"They were going to fire on the tribespeople," said Kyle. "Men, women, and children. They were going to shoot my wife."

"According to you, your wife is bulletproof," replied the general. "As for the rest, they are living in despair, starving, deprived of their lands and nobility. They are little more than beggars, living a humiliating existence, dependent on the meager compassion of their conquerors. They have no more champions. In two days' time, I will end their misery. Magic weapons or not, your Indians are going to die.

"As for you, you rode in under flag of truce. You are free to leave under the same bedsheet colors," said the general. "I thank you for the return of my men. Good night."

General Miles shouted to the lieutenant outside the office, "Lieutenant!"

The lieutenant entered the office. "Yes sir."

"Lieutenant, escort these people off the premises."

"Yes sir!" replied the lieutenant, saluting.

Kyle rose from his seat, joining Annika to leave after their unceremonious dismissal. The general looked away, refusing eye contact as the couple exited the office.

Standing Rock Reservation
South Dakota
September 27, 1890
09:20 hours
Timeline 003

A few miles from Sitting Bull's village, Annika and Kyle watched as a cloud of dust rose from the prairie to the north, announcing the approach of General Miles' army. A rumble accompanied the rising dust as thousands of infantrymen and mounted horses trooped alongside dozens of supply wagons.

Pegasus, munching dry grass nearby, lifted his head to look at the approaching prairie dust storm. Annika scanned the hulking army through her binoculars. Hoover lay on his side under a tree, sound asleep.

"Which do you want first?" Annika asked. "The good news or the bad news?"

"Let's start the day with some good news," Kyle replied.

"The good news is that the Massacre of Wounded Knee is not going to happen," she said. "The bad news is that it will be called the 'Massacre of Grand River.'"

"I'm seeing the flags of the…let's see…the 6th, the 7th, the 8th, and the 9th Cavalries, combined with the 1st, 2nd, 7th, 8th, 17th, and…wait for it… the 21st Infantries. Hold on…also joining us for tomorrow's massacre are the 1st and 2nd Artilleries. I'd say 5,000 men, give or take.

"It gets even better," she said. "Take a look at the last couple wagons."

Annika handed the binoculars to Kyle. He adjusted the focus, zeroing in on the objects of Annika's interest. Two small cannons jostled in each of the two rear wagons.

"Hotchkiss guns," Kyle observed.

"Hotchkiss guns," confirmed Annika.

In 1890, the Hotchkiss gun was a weapon of mass destruction. It was a small breach-loaded canon, capable of firing 50 grapeshot canisters per minute, shredding flesh and shattering bones with a spray of half-inch lead balls shrieking through the air at 1,300 feet per second. Kyle and Annika's submachine guns were short-range weapons, incapable of harming General Miles' army from a distance. His Hotchkiss guns could stand off more than a half-mile from their targets, annihilating every living thing in the village in minutes.

"The Chimera," Kyle said grimly under his breath.

"What?" asked Annika.

"Nothing," Kyle said, handing the binoculars back to Annika.

"They'll make camp, have a nice dinner, then they'll butcher us at dawn," said Annika.

Kyle glanced at his watch. "That gives us 20 hours to finish our preparations. We'd better get back to the village."

They walked toward Pegasus, who had wandered off to dine

on greener pastures.

"Kyle," Annika began, "are you ready for this?"

Kyle's expression was puzzled. "I don't understand the question. None of us are ready for this. Construction of the barricades isn't finished, personnel to set the fireworks haven't been selected, and our army mobilization plan isn't really a plan so much as it is a concept… We're not ready, so I'm not ready. Am I missing something?"

"I think you are," said Annika.

"Are you asking me if I'm ready to die?" asked Kyle.

"I don't think that's your problem," said Annika. "I'm asking you if you're ready to kill."

Kyle stopped. He looked down and sighed deeply. Annika had read him perfectly. He pined for his wife. Though he had skillfully executed the motions of preparing for battle, he was actually preparing for his death.

"Because it's a real problem if you're OK with dying tomorrow," she said.

Kyle was silent.

"How are things between you and the little missus?" Annika asked. "I hear you're sleeping in separate tipis."

Kyle looked at the ground. His face scrunched in anguish.

"I think my wife has PTSD," he said.

"Why is that?" asked Annika.

"She likes to kill people."

"Me too," said Annika, smiling and batting her eyes.

"I guess you two have something in common after all," he said, resuming his walk toward Pegasus.

Annika swung in front of Kyle, grabbed his face, and kissed him. Kyle returned the kiss. She sighed, holding her forehead against his, her eyes closed.

"Annika..." he started.

"You don't have to say anything," she said. "I just needed to know if what you said about us was really true."

"What's the verdict?" he asked.

Annika patted him on the chest, then picked a stone off the ground and threw it toward the approaching army.

"The verdict is that after we're done with this, I'm not going to kill you," she said.

"Very kind of you," he said, no longer caring about his fate.

They both paused, turning to look at the army in the distance. They could hear drumbeats marking the troops' cadence.

"This is not like me," Annika started, already regretting what she was about to say. "If things don't work out with your wife, I'd like to...I'd like to."

"Date?" asked Kyle.

Annika rolled her eyes. "I was trying to find a better fucking word, goddammit!"

Kyle was silent, searching for the right thing to say.

"I just put it out there," Annika said. "You need to fucking say something!"

"OK, here it is," he said. "The fact is that I fucked up everything. I brought my wife back to life, and then proceeded to destroy her life. I'm on a highway to hell that is well paved with good intentions.

"I shouldn't have disobeyed my orders. I should have left my wife alive in 2001, and I should have left you dead. None of this would have happened if I had done what the general told me to do. I should have fixed 9/11 and returned to the Time Tunnel.

"I love my wife, and I also love a version of you that I used to know. But I don't…"

"Wait, back up," Annika said. "You said you love me?"

"I said I love the other you," he said. "The dead one."

"A live Annika is better than a dead one."

"The dead one doesn't talk as much."

She slugged him in the shoulder.

"I can still kill you…with a teaspoon."

"At least do it with a butter knife. Show a little respect."

The two caught up with Pegasus. Kyle took the reins and leapt on his horse's back. He reached for Annika's hand. With a hop, she swung onboard Pegasus. She wrapped her arms around Kyle's waist, enjoying the feel of his body against hers. Kyle held the reins with one hand and placed the other on Annika's hands, clasped around his center. She took hold of his free hand.

"Let's go…fast," she whispered in Kyle's ear.

Kyle cued his horse with his leg. Pegasus broke into a full gallop. Hoover chased after him. Kyle permitted himself to enjoy the moment, flashing a smile. Annika laughed as they dashed across the prairie toward home.

Standing Rock Reservation
South Dakota
September 27, 1890
12:10 hours
Timeline 003

"Please."

"*Chanl wah-shday.*"

"Thank you."

"*Pee-lah-mah-yah-yea.*"

"Hungry."

"*Loh-chee.*"

"Friend."

"*Loh-lah.*"

"Very good, Messiah!" said Takoda. "You are *very* smart."

"*Pee-lah-mah-yah-yea,*" replied Padma, beaming.

They sat on the bed in Padma's tent. Hundreds of villagers huddled outside, waiting for the Messiah to emerge.

"Horse."

Padma furrowed her brow. "*Shuen-kah-wah-kahn.*"

"Buffalo."

"*Dah-dahn-kah.*"

"Very *very* good, Messiah!" exclaimed Takoda.

"Please, Takoda, call me by my real name," she said.

Takoda hesitated.

"I want to hear you say it," said Padma. "*Chanl wah-shday.*"

Padma looked into Takoda's beautiful brown eyes.

"Very good, *Padma,*" he said. "*Lee-lah wah-shday.*"

Padma put her hand on Takoda's cheek. "*Chanl wah-shday.* Please."

Takoda took her wrist and kissed it. Padma felt her heart race.

"*Wah-shday che la ke,*" he said.

Tears welled in Padma's eyes.

"I love you too," Padma replied.

She leaned to kiss him, placing a hand on his bare chest. He returned the kiss.

"Put your hands on me," she said between kisses.

Takoda wrapped his arms around her and kissed Padma's neck. He felt her body through her doeskin dress.

Padma stopped and put a hand on Takoda's chest. Looking him in the eye, she stood and untied her Concho belt, letting it drop to the floor. She pulled her dress over her head, standing naked in front of him. She pushed between his legs.

Takoda stared at Padma. She was the most beautiful woman he had ever seen. He placed his hands on her waist, and kissed her belly.

He paused, pushing her away.

"Padma, I can't," he said, retreating.

"Why not?" replied Padma. "I want you to!"

"Padma, I love you," Takoda began. "But I have shamed myself twice already. I failed to protect you twice as I swore to do. You are another man's wife. I can't shame myself a third time."

Padma shook with rage, then grabbed her dress and pulled it back on, slapping the beaded yoke on her shoulders and grabbing her belt as she charged out the door. Takoda heard her scream at her multitudes crowded outside the door.

"Get out of my fucking way!"

Takoda hurried after Padma as she marched toward Kyle and Annika's command tent. Padma flung open the tent flap. Inside, Kyle and Annika were poring over their map, pointing at a series of barricades being erected between the village and the army encampment. They looked up as Padma whipped into the tent, holding her Concho belt in her hand. She threw the heavy leather and silver belt on the map table, scattering the war craft objects onto the ground.

"I need to talk with you—*now!*" Padma yelled at Kyle.

"This looks like the perfect time to check on the barricades," Annika said as she retreated from the tent.

"I am in love with Takoda," Padma announced. "There, I've said it. I'm in love with Takoda."

Kyle stared at Padma.

"I require your permission to sleep with him," said Padma.

"What do you need my permission for? You're a grownup messiah. You can sleep with whoever you want."

"*He* needs your permission," replied Padma.

"I beg your pardon?" asked Kyle, stupefied.

"He is ashamed. He needs your permission."

"Ashamed to sleep with my wife? I can't imagine why."

Kyle bellowed to the tent opening, "Takoda!"

Takoda appeared in the entryway.

"Takoda, you have my permission to fuck my wife," Kyle said, returning his gaze to the map.

Takoda was stunned.

"No! No! That's not right! That's not right!" shouted Padma, frantic. "You have to say it like you mean it!"

Kyle looked up from the map. "In order for me to say it like I mean it, I would actually have to *mean it!*"

Kyle walked around the map table to Padma. "Can't you see that's an impossibility?"

He grabbed the wrist of her ring hand with a firm fist and held it up. "I spent every cent I had to buy you this ring. I would give you *anything*, including my life. Can't you see that I can't just hand you off to another man? Can't you see that everything I've done, everything, the really good things and the really royal fuck-ups, have all been because I am completely, totally in love with you? Can't you see that? *Don't you know who I am?*"

Kyle pulled his MP7 from his holster, clicked the safety off and placed it in Padma's hand. He raised the gun barrel to his chest, placing the red laser sight over his heart.

"I can solve both our problems right now," Kyle said. "Just pull the trigger, and we both get what we want."

Padma's expression was shock. Her eyes were wide. She raised her other hand to clutch the gun with both hands.

"I'll do it!" she shouted. "I'll kill you!"

The gun shook in her hands. She gritted her teeth and touched the trigger. She began to lower the gun, then grunted with frustration as she raised it to Kyle's chest again.

Padma dropped the gun and released a blood-curdling scream that could be heard throughout the village. She fell to her knees and began pounding the ground, screaming every time her fists hit the earth. Several of her followers rushed through the tent flap, straight into Takoda's blocking hand. He shook his head, dispatching the uninvited.

Kyle brushed past Takoda, giving him a hard look on his way out of the tent.

Standing Rock Reservation
South Dakota
September 27, 1890
12:52 hours
Timeline 003

Kyle sat on the riverbank, watching the river roll slowly by. He knew he should be helping Annika complete the battle preparations, though he wasn't entirely sure why. He felt the iron weight of the depression he had known years earlier after losing Padma on 9/11. Losing her a second time confirmed what he already knew—that he didn't want to live without her.

He understood well that he was committed to carrying out the plan to save the Lakota people. As a creature of duty, he took his obligations seriously.

He also understood that the Lakota people had taken his wife.

From that perch on the riverbank that Kyle and Padma had shared during their visit to 1890, Kyle contemplated the river and the water that had flowed by that spot over the past weeks. He reflected on how much had happened on shore while the water had washed by.

I traveled to the year 1890
I met Sitting Bull

I visited ancient Deadwood

I lost my wife

His mind replayed the only words that mattered:

I lost my wife

Kyle realized that none of what had occurred onshore had moved the river. The water flowed in precisely the same way. Regardless of whether he changed the course of history in the battle to come the following morning, the river's course would remain the same. Neither would the tracks of his tears alter the river's flow.

He heard footsteps approaching. He turned to look—it was Padma. She carried Kyle's gun in her right hand. She sat next to him, then set the gun on the ground. Her face was puffy and red from crying. She looked exhausted.

They both stared at the river. After a long time, Padma spoke.

"I know that I'm messed up," she said, nodding her head. "I know that. I know I can't trust my choices anymore. I can't trust my feelings."

She took a breath and sighed. "I have not been able to find my love for you," she said. "I've tried to remind myself that I am supposed to be head over heels, impossibly in love—with you. But I haven't felt it. I haven't been able to summon those feelings."

Kyle sighed. "I don't want you to try to feel something you don't."

He stood up. "All I've ever wanted is for you to be happy, and all I've done is fuck things up. If Takoda will make you happy, then I will step aside."

Kyle pulled off his gold wedding ring and handed it to Padma.

It was the first time he had removed his ring. Padma took the ring in the palm of her hand and closed her fingers over it.

"Please sit," she said.

Kyle hesitated.

"Please."

Kyle sighed, then sat.

Padma continued, "I couldn't summon my love. I thought it was gone. It terrified me. I tried to replace it."

She began to cry.

"I was so wrong, and I am so *very* sorry, husband. I am so deeply ashamed. I have wronged you."

She turned to face him, tears streaming down her cheeks. "The monsters...they didn't get inside my body, but they got inside my head. My love for you was always there. I just couldn't see it."

She broke down, sobbing.

"They got in my head, and they hid my love for you. I couldn't find it!"

She held up her ring. The diamond sparkled in the sunlight next to the glittering river.

"This diamond...it's a perfect stone, but that's not what makes it special," she said. "It's special because of how it came to me. It is beautiful because it was given to me by the most beautiful man alive. Somehow, you let me see that again. You gave me a beacon to find my love.

"I see it now. It is so beautiful. It is even more beautiful than you know. I found my love...and I found my shame in the same place.

"I don't deserve your forgiveness, but I am begging you for it anyway. Your love is worth fighting for, Kyle. It's worth dying for, and if we die tomorrow, I don't want to die without my husband at my side. I want to die as Mrs. Kyle Mason."

Padma handed Kyle's ring to him.

"Please let me have that privilege," she said. "Please make me the happiest woman on Earth. Please make me the happiest woman of all time…of any time."

Kyle looked at the ring in Padma's palm for a moment. He extended his left hand, palm down.

A relieved smile broke across Padma's face. She slid the ring back onto Kyle's finger. They embraced.

"There is nothing to forgive, love," he said. "You're already Mrs. Kyle Mason. And I am so very proud to be Mr. Padma Mahajan."

"Thank you. Thank you," she said, crying into his shirt. "I am so sorry, my husband."

"But I'd rather live than die, if that's OK," Kyle said.

"Yes, that's OK," Padma said, laughing through her tears. "Living is good if I'm with you—even in this shit hole. I don't want to be the Messiah anymore. I'm tired of being the Messiah."

"After tomorrow, you won't be," Kyle said. "One way or another, your job here will be done."

Padma nodded, sniffling. "Yes."

She took his hands, squeezed them tight, and kissed them.

"I made you a gift," Kyle said.

Padma smiled, surprised, wiping away her tears. "You did? What is it?"

He reached into his pocket and fished out a wadded roll of

paper. He handed the mangled hand-rolled cigarette to Padma. She burst out laughing.

Kyle pulled a matchbox out of his pocket. "Need a light?"

Padma inserted the crooked cigarette between her lips. Kyle lit it up. Padma took a draw and exhaled.

"Oh!" Padma said. "That is disgusting! It's also the best smoke I ever had," she added, kissing him.

. . .

Blam!

Padma gasped as she and Kyle stared at each other in surprise.

Blam! Blam! Blam!

Four cannon blasts shook the ground, followed by the screams of women and war whoops of the braves.

"Just when we were having a moment," Kyle said, picking his MP7 off the ground. "Let's go."

They ran through the cottonwood trees to the village. Annika met them.

"Our friends are rattling their sabers," she shouted. "C'mon!"

They ran through tipis to the northern edge of the village. A series of cottonwood barricades stood between them and the massive federal army. The barricades had been erected by the tribespeople as part of Kyle and Annika's plan to defend the village. The army was encamped over a mile to the north, across the creek that formed the northern boundary of the village. Kyle and Annika couldn't see what was going on through the barricades, though percussion from the rapid cannon fire rattled the ground.

"We need to get a forward position to have a look," shouted Annika.

Kyle nodded. At that moment, a dozen tribesmen rode up on horseback, preparing to attack.

"If they attack, they'll be slaughtered!" shouted Kyle to Padma. "Turn them around and round up the war council. We'll be back in 30."

Padma nodded and waved to the warriors as Kyle and Annika ran north through the barricades.

The barricades were a series of parallel walls that arced in a half moon around the village. The timber ramparts of piled limbs and branches were 8 feet tall and 20 feet deep at the base. They each stretched for over 100 yards, encompassing the hive of tipis backed into the corner juncture where the Grand River flowed into the Missouri. As the tipis hugged and protected their children, the fortress embraced the tipis.

Each of the cottonwood tree walls had openings 30 feet wide, through which Kyle and Annika ran to advance to the next barricade. The cannon fire grew louder. The blast percussions rattled Kyle's and Annika's chests as they ran to the forward barricade.

When they arrived, they peered around an opening in the barricade. Annika lifted her binoculars just in time to see the muzzle flashes of four Hotchkiss guns.

"Incoming!" she shouted as they hit the deck.

Four shells hit the barricade, blowing holes in the battlements. Cottonwood branches and twigs blew into the air, showering the pair.

"Out of range," Annika observed. "They can do some damage to the barricades, but they can't hit the village from across the creek."

"They were hoping they'd get lucky," Kyle said. "Or maybe draw the tribesmen into a fight on the open field."

"We'll keep our powder dry and make them come to us," said Annika.

"Let me take a look," he said, reaching for the binoculars.

Through the binoculars, Kyle spied a fearsome army. Thousands of men in blue uniforms were mustered on the opposite side of the creek, with hundreds on horseback. Dozens of company and regiment flags fluttered in the breeze along with the American flag. Some companies drilled while the Hotchkiss guns fired. Other soldiers tended to the requirements of the camp, setting up tents, cooking, and cleaning their weapons.

"That army looks a lot bigger close up," Kyle said.

"Funny how that works," replied Annika.

The ground thundered again. Another round of shells slammed into the barricade, pelting the pair with cottonwood tree branches.

Annika slapped Kyle on the shoulder, grinning. "This is fun, right?"

The cannon fire ceased. Kyle and Annika brushed off the foliage. Annika grabbed the binoculars. Horse-drawn flatbed wagons had pulled up next to the Hotchkiss guns. The gun crews were loading them onto the wagons.

"They're loading up the guns," Annika reported. "Let's see where they take them."

The pair watched as the guns were loaded and secured on the wagons, along with cases of ammunition. A company of cavalry soldiers escorted the wagons. The wagons then rolled west along North Creek. Several hundred yards upstream, the wagons and their escorts turned south.

"They're crossing the creek," said Annika.

The water was four feet deep, rising to the horses' chests. After several minutes, the detachment cleared the creek and continued to move south toward a series of plateaus to the northwest of the village.

"They're headed for the plateau," reported. Annika. "We guessed right."

"Well, if we're going to be dead, we might as well be right," said Kyle. "Let's get back to the village."

Standing Rock Reservation
South Dakota
September 27, 1890
16:30 hours
Timeline 003

Kyle and Annika navigated the barricade maze back to the village. They emerged from the inner barricade into a scene of pandemonium. Warriors gathered snorting, galloping horses spooked by the cannon fire. Women herded crying children into their tipis. They could hear Yellow Bird singing. He stood in front of a very large tipi in the center of the village. The structure was the council lodge.

Kyle and Annika ran to the lodge. Its hide coverings were peeled back to reveal the interior, where Padma had gathered some 100 chiefs and distinguished warriors. The lodge was huge compared with the surrounding tipis. The central tree pole of the council lodge was 30 feet high. The lodge's base had a diameter of 60 feet.

Padma's back was to the lodge entrance. As she heard Kyle's running footsteps, she turned. A relieved smile flashed across her face as she saw him. She ran to him, threw her arms around his neck, and kissed him.

"That's more like it," Kyle said between kisses.

"Tell me," she said.

"It looks like we've got ourselves a war," Kyle replied. "We should get started."

Padma nodded and motioned for the chiefs to sit. Everyone sat in a circle around the inner circumference of the lodge.

Padma and Annika flanked Kyle. Takoda sat next to Annika, opposite from Padma. Padma and Takoda avoided eye contact.

The council members could hear General Miles' army in the distance. Though the cannon fire had ceased, the army was still making plenty of noise in preparation for the morning attack. The sharp reports of rifle drills mixed with bugle calls and snare drums. Those martial noises played against a background of camp sounds. Hundreds of white tents were erected, horses were untacked, and fires blazed to cook dinner for thousands of soldiers.

A 5,000-man army on the village doorstep was an impossible distraction for the council, like making dinner plans in the shadow of a falling skyscraper.

All tribal chiefs sat in the council circle, including Sitting Bull, Red Cloud, Spotted Elk, and Kicking Bear. The chiefs were lords and masters over their individual tribes. Inter-tribal cooperation was challenging enough. Securing the agreement of all tribes to sign off on a plan with the level of intricacy proposed by Kyle and Annika was unprecedented. The Messiah was the glue that temporarily held the alliance together.

Takoda struggled to translate Kyle and Annika's English. Translating in real time was already mentally exhausting. Compounding the task with love sickness pushed fatigue to fracture. Takoda was forced to stop frequently to catch up or correct words lost in translation.

Though Kyle felt the thick awkwardness in these close quarters with Takoda and Padma, he felt sorry for his former rival. Having lost Padma twice in one lifetime, he knew well the pain that Takoda was feeling. He was patient with Takoda, giving him time to complete each sentence. Life and death hung on these words. Precision was essential.

"As Colonel Wise and I expected, the army has made camp on the opposite side of North Creek," Kyle said, drawing a circle in the dirt to represent the army opposite a line drawn for the creek. He drew another line to the south, parallel to the creek, representing the Grand River. He then crossed the two lines with a third line to the east, representing the Missouri River, into which the creek and the Grand River flowed. He then drew several pyramids, representing tipis, in the corner formed by the "L" where the Grand River met the Missouri River.

"As Colonel Wise and I advised, you have moved the village here, out of range of the army's Hotchkiss guns."

Kyle drew a small circle to the west of the village.

"As you already know, we determined that the best site for a gun battery is here—this plateau, 1,000 yards to the west of the village. From this point, the gunners have an excellent vantage.

"It appears that the army has reached the same conclusion. We spied wagons with Hotchkiss guns being hauled up to the plateau. We expect the gun batteries to be operational by dawn.

"One aspect of our plan involves setting fires here and here..." Kyle said, pointing at different points on his dirt map.

"...and setting off charges here. Colonel Wise and I will be with our forward army. We need a volunteer to light the fires and set off the charges. This mission will be dangerous," he added.

Several warriors stood to volunteer. Takoda stood up. He stepped in front of Padma, seated with her legs tucked to the side. Padma looked at the ground.

"Please," said Takoda. "Let me do this. *Chanl wah-shday.*"

Padma did not raise her eyes to meet Takoda's. She shook her head. "No," she said.

"You're too important," Kyle said, trying to take the edge off Takoda's humiliation. "We can't afford to lose you."

Takoda sighed, hung his head, and returned to his seat. Kyle pointed to another warrior—a muscular, bare-chested man with two long braids and three eagle feathers in his hair.

"Ogaleesha," Padma said. She turned to Kyle. "His name means 'wears a red shirt.'"

Ogaleesha approached Padma. His expression was deadly serious.

Kyle opted not ask why the bare-chested warrior wasn't wearing a shirt—red or otherwise.

"Ogaleesha, you volunteer for this mission?" Padma asked. Takoda translated without lifting his gaze from the ground.

"*Han!*" Ogaleesha replied. "Yes."

"You understand this is dangerous?" Padma asked.

"*Han.*"

"How can I know you will succeed?" asked Padma.

Ogaleesha raised his hands to his chest and slapped his Sun

Dance scars.

"*Lee-lah wah-shday*," Padma said, nodding. "Very good."

A middle-aged Lakota man approached the lodge, wearing fringed deerskin pants and matching shirt with blue, red, and yellow beads. He wore an eagle feather in each of the two braids that framed his troubled face.

The chiefs turned to look at the man. It was Chief Gall.

"I ask permission to join the council meeting," he said.

Sitting Bull stood to face Gall. "You are welcome here."

"I would rather die as a Lakota warrior than live as a white farmer," Gall said. "Please tell me how I can serve my people."

Sitting Bull looked into the faces of the other chiefs. They nodded in approval.

"We do not want you to die," Sitting Bull said. "We want you to live…as the commander of our army."

Standing Rock Reservation
South Dakota
September 28, 1890
06:45 hours
Timeline 003

General Miles' valet tied a crimson sash around the general's waist, then fastened the general's sword belt around the sash. His brass sword scabbard gleamed on the general's thigh in the lamplight. The sword's pearl handle peaked the scabbard. A Colt pistol, in its shiny black leather holster, hung on the general's left hip.

The general extended his arms slightly back to assist his valet as he slid on a dress coat with a major general's shoulder boards. Columns of gleaming brass buttons paraded down the general's chest. The general pulled on his tan deerskin gauntlets. The valet handed him his navy broad-brimmed hat with its brilliant gold cord. The general placed the hat on his head with precision. Satisfied with his attire, General Miles nodded to his valet, who held open the tent flap for him to exit.

The general stepped into the cool pre-dawn air. A corporal standing to the right of his tent door saluted. Ten feet in front of the general's tent, his aide-de-camp, Major David Hollingsworth, and his second in command, Colonel Joseph Reynolds, saluted in tandem. General Miles returned both men's salutes. To the east, he saw a glow over the Missouri River as the sun approached the horizon.

"Good morning, sir," said Colonel Reynolds.

"Good morning, Colonel," replied the general. "Report."

"The men are mustered and prepared for the attack," reported the colonel.

"What is the status of our artillery?" asked the general.

"The Hotchkiss gun batteries of the 1st and 2nd Artilleries are stationed on the southern plateau," replied the colonel. "They are fully operational. Awaiting your orders, sir."

"Very well."

General Miles surveyed the dark landscape. To the left of his tent was the Missouri River. A glow over the river to the east signaled the approaching dawn, illuminating wisps of fog on the water. The river's creek tributary, which separated the army camp from the Lakota village, was 100 yards directly in front of him. The general turned to his right. In the ascending pre-dawn light, the murky shapes of thousands of mounted cavalry soldiers, punctuated by hundreds of lanterns and torches, began to crystallize into sharper relief. Thousands more infantrymen stood at the rear of the cavalry. As the sun began to peek over the horizon, it threw its first beams of yellow light on the flags of the United States and the cavalry regiments, flapping gently in a light river breeze. Beyond the soldiers stood hundreds of tents.

The bucolic morning sounds of the peaceful river were oppressed by a legion of snare drums, peppered with bugle calls.

The general, Hollingsworth, and Reynolds strode toward the creek. A dozen men, the general's senior staff, waited on the creek shore. Four of the men examined the village across the creek through brass scopes. The general noticed orange flames erupting from the barricades on the opposing shore he had observed the previous day. His staff turned and saluted. General Miles returned the salute.

As the sun rose, the men could see that the fires belched black and white smoke into the sky. They could scarcely see the distant village tipis through the thick smoke.

"Good morning, General," said Colonel William Munroe.

"Report, Colonel," said General Miles. "What are the savages up to this morning?"

"As you can see, sir, they've set fires to the timber barricades surrounding the village," replied Colonel Munroe. "As reported yesterday, the Indians have relocated their tipis to the southeast, where the Grand River meets the Missouri River—approximately 2,000 yards south of our camp.

"From what we can observe, the barricades are a series, set in parallel, between our forces and the village," Colonel Munroe continued. "Indians may be hiding behind them. We have not observed any other activity. The village appears quiet."

"Madness," replied General Miles. "This man Mason claims to be an army colonel, and yet he's backed his army against the junction of two rivers with no means of retreat."

"Yes sir, I concur," replied Colonel Munroe.

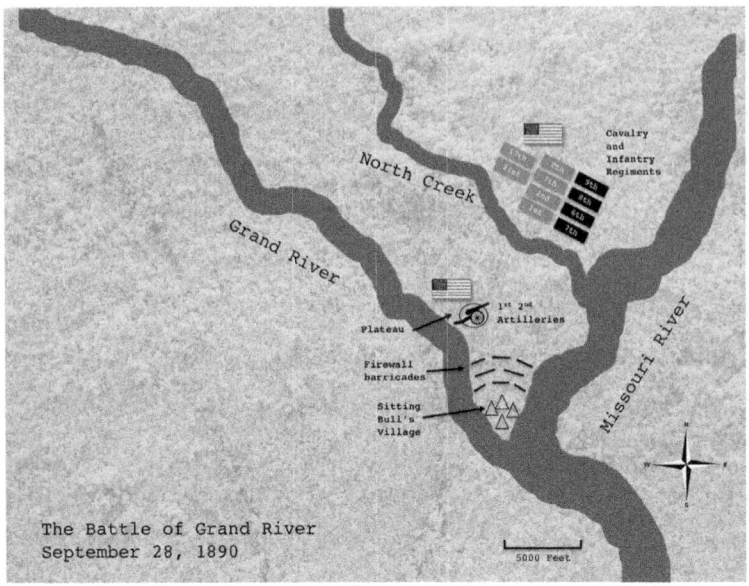

The Battle of Grand River
September 28, 1890

At that moment, they saw a plume burst from the western edge of the village smoke bank. The officers trained their scopes on the hurdling object at the head of the smoke trail. It was a decorated warrior on a painted bay horse, galloping at high speed. The equine comet was on a trajectory toward the plateau, where the Hotchkiss gun batteries prepared to fire on the village.

"What the devil is he up to?" asked the general.

The men watched warily as the warrior closed on the plateau.

"Your orders, sir?" asked the colonel.

"Signal the gun battery," the general commanded. "Artillery commence fire."

"Yes sir, artillery commence fire."

The colonel turned to a lieutenant, who ran to a nearby campfire. He pulled a torch out of the fire and began to wave it in the air.

Two miles to the southwest, atop a 1,700-foot plateau, Major James Franklin stood with a company of soldiers from his artillery regiment. Before him, four Hotchkiss gun cannons oversaw the village from half a mile away. Hundreds of village tipis were packed into the corner formed by the intersection of the Grand River to the south and the Missouri River to the east.

Major Franklin observed that the plain between North Creek and the huddled tipis had erupted in flame and dense smoke. A series of parallel barricades belched fire and smoke into the dawn. Smoke also poured from the tipis, obscuring the battlefield with a thick haze.

The major shifted his gaze to the left, scanning the thousands of assembled cavalry and infantry with awe. It was probably the largest assembly of soldiers he would witness in his lifetime. A pang of guilt tugged at him. He knew he was about to witness a slaughter. The natives stood no chance.

Crews stood by each of the four Hotchkiss guns. Soldiers stood nearby with crates of ammunition, canisters of grapeshot shrapnel that would shred the village and its inhabitants in a matter of minutes. With such awesome firepower, the major knew there would be nothing left for the massive cavalry and infantry to do except count the dead.

A blinding sun peaked over the Missouri River to the east and slightly to the left of their line of fire. The major noticed a trail of dust and smoke approaching the plateau. He picked up his scope. A lone warrior had emerged from the sea of smoke. He was riding toward the plateau at breakneck speed—within 200 yards and closing rapidly.

"The signal, sir!" shouted a lieutenant as he saw the waving torch from camp. "Your orders?"

"Gun crew one," replied the major, "load grapeshot canister. Make that bad Indian into a good Indian. Commence fire."

"Yes sir," replied the gunnery soldier as his crew opened the breach of their Hotchkiss gun and loaded a metal canister. Once secure, the men stepped away.

The warrior closed within 100 yards of the plateau. Major Franklin noticed that the tribesman appeared to be wearing a bowler hat.

"Ready," shouted the gunnery soldier.

"Fire!"

The soldier pulled the gun lanyard. A sharp blast blew from the gun as it recoiled back, rocketing a spray of lead balls toward the approaching warrior. The major watched the warrior as he and his horse were cut down in midstride. The force of the shrapnel blew the warrior off the horse's back. He tumbled to the ground before coming to a dead stop.

At the base of the plateau, Takoda's body shrieked with pain from the shrapnel. Blood gushed from multiple wounds. A piece of grapeshot had smashed his left cheekbone. His bay horse lay on his side, kicking and squealing from the pain of his wounds. Gushing blood mixed with the brilliant yellow, red, and blue paint on his bay skin.

In his hand, Takoda held the wireless detonator he had taken from Ogaleesha.

"Padma, *wah-shday che la ke*," he said as he pressed the detonator button.

The plateau erupted into a fireball as C4 charges and dynamite planted beneath the soldiers' feet detonated in an explosion that rattled the countryside. Men, guns, wagons, and horses were blown high into the air, then rained off the plateau. Kyle and Annika had correctly guessed where General Miles would park his big guns.

Takoda laughed through his excruciating pain as he watched the massive explosion light up the dawn sky. He was overjoyed that his dying sight had permitted him this vision—a knife thrust deep into the invincible white army.

As fragments of smoking artillery, ammunition, and body parts rained down around him, Takoda crawled to his suffering horse. He cradled the animal's head with one arm, and drew his knife with the other. He looked into his horse's eyes, wide with pain and fear. With a quick stroke, he slit his horse's throat. His horse squealed, then quickly bled out. He noticed his bowler hat lying next to him. He reached for it, pulled it on, then rested his head on his horse's warm belly. Satisfied with his life, he closed his eyes, released his final breath, and died.

The percussion of the plateau explosion hit the army camp with a thunderclap. Startled cavalry horses jerked and snorted in reaction to the blast.

General Miles and his senior staff were aghast. Like Major Franklin, they had assumed the artillery gun crews would obliterate the village, leaving little for the cavalry and infantry to mop up. The general's shock turned to rage with the realization that his primitive opponents had managed to land a serious blow to his massive army.

"Score one for you, Colonel Mason," said General Miles. "You should enjoy your moment while you can."

"Beg your pardon, General?" asked Colonel Munroe.

"Order your regiments to attack," commanded the general. "Give no quarter. Kill them all."

"Attack. Yes sir!" replied the colonel. He turned to a lieutenant and ordered the attack. Bugle calls signaled the order to the troops. Roars rose from the regiments as their commanders exhorted their soldiers to wage a battle that was a certain victory.

Colonel James Forsyth sat on his quarter horse at the lead of the 7th Cavalry, commanding 12 companies totaling 1,000 men. Mounted flagbearers stood next to him, holding the cavalry's colors as well as those of the United States and the companies on the regiment's leading edge. Forsyth was a pudgy man of 55 years. His pasty face was easy for his troops to recognize, even in the faint dawn light. A graying brown mustache covered his upper lip, appearing unnatural on his face, as though it had been carelessly glued there.

The men of the 7th had a special axe to grind against Sitting Bull, whom they held responsible for the slaughter of their cavalry's Colonel George Armstrong Custer, along with 267 of his soldiers.

"Gentlemen!" Colonel Forsyth shouted, pulling his sword and holding it high, "do you remember the Little Big Horn?"

"Yes!" roared the soldiers.

"Do you wish to avenge our fallen brothers?" he shouted.

"Huzzah!" roared the troops.

"Then follow me, men!" shouted Colonel Forsyth. "Follow me to victory!"

The men cheered wildly as Colonel Forsyth galloped into North Creek, holding his sword aloft as thousands in his fellow cavalry regiments joined him in the charge.

Upon reaching the opposite bank of the creek, the cavalry charged toward the first flaming barricade at full gallop, crossing the 2,000 yards of flat plain in minutes. Thousands of infantrymen ran behind the cavalry, roaring as they approached the enemy village.

The leading edge of Colonel Forsyth's cavalry reached the first of the series of flaming barricades. Forsyth observed something odd about it. The barricade wasn't a solid wall. There were two openings in the wall, 100 yards apart. The gateways were 30 feet wide, allowing five cavalrymen through at a time. The cavalry split at the middle of the first barricade to drive through the two entrances. The soldiers pulled their pistols as they drove through the barricade, expecting an ambush on the other side.

The first soldiers who cleared the barricade entrances scanned for trouble. There was none. They faced a second wall of flaming, smoking cottonwood tree branches and brush. The riders split their regiments again, trotting along the corridor between the two barricades to find openings in the second barricade. This one offered three gateways—one in the center and two at the outer edges.

Colonel Forsyth grew increasingly concerned. The barricades were not designed to repel the army. They were intended to manage it.

The army repeated the drill through an additional two barricades. The maze split the charging cavalry again and again, dissolving the orderly columns into increasing confusion. By the time the cavalry cleared the final barricade, it had devolved into an undisciplined mob of horses and men riding headlong into a thick, smoky fog.

Through the heavy smoke, the leading riders could see the cone shapes of dozens of tipis in front of them. Smoke belched from tipi openings. The dense smoke and dim morning light blinded the soldiers. The first cavalry soldiers made out tribespeople standing by their tipis. They opened fire, shooting the tribespeople and their tipi homes. When the infantry soldiers caught up with the cavalry, they joined the melee, firing at anything standing. The stampeding horde of cavalry riders and infantry soldiers drove deeper into the village, approaching the tipis that bordered the Grand River to the south. The rush of confident exhilaration the soldiers had felt as they rode into battle mutated to a chilling fear in the blinding smoke as they heard the first screams of wounded soldiers.

The cries of the wounded, hit by gunfire, punctuated the yells of officers and soldiers attempting to establish order in the chaos. Soldiers panicked in the murderous fog, shooting indiscriminately. A chorus of thousands of gunshots and wounded, terrified, screaming soldiers gave a voice to the ocean of smoke, now blindingly bright in the piercing dawn light.

As Colonel Forsyth and the leading edge of his cavalry emerged from the village on its far edge by the Grand River, something tripped their horses, pitching hundreds of riders onto the ground.

Forsyth flew over his horse's head, crashing to the ground on his right shoulder. He pulled himself to his feet. His right shoulder was dislocated. Around him were hundreds of fallen cavalrymen. Riderless horses bolted, snorting with fear as they galloped through the village. Colonel Forsyth pulled his Colt revolver with his left hand as his right arm hung useless at his side. He noticed that something strange was happening to the tipis—their buffalo hides were sliding off their wooden frames. The horses had snagged tripwires, throwing their riders while simultaneously releasing the tipi covers, which fell to the ground. Spooked, thousands of soldiers fired into the skeletons of the animated tipis. Hundreds more soldiers fell to the ground, wounded by crossfire. Individual soldiers, realizing their slaughter was the result of the Messiah's sorcery, began calling her name. The chilling epiphany metastasized throughout the mob into a collective terror.

Forsyth was dazed in a maelstrom of smoke, gunfire, and the screams of the wounded. His disorientation was compounded by the pain of his dislocated shoulder. He walked aimlessly in the smoke, trying to avoid being shot by fellow soldiers or trampled by panicked horses.

In the haze, Forsyth tripped on something at his feet—it was the body of a fallen Lakota brave. He kicked it. Something was wrong. The body was light. He heard the crunch of grass hay. He looked more closely—it was a scarecrow!

Through the smoke, the colonel saw other bodies scattered around the tipis. He ran to one and kicked it—another strawman!

"Cease fire!" he shouted. "Cease fire!"

Only the closest soldiers could hear the colonel through the gunfire, screams, and shouts. Other soldiers and officers began to repeat the colonel's order through the regiments. The gunfire died down, then ceased. Only the cries of wounded soldiers could be heard through the fog.

Forsyth smelled an odd scent in the air. It was familiar—the smell of almonds. He felt his pulse quicken. His breathing accelerated with his heart. He assumed the excitement of battle and the shock of his injury propelled his heartbeat. He approached one of the denuded tipis to take a closer look. A smoke fire burned inside the tipi frame. Through the smoke, he saw the shards of a large broken clay jug, which had been shattered by the gunfire. The jug had been suspended by twine from the tipi's apex. Beneath the clay fragments was a large wooden bucket partially buried in the ground. When the jug was shattered, whatever it contained had spilled into the bucket, producing a bubbling slurry when it reacted with the bucket's contents.

"Colonel!" shouted a soldier.

Forsyth spun around. The terrified face of the soldier who stood before him was beet red. The soldier fell to Forsyth's feet. Forsyth looked around. Hundreds of soldiers and horses lay on the ground, convulsing. In moments, Forsyth's vision went dark as he too fell to the ground, unconscious.

Across the creek, General Miles and his staff scanned the smoke-filled battlefield through their scopes with growing alarm. Though they couldn't see anything through the smoke bank, they heard the roar of gunfire and screams crescendo, then rapidly diminish to complete silence. All the men could hear was the rustling of cottonwood leaves as a breeze blew through them from the south. The senior officers looked at each other, feeling a chill of fear. In their many years of military experience, they had never known a battlefield to go completely silent so quickly.

They scanned the village through their scopes.

"I see something," said Colonel Munroe.

They could make out the shape of a cavalry horse in the clearing smoke. The horse was motionless on the ground. As the smoke receded, it revealed the shapes of dozens of bodies—human and equine—scattered on the ground. The body count grew to hundreds, then thousands.

"Good God!" the general said.

The officers were horrified. Their army, one of the world's mightiest, had been wiped out in minutes. They had never witnessed a massacre of this proportion.

The officers felt the breeze wafting north from the battlefield on their faces. They sniffed the almond scent of the hydrogen cyanide gas cloud that washed over them. The two common agents used in the Homestake mine to process gold ore, sulfuric acid and potassium cyanide, had been combined into the world's most lethal weapon of mass destruction in 1890. The soldiers had sealed their fate when they fired into the tipis, shattering the jugs that released the acid into the buckets of potassium cyanide. The gas rendered its victims into a convulsing unconsciousness in seconds, bringing death in minutes.

The officers looked at each other's beet red faces in terror.

They instinctively looked to their general for help in their final moments. The general, wide-eyed in shock and disbelief, had few words for his men.

"I'm sorry."

He fell to the ground, unconscious, convulsing. Within minutes, the general, his staff, and every remaining human and animal lay dead on the ground, thus concluding the historic Massacre of Grand River.

The sounds of the short battle—the drums, bugles, gunfire, and screams of dying men—had evaporated to silence. The north breeze rattled the leaves of the cottonwood trees. The Grand River lapped lazily against the shore as it flowed past the bodies of thousands of men lying in the morning sun.

The Massacre of Grand River
September 28, 1890

South Dakota
September 28, 1890
07:15 hours
Timeline 003

Twenty miles west of the village, Kyle, Padma, and Annika stood with thousands of Lakota tribespeople. They faced east, watching the dawn sun with anxious anticipation as its piercing rays cleared the horizon. They had slipped out of the village after midnight, leaving only Ogaleesha behind to light the barricade fires and detonate the plateau charges.

Kyle held Pegasus' reins. Hoover sat in front of Kyle.

To the left of the sun, a brilliant flash erupted. The thunderclap of the plateau explosion rattled the plains exodus. As the blast subsided, a roar erupted from the crowd as they realized no one would be pursuing them. A cacophony of cheers, war yells, and songs swelled in the open plain.

Kyle, Padma, and Annika were solemn, a dark island in a sea of celebration. Kyle's jaw dropped as the shockwave of the blast pounded against his chest, carrying the full impact of the massacre of his design.

"My God," Kyle gasped.

Padma hugged him.

"Love, you did what you had to do," Padma said, cradling Kyle's head.

Kyle tried to reconcile his thoughts and feelings—the rationalization of the need to kill those who would have certainly killed his wife and the Lakota people against the enormity of the massacre.

Annika stood silent with her arms folded, watching the fading fireball in the east. She wrapped her arms tighter, as if to bind the feelings of fear and guilt within her. She turned to Kyle and Padma. Padma could see the pained expression on Annika's face as she fought to contain her feelings within her. Padma reached out to hug her.

"No!" Annika said as Padma enveloped her in her long arms. Annika kept her arms folded, refusing Padma's embrace.

"No—don't," Annika said.

"It's OK," Padma said softly.

Annika suddenly uncrossed her arms and wrapped them around Padma. She sobbed as Padma gently stroked her hair.

"They would have killed us," Annika cried.

"Yes, they would have," affirmed Padma. "They would have killed us all."

"It still hurts," Annika cried.

"It's supposed to," said Padma, kissing Annika on the top of her head.

Padma saw a distant puff of dust rise from the prairie to the east. She patted Annika on the back. "What's that?"

The trio looked as the dust cloud grew closer. Annika wiped the tears from her face and reached for her binoculars.

"Is it the army?" Padma asked.

The Lakota's celebration died down as the tribespeople noticed the approaching dust storm. Warriors mounted their horses and galloped to repel the invaders.

Annika focused on the cloud. A warrior on a roan mustang emerged from the dust cloud.

"It's Ogaleesha," Annika reported.

"That's impossible!" Padma said. "Something's wrong. There's no way he could have gotten here this fast."

Padma felt a pang of fear. She looked around the crowd, trying to find Takoda. She had lost track of him during the midnight escape.

"*Due-kdayl* Takoda?" she asked the tribespeople. They shrugged.

Ogaleesha raised his rifle high in the air to greet the approaching warriors. They raised their rifles in return and turned their horses to flank Ogaleesha as they rode back to the awaiting crowd. Ogaleesha halted his horse in front of Padma.

He reached down from his horse to hand Padma a folded piece of paper. When she took it, he rode away.

Padma unfolded the farewell note from Takoda. After a few moments, she crumpled it in her hand.

"I killed him," she said.

Kyle hugged her as she cried softly into his shirt.

The tribespeople slowly began to mobilize, turning away from the destruction. Those with horses mounted them. Those on foot continued their slow journey west across the prairie. The brilliant morning sun ascended at their backs, bringing with it a new day.

Deadwood, SD
October 1, 1890
08:30 hours
Timeline 003

It was a beautiful morning in Deadwood. The citizens began their day with their customary routines. Businessmen walked purposefully to work. Shop owners unlocked their doors. Mine workers pulled on their boots and hurried off to another day of hard labor cracking rocks. Bacon sizzled in iron pans in the town's restaurants and hotels. The warm yeast scent of freshly baked biscuits wafted from ovens. In the saloons, barkeeps wiped their countertops and glasses.

In Chinatown, shops, laundries, and opium dens shook off the night's slumber and prepared for the day.

Caucasian and Chinese men and women strolled down the Main Street thoroughfare in their suits, bustled dresses, and long Changchun shirts, stopping in their tracks as they heard a sound that did not belong in their routine Deadwood morning. From the hills surrounding the town in the south and east rose a deafening high-pitched roar. They looked to the hills—to their horror, they saw a massive army of Lakota warriors on horseback, lofting rifles, feathered spears, and bows. As the thousands of warriors galloped their horses down the hills, it appeared as though a waterfall of brilliantly colored war paint and feathers was washing over the hills to flood the town.

The 5,000 Lakota warriors descending on Deadwood were more than double the town's population. As the warriors bore down on the town, hundreds fired their rifles. Screams and shouts erupted from the men and women on the thoroughfare as they panicked and ran north up Main Street, away from the galloping horde.

People in shops and cafes heard the gunfire and watched as hundreds of terrified citizens ran past the glass windows. Some joined the Main Street exodus, some exited out back doors and ran away. Some, frozen in fear, hid behind bars, desks, and counters.

Seth Bullock grabbed his rifle and bounded out of his sheriff's office, where three of his deputies serpentined through the fleeing mob to meet him.

A man in his thirties, with a brown beard and brown felt hat, looked up from the street at the sheriff. "What do we do?" he asked.

Sheriff Bullock looked down Main Street at the approaching army. The warriors were less than 30 seconds away from the downtown. He knew there was nothing a handful of men could do in the face of the painted tsunami.

He shook his head at the impossible options. "You men save your families. I'll tend to mine."

The deputies tipped their hats to the sheriff and disappeared, swept downstream in the rushing mob.

Those cowering inside Main Street businesses peeked from behind their hiding places to see the first of the warriors as they passed by the front glass. The warriors and their horses were spectacularly decorated. The men's faces were painted with streaks of red, yellow, and blue. They wore feathers in their hair—the chiefs wore feather bonnets. Most were bare-chested—some wore bone breastplates. Their pants were fringed deerskin. Their horses also wore feathers in their manes and tails. Painted handprints blazed from their horses' hindquarters.

From his hiding place on the cherry wood floor of his bank, Daniel Dickinson raised his head above his desktop to glimpse the scene on Main Street. Through the bank's front window, he watched with combined terror and awe as a chief, wearing a full feather bonnet, bone breastplate, and fringed leather pants, reared his painted black and white mustang high in the air.

Chief Gall waved a feathered spear. After years of humiliation in the shadow of the whites, the chief burst with enormous pride. He shouted and pumped his spear, extolling his troops as his horse reared back and struck at the air with his front legs.

When the warriors arrived, they scanned Main Street for people—the street was empty. Chief Gall held up his hand. The thousands of Lakota tribesmen who packed the street went silent. Kyle and Padma sat astride Pegasus at the front of the army. Annika rode her black mustang next to them. Kyle noticed they stood in front of the Gem, where he had said goodbye to Margaret days before.

Padma stood up on Pegasus' back, steadying herself by placing her hands on Kyle's shoulders.

"People of Deadwood," Padma shouted. "The Lakota people

reclaim the land that was stolen from them. We have killed your army. No one is coming to save you.

"You have five minutes to leave town. Anyone remaining in five minutes will be killed. Leave now or die."

Kyle set the timer on his watch. The warriors scanned the Main Street businesses for activity.

The saloon doors of the Gem swung open. Al Sweringen walked out. He glared at Kyle.

"I should have killed you when I had the chance," Sweringen said.

"I'm glad you didn't," replied Padma, patting Kyle's shoulders.

Sweringen spat at Pegasus' feet and turned away, joining the diaspora as Deadwood's remaining inhabitants, their worlds inverted, walked north on Main Street on their way out of town. The army of warriors roared in their wake.

Kyle turned Pegasus. Padma looked out upon a sea of painted faces. The warriors went silent.

Padma began to recite a Lakota prayer Takoda had taught her.

"*O' Wakan Tanka…*

Oh, Great Spirit, whose voice I hear in the wind,
whose breath gives life to all the world.

Hear me; I need your strength and wisdom.

Let me walk in beauty, and make my eyes
ever behold the red and purple sunset.

Make my hands respect the things you have
made and my ears sharp to hear your voice.

Make me wise so that I may understand the

things you have taught my people.

Help me to remain calm and strong in the
face of all that comes towards me.

Let me learn the lessons you have
hidden in every leaf and rock.

Help me seek pure thoughts and act with
the intention of helping others.

Help me find compassion without
empathy overwhelming me.

I seek strength, not to be greater than my brother,
but to fight my greatest enemy—myself.

Make me always ready to come to you
with clean hands and straight eyes.

So when life fades, as the fading sunset, my
spirit may come to you without shame."

Padma paused. Tears flowed down her face. She saw that some of the warriors wept as well.

"*Wakan oyate wan waniyang u ktelo!*" Padma shouted. "A sacred nation is appearing!"

"*Wakan Tanka!*" roared the warriors. They began walking their horses in procession on both sides of Pegasus, reaching for Padma as they passed. She extended her arms. Hundreds touched her hands and her doeskin dress. She beamed as they rode past. As the last warrior walked by, Padma turned to Kyle.

"Help me down, love," she said.

Kyle eased her off Pegasus, then dismounted and tied his horse to the hitching post in front of the Gem. Annika slid off her horse and joined them. Many of the warriors rode out of town to collect their families waiting in the hills. Others began to explore the town.

Padma looked at Kyle and Annika with a lost look on her face.

"I don't know what to do now," Padma said.

"I don't know about the two of you, but I could use a drink," said Annika, turning toward the Gem.

Padma shrugged at Kyle. "Good idea."

Annika blew through the swinging bar doors into the empty saloon. A smile lit up her face as she surveyed the Wild West bar. Half full glasses of whiskey and beer sat on the bar and tables. A smoke trail rose from a cigar resting on the edge of the bar. Four poker hands lay on a table, surrounding a pile of coins and crumpled paper bills—abandoned by the players who had fled without their stakes. One of the game table chairs was knocked on its back on the floor.

As Kyle and Padma entered the Gem, Annika put a hand on the bar and leapt over it effortlessly with a scissor kick. Padma marveled at the tiny woman's ability to defy gravity with such a simple motion. Kyle unslung his back and set it on the bar.

Annika reached under the bar and produced three shot glasses and a bottle of whiskey.

"Belly up!" she said. Annika uncorked the bottle and began to pour.

"Well, I guess they're going to have to find another place to put Mount Rushmore," she said.

The trio held up their glasses.

"What shall we drink to?" Annika asked.

"To the new world," Padma said.

Annika flashed a bright smile. "To the new world!"

The clinked their glasses and downed the whiskey. All three mangled their faces as the ragged-edged whiskey went down.

"That is horrible!" exclaimed Annika.

All three laughed.

Annika turned to the door behind the bar that led to a storeroom. "I'm gonna see if they've hidden the good stuff in the back."

As Annika disappeared into the storeroom, Kyle and Padma heard the creaking of the swinging saloon doors. They turned to see Sitting Bull. He was wearing fringed buckskin from head to toe, brilliantly beaded in blue, red, and yellow. Unlike the other chiefs, he did not wear a feather bonnet. Instead, a sole eagle feather rose from a knot in his hair.

As he approached Padma, he reached for the feather and pulled it out of his hair. He extended it to her.

"Oh no," Padma said. "I can't. It's too much! *Hiya.*"

Sitting Bull shook the feather at Padma, insistently. She took it, reluctantly.

"Thank you very much," Padma said. "Pee-lah-mah-yah-yea."

Sitting Bull did not acknowledge Padma's thanks. Instead, he stared at her. His expression was one of expectation.

"I don't understand," said Padma, looking to Kyle for guidance. "What does he want?"

Kyle mirrored Padma's confusion, "Maybe a trade?"

Padma reached into her backpack slung around her shoulder.

The only meaningful item she could find was her small blue Krishna figurine—the one that had enshrined Kyle's death years before. Somehow, the little blue ceramic deity had survived the war. She extended it to the chief, hoping he would find it an acceptable trade.

Sitting Bull slapped her hand away. The Krishna figurine shattered on the floor. The chief seemed insulted. Kyle took a step forward—Lakota legend or not, no one was going to slap his wife.

At that moment, Kyle felt the floor vibrate. A low hum began to rise with the vibration. Kyle reached into his pocket, pulling out his transponder. While he had hidden Annika's transponder as he had claimed, his own transponder had never left him. He flipped it open. The red light was on. On the display, a single word appeared.

"ACTIVE"

Kyle grabbed Padma by the waist and pulled her close. He grabbed Hoover by the scruff of his neck. As the light began to rise with the hum, they saw Sitting Bull nod affirmatively. The moment before the light washed out the scene, they saw Annika explode through the storeroom door.

"NO!" she screamed.

Annika's scream and panicked face faded into the blinding light and teeth-rattling hum of the Time Tunnel.

As the light and vibration faded away, Kyle and Padma found themselves in the Time Tunnel's glass sphere. The vault door to the chamber opened. Technicians and a dozen armed soldiers rushed in. The soldiers pointed their assault rifles at Kyle and Padma as the technicians moved the stairs into place.

"Oh my God!" Padma shouted, covering her face.

Kyle knew it was pointless to reach for his holstered MP7.

Hoover gnashed his teeth, barking wildly at his new world.

A technician in white clean-room garb climbed the stairs to the glass sphere and opened the hatch, gesturing for Kyle and Padma to come out. As they did, one of the soldiers shouted at the couple.

"Put your fucking hands on your head—right now!"

Kyle and Padma obeyed, putting their hands on their heads as they descended the stairs. The technician slammed the door on the glass chamber, locking Hoover inside.

The soldiers grabbed Kyle and Padma and threw them both to the floor, pulling their arms behind their backs as they locked their wrists in handcuffs. Padma clutched Sitting Bull's eagle feather in her shackled hand. A soldier pulled it away and tossed it aside.

"No!" she screamed.

The soldier grabbed a fistful of hair and pulled her head off the cement floor, straining her neck.

"You do what we tell you to do!" the soldier shouted.

"Kyle!" Padma screamed.

Kyle fought to get up. A soldier smacked him on the back of his head with the butt of his rifle.

The soldiers disarmed Kyle and patted down every inch of both their bodies. Hoover jumped against the glass walls of the Time Tunnel chamber, barking and snarling. One of the soldiers climbed the steps to the chamber. He unholstered his pistol and put his hand on the chamber latch. Kyle could see he was about to shoot Hoover.

A deep voice spoke over the PA system, "Don't hurt the dog." Kyle recognized the voice as General Craig's.

The soldier holstered his pistol and trotted down the steps to Kyle and Padma. The two were hoisted to their feet. A soldier poked Kyle hard in the back with his rifle barrel.

"Move!"

The couple was escorted at gunpoint to mission control. The vault door swung open to reveal General Craig, wearing his uniform.

The general's eyes went wide in reaction to Padma's native dress.

"Which General Craig are you?" Kyle asked.

A flash of confusion crossed General Craig's face. "I'm the General Craig who's going to kick your insubordinate ass!" he said.

Kyle looked around the mission control amphitheater. At the mission director station stood Gus Ferrer.

We're in Time Tunnel 1! he realized.

"How…" Kyle began.

"How did we catch you?" the general finished. "Our Zhang was able to repair the damage her double caused. Strangelove used your graviton trick to track your transponder. We figured out how to activate it remotely."

The temporal variance alarm sounded. The pink TVA cube flashed on. Roger Summit, Aysha Voong, and their team dove into their computers to learn how time had changed. In moments, they looked at each other in disbelief. Roger raised a hand to his chest.

"Guard them," the general said to the soldiers as he descended the steps to the historians' hive. The history team was shouting at each other as they pointed at each other's computer screens.

"What is it?" the general asked Roger.

Roger was hyperventilating.

"I...can't...breathe," he said.

The general signaled to Lara Meredith to tend to Roger. He turned to Aysha.

"What is it?" he asked.

Aysha swiveled her chair to face the general. She took a breath.

"General," Aysha began, "where and when was the first atomic bomb used in battle?"

The general looked confused. "Hiroshima, Japan. 1945."

"No," Aysha said. "Try Chicago. 1938."

The general's jaw dropped.

Aysha swiveled her chair back to her keyboard and began typing. On the colossal mission control screen, a grainy black and white image of the ruins of Chicago appeared. The limestone Chicago Water Tower, one of the few surviving structures of the great 1871 Chicago fire, also somehow managed to survive the 1938 nuclear cataclysm.

"There's more," Aysha said.

She continued typing on her keyboard. A globe map appeared on the big screen. It rotated to the western hemisphere. The United States was colored blue.

"This is where the United States is supposed to be," Aysha said.

She clicked a button. A red hourglass on a black background washed over North and Central America, replacing the blue.

"There is no more United States," Aysha said.

"This," she said, "is called the 'Annikan Empire.'"

"Annikan…as in Annika Wise?" the general asked.

Aysha nodded. "There's more."

She typed on her keyboard. The globe spun to the opposite hemisphere. A swastika covered all of Europe, the United Kingdom, and North Africa. The red circle and rays of the Japanese rising sun flag spread across Asia and Australia.

Stunned silence. The general dropped into a chair.

"My God."

Roswell, NM
July 5, 1947
22:49 hours

Hundreds of soldiers stood in the New Mexico desert looking up at the partly clouded night sky. Lightning flicked from cloud to cloud. The blue-white bolts lit up the soldiers and the desert landscape dotted with scrub and yucca. The soldiers wore charcoal gray uniforms, tall black boots, and tunics with a row of gleaming silver buttons running up the left breast. Dozens of tanks were parked nearby, along with trucks and earthmoving equipment at the ready to collect the wreckage of a strange craft that was prophesized to fall from the sky in the coming moments. The black vehicles bore the same emblem that waved on a large flag that flapped lazily in the breeze—a red hourglass against a black background.

A tiny woman in a wheelchair looked up at the sky expectantly. The woman, in her nineties, wore the same charcoal gray tunic as the others. Five gleaming silver discs on her left shoulder distinguished her superior rank. Her white hair was worn in bangs, with a ponytail down her back.

The woman had waited over half a century for this moment.

The catastrophic accident that caused the crash of a UFO in Roswell had happened long before the woman was born.

Abandoned in the past, she had lived just long enough to witness history.

A brilliant blue-white explosion erupted in the sky, momentarily blinding the soldiers as it lit up the desert. Two lights and smoke trails descended from the blast point in the sky.

Annika Wise clapped and cackled excitedly as she watched the wreckage of a time machine from the future hurtle toward earth.

— END OF BOOK 2 —

Annika Wise will return

ABOUT THE AUTHOR

RICHARD TODD is an entrepreneur, author, and inventor. As a contributor to the *Huffington Post* and the *San Francisco Chronicle*, he has written on a variety of subjects, including climate change, education, and economics.

His interview subjects include astrophysicist Neil deGrasse Tyson, founder and chairman of the Virgin Group Sir Richard Branson, economist and EU advisor Jeremy Rifkin, astrophysicist Brian Greene, Apple co-founder Steve Wozniak, Pulitzer Prize-winning author Jane Smiley, IBM "Watson" supercomputer team leader David Ferrucci, and *Who Killed the Electric Car*'s Chelsea Sexton.

Richard Todd holds four patents in the field of information technology. He lives on a ranch in Carmel Valley with his wife, Laura, and the many rescue animals under their care.

Made in the USA
Las Vegas, NV
02 November 2021